PRAISE FOR CHRIST..... .. ..

"If you believe *Die Hard* is a Christmas movie, then you will LOVE this anthology. All three stories kept me turning pages long after I needed to sleep. Romance, characters, team dynamics, and suspense to die for!"

KARISS LYNCH, AUTHOR OF HEART OF A WARRIOR SERIES

"I can't imagine a better combination than the Elite Guardians and Christmas. *Christmas in the Crosshairs* is nonstop action and 5 stars!"

CHELSA W., GOODREADS

"Filled with suspense and danger, *Christmas in the Crosshairs* will keep you on the edge of your seat and flipping the pages until the end."

ALLYSON A., GOODREADS

"*Christmas in the Crosshairs* was an outstanding collection of three interwoven stories. I absolutely enjoyed the suspense and adventure that filled each page. From the first page to the last, this three-story collection exceeded my already high expectations."

CLAIRE, GOODREADS

CHRISTMAS IN THE CROSSHAIRS

LYNETTE EASON PRESENTS AN ELITE GUARDIANS ANTHOLOGY

KATE ANGELO   KELLY UNDERWOOD

SAMI A. ABRAMS

sunrise
PUBLISHING

The Elite Guardians Anthology is dedicated to the memory of Susan Snodgrass. Authors all need a cheerleader, someone who comes along beside them and gives them a reason to continue writing. Susan touched the lives of all of us with her encouragement, book reviews, and her passion for reading. We are saddened by the loss but know that one day we'll see her in heaven, probably with a good book in her hand and telling everyone about it.

CHRISTMAS IN THE CROSSHAIRS

It's Christmastime and love is in the air. But when these three Elite Guardians walk into the crosshairs of trouble, they find themselves fighting not just for justice, but for the lives of the men they love in this riveting thriller collection!

DEADLY HOLIDAY HIJACK BY KATE ANGELO

"Come out to Savannah, she says. It'll be fun, she says. Boss can be in the nativity pageant, she says," Yeah. Great idea.

Bodyguard Christina Sherman and her fiancé, former spec ops air commando Grey Parker just want to sneak away to beautiful Savannah, attend a Nativity Pageant, maybe set a wedding date. But when a group of terrorists take over the church and the whole thing is live streamed, they find themselves in a hometown version of a Die Hard Christmas movie. But will they make it to the happy ending?

SILENT NIGHT SIEGE BY KELLY UNDERWOOD

Billionaire Preston Whittaker and bodyguard Laila Rabbinowitz just can't get a break. Not only are their schedules so crazy they've put their relationship on simmer, but on their way to the mountains for much-needed togetherness...yep, their plane crashes. Suddenly they're stranded on a remote mountainside in freezing temperatures, minimal food, wildlife, and no hope of rescue.

And then, the real danger starts. Someone deliberately caused the wreck, and that person is hunting them through the wilderness.

Now, it'll take more than togetherness to survive...

CHRISTMAS SNOWSTORM STANDOFF BY SAMI A. ABRAMS

It's finally time for bodyguard Lizzie Tremaine to tie the knot with the man she's loved for years—fellow bodyguard Charlie Lee.

But maybe fate is still against them, because on the eve of their big day, a snowstorm hits. And, while it's kept the guests away, it's brought trouble in the form of a woman from Charlie's past. More, she's on the run from a killer...

A man who will stop at nothing to make sure Charlie and Lizzie never make it to the altar.

Now Lizzie and Charlie must battle the storm, stop the killer, and defeat the doubts that suddenly have them wondering if they are truly meant to be.

Three epic love stories. Three edge-of-your-seat thrillers. Three Christmases caught in the Crosshairs inspired by best-selling author Lynette Eason's Elite Guardian series.

A NOTE FROM LYNETTE EASON

Hello wonderful readers,

Welcome back to more adventures with the Elite Guardians. I can't tell you how fun these projects have been. Working with Kate, Sami and Kelly has been an amazing adventure, and I've been honored to get to know the ladies who've brought characters back to life and breathed life into new ones.

So, the Guardians are off once again tumbling headfirst into danger and love. This time we get the added fun of Christmas and a wedding—and a few killers who get what's coming to them. Thank you for being so wonderful about supporting these authors and being excited about the stories they're bringing to you.

I'm so excited you have your hands on a copy!

Oh, and Merry Christmas! Stay safe and warm, snuggled under a blanket, sipping your tea or coffee, in front of the crackling fire while you dive into the new Elite Guardians adventures.

Happy Reading,

Lynette

DEADLY HOLIDAY HIJACK

KATE ANGELO

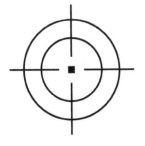

ONE

When someone stabbed Tomás Muñoz in the back, he turned around and stabbed them in the face. There was a price for betrayal, and tonight they would pay.

With a flick of the wrist, Tomás swiped his stolen key fob on the access box and strode through the side entrance of Hillspring Church. The one marked *Private*. Strictly reserved for the lead pastor and special celebrity guest speakers, the entrance always had extra security. So when he saw retired highway patrolman Bruce Martin marching down the hallway toward him, Tomás simply smiled and offered a polite wave.

At first glance, Bruce looked like every other church attender. Olive pants, black polo shirt, and black shoes, packaged tightly for an all-around clean-cut appearance. Beneath the surface, Tomás could see the truth. Those black shoes? Military combat sneakers. The olive pants? Tactical. Of course, the nylon duty belt holding his Maglite, taser, handcuffs, and the sidearm all screamed *security* louder than the reflective word printed on his back.

"Excuse me, sir, this is a private area," Bruce declared in a deep authoritarian tone.

They walked toward each other.

Only twenty feet apart.

"Oh? It is?" Tomás used his kindest voice.

"How'd you get in here?" Bruce boomed.

Ten feet.

Tomás jerked his thumb over his shoulder and made an appearance of looking behind him. "I came right through that door."

Bruce placed his hand on his gun holster and unsnapped the safety latch. "Sir, I need to see some identification."

Six feet.

"From me?" Tomás placed a hand on his chest and flashed a grin. "I think there's been a mistake. I'm a very special guest and I'm meant to be here. My name is Tomás. Tomás Muñoz."

He offered his hand to the security officer.

Bruce hesitated, studying Tomás's face. Like most churches, treating guests with friendliness was the highest priority, and Hillspring Church prided itself in making everyone feel welcome. Tomás could see suspicion in Bruce's eyes.

Finally, good fellowship won out, and Bruce mirrored Tomás and stretched his hand out for a greeting.

Three feet.

Tomás closed the distance and pumped his hand.

"I'm sorry, Mr. Muñoz," Bruce said. "I hope I didn't appear rude. We take security around here very—"

Tomás jerked Bruce forward, dropped the handshake, and grabbed Bruce by the top of his head and chin. He twisted hard. In a crunch of bone and cartilage, Tomás heard Bruce's vertebrae snap beneath his hands. He smiled and relaxed his grip until the lifeless body dropped to the floor.

Out of habit, Tomás twisted his own neck until he heard the satisfying crack. He smoothed his suit and tie. Behind him, the VIP door opened. His men poured through.

Show time.

TWO

M egachurches topped the chart of Christina Sherman's list of worst nightmares.

Attending the night of a special holiday event? Absolute insanity.

A rumble of excited energy blended with Christmas music and echoed throughout the expansive atrium of Savannah, Georgia's Hillspring Church. So many people all in one place had Christina's bodyguard senses heightened. She tightened her grip on the leash in her left hand and surveyed the horde congregating in the lobby.

A line of antsy children and frazzled parents waited their turn for a family photo in front of the massive Christmas tree. A group of young adults mingled in the open café and sipped specialty drinks from disposable cups. To pass time, shoppers roamed around the bookstore snagging last-minute gifts.

"Is it just me, or did this place look bigger when we did the security check?" Grey asked.

Christina's fiancé, Grey Parker, navigated his wheelchair

through the channel created by three men chatting near the life-sized nativity scene.

"They expect five hundred people to attend the Christmas pageant this year," Christina said. "I think they're all standing right here."

"Relax, Agent. You're not an Elite Guardian bodyguard today." Grey beamed a smile. "You're a proud aunt here to watch your nephew and best dog, Boss, in the play."

Christina smiled at the man she loved with the blond hair and gray eyes. "I'm always a bodyguard, Captain."

They'd taken to calling each other the nicknames after the comic book hero Captain America and his love for Agent 13. She didn't claim to fully understand it, but Grey liked it, and they weren't the ooey-gooey-pet-name type people anyway.

The crowd pressed in all around them and, when zigzagging didn't work, Christina and Grey took turns saying *excuse me* and *pardon me* to get to the sanctuary.

"You think we're making a mistake letting Boss be in the show?"

"Um, yeah, I do think it's a mistake. He'll be humiliated wearing that ridiculous camel costume you picked out for him."

Christina gasped. "No, he won't! He looks adorable! Don't you, Boss?"

The Belgian Malinois tilted his head and studied her with watery brown eyes. The braided cord with gold tassels adorned his head in a makeshift bridle. She'd sewn tiny gold tassels along the edge of a purple silk square and draped it over his back. The saddle consisted of a fringed pillow that also served as a hump. With his long legs and tan coat, he fit the camel role well.

"Boss is a highly trained military working dog. He's not supposed to be *cute*."

"*Retired* military working dog, remember?"

"Once a soldier, always a soldier," he said.

Christina followed Grey and the throng of others through

the sanctuary doors and down the center aisle. Around them, guests filled in sections of the tiered seating. She scanned the sanctuary for Bruce Martin and Nolan Fry, the armed security guards employed by the church. Didn't see either man. Probably securing key areas of the building before the pageant began.

When her sister, Alana Flores, began attending the church with her son Rocco, Christina had balked. Megachurches seemed so impersonal and utterly overwhelming to her. It wasn't her style. She preferred more intimate worship. But she had to admit, the church did everything with the utmost excellence.

The curved LED video wall behind the pulpit displayed a desert night sky with a glowing star in the center. A black curtain concealed the baptistry window above the video wall. Instead of a wooden stable, the stage designers had built a cave that appeared to be constructed from real stones. The manger— an old wood feed trough. Straw and sand covered the floor, and a realistic-looking ox slept in the back of the cave.

"Broadway would be jealous of this set," Christina said. "It's like stepping into Bethlehem."

"Yeah...wow," Grey said. "I think they used real sand for the desert."

"I'm sure we'll find out when Rocco and Boss come home covered in it. At least they aren't using any other real animals."

"Could you imagine real camels? Talk about stinky." Grey chuckled. "Now I know why the wise men brought frankincense and myrrh to baby Jesus. To cover up the animal smells."

She chuckled. Grey was always doing that. Making her smile or laugh.

"You know..." He sighed. "This would be an incredible place to get married."

Christina's heart skipped a beat. He wanted to have their wedding *here*? They didn't even live in Savannah. They were only here because Alana had agreed to move from Los Angeles to Georgia and open a new branch of the Elite Guardians Agency.

Besides, Grey had proposed months ago, and they still hadn't set a wedding date. The timing never seemed right. Not while Grey recovered from his experimental surgery and focused on the treatment program tailored to help him walk again. She didn't mind waiting, but did he plan to have that conversation right *now*?

"It, um...it's lovely—"

"Aunt Christina!" The face of her nine-year-old nephew lit up when he saw them. "You guys made it!" He flung himself into a hug with such force it knocked her back a step.

She squeezed him tight and kissed the top of his head. "Of course, Rocco. We wouldn't miss this for the world."

Rocco released her and turned to Grey. "Did you hear? I'm playing Balthasar! He's the best magi to play because he has the most lines."

"My man!" Grey fist-bumped Rocco. "You're going to be the best Balthasar since the real Balthasar."

"Don't get him started," Alana said, pausing to give Christina and Grey a hug. "He'll chew your ear about the biblical version of the nativity story, which never even named the wise men."

"Yeah, and no one even knows how many there were!"

Alana placed her hand on Rocco's shoulder. "Okay, okay. We can have the history lesson over dinner."

Christina smiled at her nephew's enthusiasm. "Sounds like you're learning a lot about the Bible in your new church."

Rocco nodded. "I have the best Sunday school teacher. He's from Africa!"

"You know, Boss has been to Africa," Grey said.

At the sound of his name, Boss twitched an ear and glanced at Grey.

Rocco inhaled sharply and his eyes went wide. "That's so cool! I wonder if they know each other."

"Boss *looks* like he came from Africa." Alana knelt and scratched the dog's face. "Like a camel right out of Egypt, but cuter."

Christina grinned at Grey and he rolled his eyes.

Alana gave Boss a final head pat and stood. "Okay, I need to get Rocco and Boss backstage. You guys wanna grab seats?"

"Can Aunt Christina and Grey take us, please?" Rocco whined and clasped his hands in a begging gesture.

Alana put her hands on her hips. "What did I tell you about whining?"

Rocco dropped his hands. "Sorry, Mom." He flashed brown eyes at Christina. "Will you please escort us backstage?"

"It'd be our honor," Christina said.

Boy, that woman could get him to agree to just about anything. Grey watched Rocco skip down the hall, holding the rope reins on Boss's halter. The boy chattered to the dog, telling him it was okay to be nervous. The so-called vicious military dog simply trotted beside Rocco, tongue out, looking like a kid himself. The fake hump Christina had secured on his back swayed with each step—as did the hundreds of tassels.

The only person in the world who could talk him into dressing his dog like a camel was Christina.

Of course, he hadn't made it easy on her. There'd been logistics to consider. And he wasn't sure Boss was ready to be on stage in such a public venue after being kidnapped as a priceless asset to sell on the black market. Even though more sniffer dogs were in training to track the same chemical weapon Boss could detect, he was still considered a high-value target.

But the pageant was only an hour long, and it meant the world to Rocco. Grey trusted Christina. Knew she'd memorized the building layout and verified all background checks were clean. And with two Elite Guardians on site, Boss would be well protected.

He stole a glance and caught her studying Rocco. The slight smile in her soft lips made his pulse flutter. Oh, how he loved Christina. And…he thought she loved him. So why hadn't they set a wedding date? He'd brought the conversation up numerous times, but she always seemed to go quiet or change the subject. Was she having second thoughts?

"Isn't that right, Grey?" Rocco said, glancing over his shoulder.

"Oh…um," he stammered.

Christina touched Grey's shoulder. "Rocco was saying that Boss is smart enough to play Joseph and Mary's donkey."

"Ah." Grey laughed. "You're probably right, but I think the camel costume is enough for now."

"Yeah, and his fur is even tan like a camel!" Rocco ran the last few feet to the backstage door. His hand hovered over the accessible push button. He looked at Grey hopefully. "May I do it?"

"Sure, little man." He suppressed a smile.

When he'd first met Rocco, the boy had been quiet and reserved. He'd opened up after the first few days and revealed himself to be a highly intelligent and happy child. Now that Alana and Rocco lived only a few hours away, Grey could see himself as a strong male role model for the boy and couldn't wait to become his uncle. Whenever that would be.

A dark passageway led backstage where cast members and stagehands moved around. Black paint covered the walls and the open ceiling. Long, thick curtains hid the offstage area from the audience. Rocco found his costume, and Christina helped him pull the green robe over his head.

A woman with a protruding belly turned and bumped into Grey's knees. "Oh, I'm so sorry, sir." She wore a white gown with a blue shawl covering her long, dark hair.

"You must be the Virgin Mary," Grey said.

"Well, yeah." She patted her round belly. "Ironic, since this isn't exactly a costume. My name is Gail Moore."

"I'm Christina Sherman and this is Grey Parker. We're here to drop off Balthazar and Boss the camel."

"Rocco, you look like the real Balthazar in your robe." Gail sucked in a breath when she saw Boss. "Oh my goodness. Boss is so cute in his camel costume!"

Grey looked at Christina. She shrugged and suppressed a smile.

"Have you seen Nolan Fry, the security officer?" Christina asked. "He's supposed to keep an eye on these two for us."

"He was here earlier." Gail turned and searched the crowd. "I don't see him now. But go. Find your seats and enjoy the show. I'll look after them until Nolan gets back."

Christina knelt and fussed with Boss's halter. She smoothed the fur around his ears. "It's okay if you're nervous, Boss. I'd be nervous too. But I know you'll do great, so have fun."

Grey knew she really meant her words for Rocco but didn't want to embarrass him.

"Rocco, you remember all the commands for handling Boss like I taught you?" Grey asked.

"Yes, sir."

"Good man." Grey gave him a fist bump and ruffled Boss's head. "You be a good dog for Rocco."

"We'll be right out front if you need us. Just a phone call away," Christina said.

"But I don't have my phone. Mom took it."

"What about your glucose monitor? I thought you needed your phone nearby for alerts."

"The play isn't that long, and with my insulin pump..." He

patted his hip. "I'll be fine. Mom said she would sit at the front so when I'm on stage I'll be close enough to transmit to my phone."

"Well, you've got everything under control, so we'll go find your mom." Christina hugged her nephew. "You're so brave, Rocco. I love you."

"Love you too, Aunt Christina."

Once they were in the hall, Christina took Grey's hand. He pushed his chair with his left, and Christina pulled and steered him while holding his right.

Together, they headed back through the labyrinth of hallways toward the sanctuary. The diamond engagement ring on her left hand sparkled. Five months ago he'd given her the ring in front of friends and family. Should he bring up the subject of planning their wedding?

If he didn't do it now, it would be a while before they could be alone again. Plans with Alana and Rocco would keep them in Savannah until Charlie and Lizzie's wedding on Christmas Eve. Then New Year's with his family at their ranch—which was always a huge party with live music, dinner, and dancing under a white event tent. At midnight his dad and his friends went nuts with the fireworks display. They'd rope him in for sure.

No, Grey couldn't wait. He had to know why she hadn't brought up the topic of setting a date for their wedding.

He stopped pushing his chair.

She halted and turned to look at him. "What's wrong?"

"Christina..." He sighed and rubbed the back of his neck. "We need to talk—"

A massive boom sent a shockwave through the hallway. The building shook with the force and pressure of an explosion.

Grey grabbed his wheels and steadied himself. "What in the world was that?"

THREE

S he didn't remember explosions in the nativity story. Christina stilled and furrowed her brow. "That sounded like an explosion, but not the battlefield kind."

Grey clutched the wheels of his chair with both hands and spun to look down the hallway. "No, it didn't sound like—"

A secondary explosion powerful enough to vibrate Christina's bones reverberated from somewhere nearby. A smoke cloud roiled up at the end of the hallway ahead. A red-orange glow hovered behind the haze. At the other end of the hall, another smoke cloud drifted from the floor to the ceiling.

"That smoke isn't from a fire," Grey said.

No, it wasn't. Which was why her stomach clenched and her skin prickled. "We need to get Rocco and Boss. Now," she said. "Cover your face. It could be smoke to disorient people, but it might be an incapacitating agent."

"I'm following you. This place is a maze."

Another reason she didn't like megachurches. How could anyone without her keen memorization skills navigate these

14

halls and intersections as a first-time guest? The layout was a giant hexagon inside an octagon, with corridors of classrooms attached like spokes on a wheel. No matter where she looked, a sign pointed to a restroom and the main sanctuary, because in many ways, it was a giant circle.

Voices and the clatter of boots pounding the carpet banged down the hall. Men's voices shouted in Spanish.

Christina slowed. She was fluent in Spanish, but with the distance, she couldn't make out their words. Through the haze, two figures took shape at the end of the hall. Men dressed in all black, right up to the neck gaiters pulled up to cover their faces. The glow of red cast an eerie halo around them.

Christina and Grey halted.

The men carried automatic rifles.

She drew her concealed weapon. Pressed her back to the wall and crouched beside Grey's wheelchair. She prayed the men couldn't see them through the thick cloud of smoke filling the hallway.

"Not good," Grey whispered.

The taller man paused. "Did you hear something, Hector?" he asked in Spanish.

"Search the rooms. You take that side. I take this one."

They peeled apart, each on opposite sides of the hallway until they disappeared into the classrooms.

"We've gotta move." She spoke in a low voice. "We can get backstage if we go back."

Grey nodded and whirled his wheelchair around. She sprinted behind him, putting distance between themselves and the men. They found themselves in another hall that brought them to the atrium and back around to the other side of the church. The cloud of smoke drifted into the hall, and Christina's eyes burned.

"Where is everyone?" Grey whispered. "Where's the security team?"

"I don't know. Lockdown protocol?" The toe of her boot kicked a small silver canister and sent it clattering into the wall. It disappeared into the smoky haze. "Flash bang grenade," she whispered.

That explained the concussive blasts they'd heard.

"Hey!" A man's voice shouted from somewhere behind the smoke.

They didn't bother waiting to see who it was. Grey whirled his chair around and rammed his wheels forward.

She was close beside him. So close they banged elbows. A shock of pain zipped through her arm. The twinge in her funny bone was the least of her worries. The stinging in her eyes grew worse. They had to get away from the smoke before it debilitated them.

"There. Pastor Leo's office," Grey said.

Christina rushed ahead and wrenched the door handle. Breathed a mental sigh when the door opened. She shouldered through. Once Grey's wheelchair cleared the opening, she shoved the door closed and threw the lock.

Now for something to use as a barricade.

Pastor Leo's bulky desk anchored the windowless room. Far too heavy. The leather wingback chairs? Too light. The sofa was her best option. She holstered her gun and ran to the far armrest. With all her strength, she pushed. The sofa slid so fast she almost fell on her face.

"Wasn't expecting *that*."

"Leave it," Grey said. "He'll be here any second!"

"I got it. It's on sliders." She spun the end around and dragged the couch at an angle. With a final push, she rammed the armrest into the doorknob. Lifted each corner and kicked the slider out. No sense in making it easy for the guy once he got through the lock.

"That won't hold him for long."

"The vent." He pointed above the desk. "That's our escape.

You know the way?"

"Yeah…" Christina hesitated.

Grey's legs didn't always work well enough to allow him to stand, especially in high-stress situations. He couldn't reach the ceiling without standing on the desk, and she wasn't about to leave him to face that guy alone. No doubt Grey could handle himself, but two soldiers were always better than one. They could stay and face the danger together.

"Grey, we should—"

The door handle jiggled.

"Go!" He grabbed her by the waist and lifted her onto the desk. "Get somewhere safe and call it in."

A banging on the other side of the door said someone wanted in. Bad.

Grey pulled his gun from his concealed holster and slide-checked it. The sound kicked her into action. She reached up to the vent. Found the latches and slid them back. The cover dropped and she let it dangle. Blackness consumed the narrow opening. She prayed she could fit her shoulders through.

The banging turned into kicking. The handle wouldn't hold much longer.

She crouched and with all her strength, jumped for the opening with her arms up. Caught herself by the elbows and squirmed her body into the vent.

She peered down at Grey.

"Close the vent," he whispered.

She shook her head. "No way, Captain. We're in this together. Give me your hand and I'll pull you up."

"It's okay. I have a plan."

She didn't want to leave Grey behind, but if he had any chance at survival, she had to trust him.

Grey turned his chair around and fixed his eyes on hers. "I love you, Christina. Now close the vent."

GREY'S PULSE POUNDED IN HIS EARS, AND THE FAMILIAR BUZZ OF adrenaline surged through his veins. The man kicked at the office door, determined to break in. It would only be a matter of seconds before he made it inside and found Grey.

So far, they'd seen three gunmen in the church, but his gut told him there were more. The first two men hadn't seen them, and Grey said a silent prayer this guy hadn't notified the others. If he could take the assailant down without drawing anyone else to their location or revealing themselves, they'd have the upper hand.

He stole a final look at Christina before she closed the vent. The anguish on her face pierced his heart. He knew exactly what emotional battle waged war inside her head. The same one he'd have in her position. He wouldn't have left her behind either.

The handle gave way, and the door opened an inch before colliding with the couch. The man cursed in Spanish and slammed the door back and forth.

The vent clicked into place, and Grey steered his wheelchair into Pastor Leo's bathroom. The ADA-compliant wide doorway was a nice touch he wasn't expecting. He closed the door. Didn't bother locking it. Along the back wall, he found a supply closet and prayed there was something he could use. The shelves held bathroom products, cleaning supplies, duct tape, towels, and… bingo! A box of batteries.

He snatched the box from the second shelf. Two left. He stuffed one into his pocket, reached into the pouch he kept attached to his chair, and fumbled around until his fingers found the new multi-tool Christina had bought for his birthday. Twenty-one tools in one compact unit he could everyday carry. The perfect gift.

He snapped the knife open and carefully made a cut in the outer shell of the battery. Turned it so the knife sliced all the way around. He switched the tool to the sharp-nosed pliers and pinched one end, then he gripped the other with his thumb and forefinger and wrung the casing. Tugged and twisted.

"C'mon, c'mon."

With a bit of muscle, he managed to pop the casing off and expose the insides. That's what he was looking for.

From the office, he heard the man grunt with each forceful shove of the door. The couch bounced.

Nothing Grey could do about it right now. He went back to work and eased the rest of the casing off. In his hand, he held the interior of the battery. Rolled up plastic and metal soaked in chemicals. Working fast but cautiously, he unrolled the materials and separated the thin lithium metal from the paper.

"Come out to Savannah, she says. It'll be fun, she says. Boss can be in the nativity pageant, she says," he muttered to himself. Yeah. Great idea.

More Spanish cursing, then a crash.

Grey finished folding the metal strip into a dense square. Took a deep breath and stilled himself. Air trickled from his nostrils.

Footsteps approached.

Grey tensed. A shadow moved beneath the threshold. He shifted his gaze to the door handle.

It turned.

Grey tossed the lithium square into the toilet. Leaned back and sat ramrod straight. Instantly, the water in the toilet sizzled. The metal reacted with the water, and smoke billowed from the ceramic bowl.

The bathroom door swung open, obscuring Grey from the assailant. The muzzle of a rifle poked through the door first, followed by a man dressed in black tactical pants and a long-sleeved black shirt. His military boots squeaked on the tile as he crept into the room. A mop of thick, wavy black hair fell over the man's ears and forehead. A black mask hid his face.

A pink flame erupted from the toilet and mingled with the gray smoke.

"¿*Que?*" The man lowered his rifle and moved to stand over the toilet.

The tiny fire blazed into an orange firestorm dancing inside the bowl. The man gawked at the ball of flames and smoke. The water hissed and bubbled.

With the man distracted, Grey eased the door closed. The sulfuric smell tickled his nostrils.

The man sensed movement and whirled.

Grey said, "Welcome to the party, pal."

The man's eyes bulged.

Grey thrust his wheels forward. His kneecaps slammed into the assailant's shins. The force knocked the man off balance and he toppled forward. Grey raised a rigid hand high.

"I think it's time for a silent night," he said.

One forceful chop to the nerve on the man's neck and he was out cold.

FOUR

Multiple explosions from somewhere in the building brought Alana and every other parishioner to their feet and into chaos.

"Rocco!"

But she'd only made it two steps before men swarmed the room to take control. They forced everyone back into their seats and ordered them to sit with their hands on their heads. Alana hadn't bothered to draw her weapon. As a former member of the Los Angeles Police SWAT, she never pulled her gun unless prepared to use it. And she wasn't ready. Yet.

From her seat on the front row, she craned her neck to assess the situation. Where were Christina and Grey? She prayed they were in the back with Rocco and Boss.

The men taking the church hostage were dressed in all black, including the neck gaiters pulled up to mask their faces. They moved with precision to control the mass of people. A takeover of a church this size took coordination. They were organized. This wasn't a group of teens playing some type of prank.

21

It was a full-blown military operation.

Terrorists.

She counted the men. A man with an automatic rifle blocked each of the five exits. Six men with pistols. One to cover each section of seats. Two more took control of the audiovisual booth.

Her phone buzzed in her pocket. She reached for it.

A man stepped in front of her and aimed his gun at her chest. "Hands on your head," he bellowed in a heavy Hispanic accent.

Alana raised her hands and examined the embroidered gold dragon on his face mask. Ice slid through her veins.

A cry from the stage pulled her attention away. Masked men ushered the cast from backstage, still in their costumes. The man playing Joseph was her friend and Sunday school teacher, Aaron Rhodes. He held his arms outstretched to guard the group behind him.

Gail Moore, Alana's pregnant friend from the same class, pulled her shawl tight around her face and dipped her head low. Stress like this was not good for her baby.

Alana's heart skipped a beat when her eyes fell on her son, Rocco. He walked behind Gail, his hand fisted around Boss's rope reins. The dog leaned against Rocco's leg. Eyes alert and hackles raised.

"Everyone stay calm," Pastor Leo Godzich's voice boomed over the speakers from his head-worn microphone. His voice and his six-foot-six boxy frame commanded attention. "Now is the time to pray and ask God to protect us."

A man in a silver sharkskin suit stood from the front row. He smoothed his black silk tie and cracked his neck. The guards didn't stop him. Alana studied the man. Handsome, with wavy black hair and dark eyes. A sharp jaw and smooth skin. Built like a swimmer. He calmly walked up the four steps to the stage and stood toe to toe with Pastor Leo.

"You are not in charge here, Pastor!" He thumped Pastor Leo's chest. "I am in charge!"

The man's accent was a light Hispanic that mimicked her own. Either he tried to suppress it or, like Alana, he'd grown up around Spanish-speaking family and inherently picked up the accent.

Without warning, he drew his arm back and delivered a powerful punch to Leo's gut. The pastor doubled over in time to catch a hard knee to his jaw. Leo fell and rolled. His fingers clawed the carpet as if grasping for a breath with his hands.

Alana set her jaw and pressed her laced hands down on her head. A subconscious effort to keep herself in her seat. Whatever she did would only make things worse.

The man leaned over and ripped the microphone from Leo's head and placed it on himself. The receiver dangled from a flesh-colored wire, and he scooped it up and clipped it to his waist. He straightened. Smoothed his suit jacket and thrust his chin.

The screens beside the stage came to life with a video feed. Alana glanced over her shoulder. The red light on the camera glowed. They were live streaming. The camera framed the scene of frightened people dressed for the nativity production.

"We're sorry to interrupt your lovely Christmas program. It could not be avoided. My name is Tomás Muñoz. And I've ordered my men to hold the people of this church hostage until the American government pays for their release."

He turned to the masked man on his left. "Have these people sit right down here. Tie the pastor to that chair and bring another chair."

The men hurried to oblige.

Alana swallowed.

Gail wrapped a comforting arm around Rocco, and they sat on the first step with the rest of the cast. Boss tucked himself between Rocco's knees.

Never in her life had she been so thankful she was one of those crazy, overprotective moms who sat on the front row to support her child. Her son was within arm's reach.

"Rocco," she stage-whispered. "Rocco, come here."

He shook his head sharply, eyes wide.

She gave him the mom glare. "Now, Rocco. Bring Boss."

Rocco scooted down a step and paused. He glanced around and, seeing the men weren't paying attention, made a run for it. He managed two steps before Tomás grabbed Rocco by the back of his arm.

"Oh no you don't." He dragged Rocco up on stage.

Alana dove forward.

A gunman raised his rifle and pointed it at her chest. She halted and gritted her teeth. Flicked her gaze to the two men guarding the stage. Half a second and she could put a bullet in two of them, but she was outnumbered. They'd shoot her on the spot. In front of her son.

With clenched teeth, she forced herself to stay put.

A low rumble came from Boss. The edge of his lips curled to reveal razor sharp fangs. The dog turned. Snarled at Tomás. Barked and snapped his jaws in warning.

Tomás pulled a handgun out of his concealed holster and aimed at Boss.

"No!" Alana screamed. She shouldered past the guard. Sprinted up the steps and stood in front of the gun.

Tomás tilted his head and looked at her curiously.

She panted. Stared beyond the gun aimed at her stomach into the black eyes of Tomás.

Rocco clutched Boss and whispered something she couldn't hear.

Boss stopped barking but continued to emit a low growl.

Tomás smirked. "This is curious to me. You will protect the dog but not the boy?"

"You weren't aiming the gun at the boy."

He nodded and laughed. "Right, right. But this is a mongrel. You would risk your life for a mongrel?"

She had to think quick. If she let the guy know she was Rocco's mother, or how important Boss was to the world, they'd be in a whole different type of trouble.

"I didn't want the boy to see his dog shot right in front of him. No one needs to get hurt here."

Tomás stared at her for a full thirty seconds. Her body trembled.

"Maybe you're right." He spun the gun on his index finger and clicked it into his holster with the expertise of a movie cowboy. "We'll let the boy keep his dog. For now."

Her shoulders relaxed. Now all she had to do was figure out a way to convince Tomás to release these people.

A gunman stepped forward and handed a phone to Tomás. He answered in Spanish. Turned his back and murmured something to his men.

She took the split second to hold her index finger over her lips to tell Rocco to keep quiet. Her son nodded his understanding.

Tomás whirled and slammed his fist into her stomach. The force sent her breath out in a gush. She doubled over in time for a second blow to explode into her temple. She stumbled. Fell.

Blackness crept into her vision. She tried to blink it away, but her lids refused to rise.

"Mooooom!"

FIVE

Saturday, 6:57 P.M.

Wedged into the air duct, Christina held her breath and waited to hear a gunshot. From the ceiling, she'd watched the man break into the office and search the bathroom where Grey was hiding. She fully expected to hear gunfire, but so far she'd only heard the muffled sounds of fabric rustling. She checked her watch for a text or missed call from Alana. Nothing.

Quickly, she tapped out a group text to the Elite Guardians.

CHRISTINA

Gunmen at Hillspring Church. Hiding with Grey in PL's office. Status of Alana, Rocco, Boss unknown.

She verified her phone was on silent and tucked it into her back pocket. Stealth was their secret weapon. If the masked men didn't know about her and Grey, they wouldn't come after them. It gave her and Grey the upper hand.

She lowered herself from the ceiling and landed toe first

onto Pastor Leo's desk without a sound. Crouched. Gun beside her leg, she eyed the bathroom door.

Was that *smoke*?

She hopped down and closed the busted office door. For all the good it would do. The missing handle left a gaping hole. Anyone passing by would notice.

With careful placement of each step, she silently crossed the room to the bathroom. Her heart pounded, and she gripped her pistol tighter. Did she really want to see what was behind the door?

Before her fingers touched the doorknob, it flew open.

She blinked.

The masked man was facedown on the floor in a pool of water. His thick black hair appeared wet. And his clothes. Dark spots of wetness also covered Grey's shirt.

He held up a roll of duct tape. "A little help?"

"What—why is the toilet smoking?"

"Just a little science experiment," Grey said. "Let's get him tied up before we have any more visitors."

Christina caught the tape from Grey. She brought the man's arms up behind his back and worked to bind them. "Okay, but why is he wet?"

"It's toilet water from—"

"Ew! Say no more."

She rolled the man over onto his back and fingered the golden dragon embroidered on his neck gaiter.

Grey leaned over. "Looks familiar."

"It's the emblem for the militia group in Honduras. The one the American government refused to supply with weapons."

"Oh, that's right." Grey's brow furrowed. "You think they're here for Boss? He was front-page news after taking down The Scavenger. The entire world knows his special skill set makes him a high-value target."

"I don't know, but we can't wait to find out. If Boss is in

danger, Rocco might be too." She checked her watch. "I texted Alana and the Elite Guardians, but they haven't replied."

"Did the text go through?"

"Hmm." She stared at her phone. "Actually, no. The text says 'Undeliverable.'"

Grey checked his phone. "No signal here either. They probably jammed the cell signal. Check him for a phone or radio."

She patted the man down, pulling items out as she went. "Pocket knife. 9mm. Heavy-duty zip ties. Coulda used those a few minutes ago. But no phone or radio."

Grey took the items and tucked the pistol in his waistband. He dropped the rest into his chair bag. "There's a good chance he didn't let anyone else know about us, so we've got the element of surprise...for now."

"Let's secure him here and check Pastor Leo's phone and computer."

Grey handed her a necktie from the stash behind the door.

The assailant was still out cold. She used the tie as a gag and secured it with duct tape. Pulling him by the ankles, she dragged him into the shower and propped him up. Grey rummaged in the supply closet.

"What are you doing?"

He held up a can of hairspray and a lighter. "These might come in handy."

She shook her head. Grey knew more about improvised weapons than anyone she'd ever met. "Part of your Air Force Special Ops training?"

"Nope. Sixth grade physical science."

"Okay. You owe me a story later," she said. "Can you check the landline while I barricade the shower door?"

"Yup." Grey carried the rifle on his lap and rolled to the phone. "Nothing."

She wedged one of the wingback chairs under the shower

door handle and closed the bathroom door. "Check his computer."

"Password protected." He typed on the keyboard and clicked the mouse. "Locked down to guests. I have a feeling it wouldn't work anyway. These guys came prepared."

Christina chewed her lower lip. "First things first. Let's get our boys. We can assess and make a plan from there."

Grey nodded, but she saw concern in his eyes.

They were heading into a mission blind.

SIX

Alana's eyes fluttered open. She winced at the searing pain pulsating through her head and blinked several times. Her stomach churned with nausea, and she swallowed hard, willing the queasiness to subside. She took a few shallow breaths, trying to gain her bearings, and forced herself to focus on her surroundings.

From her angle on the floor, she could see the fancy brown dress shoes of Tomás. Made from some type of animal skin, no doubt. Alligator? Snake? Ostrich? For all she knew they were dragon skin.

Dragons.

The emblem on the men's neck gaiters told Alana they belonged to a paramilitary group once funded by the United States. A news article had reported on the group several months back. For the life of her, she couldn't remember their name, but recalled the group had attempted an unsanctioned military coup. As a result, America pulled the plug on the financial support.

The real question was, what did this group want with a church full of hostages?

She rolled her head to see the video wall behind Tomás. The nativity sky disappeared. A black screen displayed bold white numbers.

A clock?

No. Not a clock. A timer set for sixty minutes.

The two screens beside the stage centered on Tomás. She focused on his words.

"And I will kill one hostage every hour until the money is deposited into the account."

Alana's stomach sank even as her pulse kicked up.

The camera angle transitioned to pan the sanctuary. Hundreds of people in the seats, hands laced on top of their heads. Gunmen milled around, watching the congregation. How could Tomás take over a church with so few men?

There had to be more somewhere.

"We want the world to know that the United States of America cannot be trusted. They reneged on their agreement because they do not care about the people of Honduras. And they do not care about their *own* citizens. I will prove it to you."

Tomás gestured to the people on the steps. "We will start with these ten individuals."

The camera panned across each terrified face. Alana saw Rocco, and her skin flushed hot. Her son, her baby boy. She'd brought him here to give him a better life. Get him out of L.A. and into better schools. Even turned down the job with the state police and took the job with the Elite Guardians Agency to provide security to those who needed it most. But she couldn't even protect her own son.

Tears welled and threatened to spill over. She fought the urge to run to him.

The camera shifted back to Tomás. He took slow, deliberate

steps until he reached the last person on the stage and turned on his heel.

"Do you see these people? What are they worth to the American government?" He touched the head of the last man on the stage step. "One million?"

"Two million?" Touched the next head.

"Five million?" Touched the third head.

He was insane if he thought America would pay. The Department of Justice would not negotiate with terrorists. Period.

"One hundred million. That is what it will cost. But I am a reasonable man," he crooned. "As a show of good faith, I will release all but one hundred hostages."

Alana's heart leaped. She had to get to Rocco and Boss and make sure they were among the hostages released. Even if she had to take their place.

Tomás stopped in front of Rocco and squatted behind him. "So, I ask you, is the life of this boy worth one hundred million dollars?" He ruffled Rocco's hair and grinned into the camera.

It took every ounce of discipline she possessed not to come unglued but to stand down. Tomás walked to her and nudged her with his fancy shoe.

"Get up," he growled. "It's your lucky day. You get to leave and won't have to watch the dog die. Or the boy."

She drew herself into a sitting position. Rubbed her sore head. "I'll stay. Let the boy go."

Tomás snatched her arm and yanked her to her feet.

"You do not make the rules! I make the rules! I say who lives and who dies!" Spittle flew from his mouth and clung to his lips. He jerked her up. Hauled her to the steps and dragged her to the front row. Red-faced and eyes blazing, he shoved her into the seat.

Alana didn't speak.

"Now, when it's his turn, you'll watch the boy die." He cracked his neck and marched back to the stage. "Get those people out of here! Then rig the doors. If anyone tries to leave, the building will explode."

SEVEN

Never had Grey wanted his legs to work more than right now.

Stationed in the hall on lookout, he was forced to watch while Christina cleared each office and Sunday school room they passed. If only the experimental surgery had worked. He could have been her protector, the one shielding *her* from danger. Instead, he was helpless, forced to rely on her strength and training.

Stop it.

The still, small voice rippled through his body.

Heat flushed his head and radiated down his neck. Those demeaning thoughts were not of God, and Grey knew better than to let the enemy run wild inside his head. He wasn't a hindrance. Or a burden. No. He was Christina's battle buddy, and she relied on him as the first line of defense.

Christina exited the classroom and gently closed the door. "All clear in there."

They kept their voices low and moved with caution, taking

34

the long way to the stage doors where they'd left Rocco and Boss.

"It's a good sign we haven't found any one...alive or dead," Grey whispered.

"They must be holding everyone hostage in the sanctuary."

"I'm all turned around. Aren't we heading there now?"

"We go right at the intersection and clear the cry room."

"Cry room?"

She cast a glance that told him he should know this. "It's a soundproof room where mothers can take their crying babies and still have a view of the sanctuary through the one-way glass."

"Oh, yeah. They call it the mother's chapel at my old church." At least, that's what he thought the room was used for. He didn't exactly have his finger on the pulse of all things parenting. Of course...that could change.

Christina pointed. "It's right up here. I'll check it, then we cross the atrium with the main doors to the sanctuary."

"Is that a good idea? It will be heavily guarded."

"We can cut through—"

They froze. Voices ahead carried down the halls.

"Hide!" Grey urged. "I'll pretend I'm lost."

Christina dashed ahead and slipped inside the cry room as two black-clad gunmen rounded the corner.

They saw him. Immediately raised their rifles and ran forward, shouting in Spanish. He recognized them—the taller guy had called the shorter one Hector earlier.

"Whoa, whoa!" Grey threw his hands up in surrender. "*¡No hablo español!*"

"What are you doing?" Hector said in thickly accented English. "You must be in the church with others."

"I was using the bathroom." He dropped his hands and gestured to his wheelchair. "Takes a bit longer for me these days."

"We check bathrooms." Hector moved closer, pressing the barrel of the rifle into Grey's chest.

Bad move.

Grey grabbed the rifle barrel and thrust it upward. It slammed into Hector's face with a sickening crunch. The man's hands flew to cover his bloody nose.

Grey yanked the rifle forward. The strap caught on Hector's shoulder and pulled him off his feet. He stumbled, then fell into Grey's lap. Quickly, Grey wrapped his arm around Hector's neck and locked him into a sleeper hold. He squeezed. The man squirmed and kicked his boots at the ground, then stilled.

The second guard continued to shout in Spanish. He sighted down his rifle but didn't fire. With Hector blocking Grey, the guard refused to take a shot. But he should have been quieter. Over his own racket, he didn't hear Christina sneak up behind him. Weapon drawn.

She squared her stance. "Don't move."

He whirled.

She caught his rifle with her right hand and slammed her gun hand into his jaw. The man's knees buckled, and he crumpled to the floor.

Grey's eyebrows shot up. "K-O."

Christina winced and shook out her hand. "Yeah, but it hurt like crazy."

"I'll kiss it later," he said. "We can't stay here. Let's secure them in the cry room."

Grey left Hector draped over his wheelchair and wheeled him into the room. There, he dumped him on the floor and helped Christina secure his hands and feet with the duct tape.

"This guy won't be able to breathe through his nose, so don't bother gagging him. The room is soundproof anyway, right?"

"Right." Christina searched his pockets. "Man, don't these guys believe in comms? No radio."

She handed Grey their pistols.

He removed the clips and cleared the chambers while Christina bound the second man's hands and feet. When he finished disarming the rifles, he turned to the wall-sized window with a view into the sanctuary.

Several black-clad men led the hostages out, nudging them with rifles and forcing them to keep their hands on their heads.

"Christina, look. He's releasing hostages through the side door."

She abandoned her search and moved beside him. "Not all of them. There's Rocco and Boss on the steps, and Alana's in the front row. They're not moving."

Grey's stomach lurched. Young Rocco sat with the rest of the actors huddled on the steps. Boss was tucked between the boy's small knees. His dog scanned the crowd. Probably searching for Grey, anxious to receive the attack command.

"This stress can't be good for Rocco's blood sugar," he said.

"Or Gail's pregnancy." Christina gestured to the pregnant woman beside Rocco. "Why doesn't Alana get Rocco and Boss out while she can?"

"I dunno," Grey said. "Isn't there a way we can hear what's going on in there?"

She found a knob on the wall near the door and a speaker clicked on.

A man in a silver suit stood centerstage and spoke to the crowd. "Don't bother trying to infiltrate the building. The entrances and exits are armed with chain explosives. If even one door is breached..." The man made a fist and opened it. "Boom."

Grey's teeth clenched. The last few hostages filed out, and the door closed behind them. Two men knelt by the doors and wrapped wires around the handles. One of the men connected the wires to a green rectangle.

"They're rigging the doors with land mines," Christina breathed.

"Well, that'll make things a little easier."

Christina folded her arms and raised a brow. "How exactly?"

"How many exits does the sanctuary have?"

"Five double-wide doors plus two doors accessible from backstage."

"Not including backstage, I can see four of the exit doors from here. All of them rigged. All of them guarded with a single guard."

Christina was nodding. "They're trapped inside too. Which means at least one backstage door—"

"Is accessible," he finished. "They'd have at least one way to escape."

"Now then," the man on stage boomed. "It is time to select our first victim."

Grey's blood chilled as he watched the man gesture to the line of hostages on the pulpit steps. Rocco hid his face in Boss's fur.

Two gunmen stepped forward. One grabbed the first man in line by the arm.

"That's Alana's friend, Aaron Rhodes," Christina whispered.

Aaron wrenched himself away. The second gunman plunged the butt of his rifle into Aaron's stomach. He doubled over, and the men dragged him to the empty chair next to Pastor Leo at centerstage. They bound Aaron's hands in front of him. Zip-tied his ankles to the chair.

"Start the timer," the man boomed.

Behind the stage, the clock on the LED video wall began a countdown from sixty minutes.

The terrorist stared at his left palm and twisted his wedding ring.

"You have one hour to comply with our demands," he said, eyes fixed on his ring. "If you do not...this man dies."

CHRISTINA'S HEART QUAKED AS SHE CATALOGED THE SCENE INSIDE the sanctuary. Aaron had been first in the line of hostages on the steps. The very pregnant Gail Moore was next in line. Then...

Rocco.

Every cell in her body lit up like embers ready to set her skin ablaze. If the terrorist on the stage went in order, they only had two hours until Rocco was in that seat.

Two. Hours.

She had no idea why Alana hadn't grabbed Rocco and Boss and evacuated when she had the chance, but it was a moot point now. The doors were shut. The hostage-takers were settling in for the long haul. The remaining hostages filled a single section of seats, hands laced on their heads. Guards strolled up and down the aisles, watching closely.

Alana sat in the first seat on the front row, only a few feet away from Rocco and Boss. Like the others, her hands were on her head. Even if their phones worked, Alana couldn't call or text without the guards noticing.

As if the mere thought summoned it, Christina's smart watch and phone vibrated simultaneously. The unexpected jolt had her scrambling to answer the call. In her rush to dig her phone out of her pocket, she fumbled it. Grey caught it midair with lightning-quick reflexes and handed it to her.

She glanced at the caller ID and saw the name. Haley Rothwell. Her best friend and fellow Elite Guardian in Columbia, South Carolina. Grey motioned for her to put the call on speaker. She punched the button and held the phone between them.

"Haley, it's Christina and Grey."

"Oh, thank you, Lord," Haley said in her slight Irish brogue. "We've been trying to reach one of you since we saw the takeover on the church broadcast. We kept getting a message saying all circuits were busy. Your text came in a few minutes ago, but we've all been calling nonstop. You'll have a million messages to sort, I'm afraid."

Which meant friends and family members watching the nativity pageant online had seen the hostage situation and immediately flooded the cell towers.

"We're safe," Christina said. "For now."

"Wait—they're broadcasting this live?" Grey asked.

"Aye. We had a watch party at Olivia and Wade's house. This guy on stage says he will kill one hostage every hour if he doesn't get a hundred million dollars."

"We heard the threat, but not the amount of ransom he's asking. That's insane," Christina said. "He'll never get it. The government doesn't negotiate with terrorists."

"The families might," Grey said.

"Yeah, listen. We've got the number of the agent in charge, William Blake. As you can imagine, the FBI Critical Incident Response Group is on site along with other first responders. And by the looks of it, you two might be the only ones on the inside with access to a phone. Call him."

Haley rattled off the number and Christina memorized it. "Got it."

"And Christina…we're praying for you all."

"Thanks. We'll update via text when we can."

Christina disconnected and dialed Agent Blake. The call wouldn't send. "Great. We're back to the overcrowded circuit."

"Keep trying. I'll text."

A groan came from one of the two men. Hector rolled his head and looked at her. Dried blood tinged his nostrils. His swollen eyes slitted open. He mumbled rapid-fire Spanish.

"Hey, quiet," Christina said. "I'm on the phone."

Grey ripped a piece of duct tape from the roll. "It won't be easy to breathe, but if you can't keep quiet, I'll have to cover your mouth."

Hector shook his head and pressed his lips together. Grey

left the tape stuck to the arm of the rocking chair. A warning to Hector.

"The call is connecting," Christina said.

"This is Blake. Who am I speaking with?" The agent had a gruff voice and his tone sounded annoyed.

"Christina Sherman and Grey Parker." She made eye contact with Grey, and he gave her a wan smile. "We're—"

"We know who you are," Blake said bluntly. "We've pulled your files. Where are you? How are you able to make this call?"

"Sir, we are currently in the cry room inside the church. Our phones haven't been working."

"Yeah, yeah. We're working on clearing the airways. How did you escape?"

"We weren't in the sanctuary when they took over," Christina said. "We were able to evade the gunmen we encountered, sir."

"I need you to lay low. Let our hostage negotiator work the situation. We'll get the suspect to release the rest of the hostages."

"That could take hours," Grey said. "You expect us to what? Sit here on our hands while you talk to this psycho?"

"That's exactly what I expect, Captain Parker."

Grey shook his head, eyes ablaze. "No way. Our nephew is one of the hostages. Not only that but he's with—"

"We know about the dog, Parker. He's a high-value target, which is another reason we are ordering you to stand down. You have emotional attachments which may cloud your judgment. We can't have you interfering and making things worse."

"Agent Blake, you have two capable soldiers on the inside," Christina said. Her muscles crackled with energy. "We've already captured and incapacitated three guards undetected and without loss of life. The timer is ticking down. We were trained for missions like this. Let us help before that man kills an innocent man live on camera for the world to see."

"Gimme a sec," Blake said. He muffled the phone and spoke in hushed tones Christina couldn't decipher.

He was running it by the team. She prayed they'd see the value in having their expertise on hand. But the FBI had their protocol. Systems to follow. And Christina and Grey weren't exactly prepared with comms and Kevlar. As far as the FBI was concerned, they were two more civilian lives on the line.

But they weren't ordinary civilians. They were retired special ops. Grey still had a Defense Department contract. Agent Blake couldn't have asked for better assets on the inside. She'd rather work with law enforcement on this, but she wasn't about to sit by and let innocent people die. Not if she could help it.

A slight scratching noise came through the phone. "Okay, here's the deal. You've got Top Secret security clearance, so I can read you in. What I'm about to tell you is highly classified, do you understand?"

"Yes, sir," they said in unison.

"The man on stage is Tomás Muñoz. Former CIA counterintelligence officer. He worked in Honduras with a militia group doing the usual—training their military while covertly collecting intel. His performance was...mediocre at best. Other assets confirmed his drinking and anger issues were getting out of hand, so we exfiltrated him. Brought him back to Virginia so he could be with his family. After a few months, he was in jail for spousal abuse. He skipped bail, returned to Honduras, and got lost in the jungle. This is the first we've heard of him in six months."

"Why *this* church?" Christina asked.

"We're working on that. You may be of some help if you can get past the gunmen and remain undetected."

Grey smirked. "Hasn't been a problem so far."

"We're interviewing the released hostages as best we can, but with so many…" He sighed. "Well, you can imagine how long it's taking. They're reporting explosives and thirty to forty armed gunmen. Does that check?"

"So far," Christina said.

"As for explosives, looks like they've daisy-chained MON-50 antipersonnel mines to all exit doors," Grey said.

Christina smiled. *I knew it*, she mouthed.

"Yep, the bomb expert caught a glimpse from the live stream. Those are the Russian version of Claymore mines."

"Exactly. They could have seismic sensors and be triggered by movement or remotely by hand," Grey said.

"Or both," Christina added.

"We knew they wouldn't risk using radio-controlled detonators with so many cell signals in one place," Blake said. "Know how to neutralize the mines?"

"Of course." Grey made a *duh* face at Christina, and she smiled despite herself.

"Good. Get to the room they call Wilson's Chapel. It's the south—"

"We know where it is," Christina said. "It was the original sanctuary, but now it's used as a fellowship banquet hall. We did a complete security check and walkthrough before the event. We know our way around."

"Fine. Make it there undetected and keep the area clear. Disarm the unit on the door—if there is one. The FBI SWAT team is on standby and will infiltrate from there."

Christina glanced at the countdown timer on the screen. "We only have forty-three minutes before he kills the first hostage."

"I can see that. Just…" He exhaled audibly. "Can you do this or not?"

Christina looked at Grey. He gave her a thumbs-up.

"You can count on us," she said.

EIGHT

After a few more directions from Agent Blake, Christina disconnected the call and drew in a deep breath. There was a lot riding on reaching Wilson's Chapel. More than just Grey's life and her own if they were caught. Rocco's, Boss's, and Alana's, too.

Absently, she twisted her engagement ring.

Would they ever make it to the altar?

She was excited to marry Grey, but she hadn't pushed it. He'd said he wanted to stand beside her on her wedding day, but so far, the surgery to help him regain the ability to walk hadn't worked. She knew how much it meant to him, so each time anyone brought up their wedding, she changed the subject. The last thing Grey needed was more pressure to have his surgery work.

Yep, she wanted to be his wife and battle buddy for life. But she was willing to wait and give Grey time. Which might be soon, since he'd brought the subject up earlier.

"Hey, what's with the thousand-yard stare?" Grey asked.

She smiled. "Just thinking, Captain."

"Really? Well, tell me later so I have something to look forward to—after we stop that maniac."

"You're right. Let's go save our family." She leaned in to kiss him.

"¡Oye! ¡Déjame ir!"

They froze.

Hector killed the moment with his plea to be released. He kicked and squirmed but couldn't escape his binds.

She lasered an angry stare at the man. "Don't make me get the tape."

Hector quieted.

"We better get moving," Grey said. "Clock's ticking."

"One more thing before we go," she said.

She pulled Hector's neck gaiter up and bunched it over his eyes. Secured it with a small bit of duct tape to hold it in place, then did the same for the other man.

"They should be good for a while," she said. "Let's move."

The plan was to continue their original route leading to the atrium. If they moved with stealth, they could get to the south doors before the timer ran out. And if they encountered any gunmen along the way…well, they'd improvise.

She held the door open for Grey and slipped out behind him.

They hurried around the corner and paused, surveying the atrium. The vast space was eerily quiet. She didn't see or hear anyone, but she didn't like this one bit. Too many wide-open spaces.

She gestured to Grey, indicating they should zigzag their way around, pausing to take cover where possible.

Grey nodded and pointed to the fifty-foot Christmas tree illuminated in the center of the room.

Christina held her position by the wall and covered Grey while he crossed the open walkway.

He slid his chair to a stop behind the tree.

Two guards appeared and headed right for her.

PERFECT. HERE HE WAS, HIDING LIKE A GIFT UNDER THE TREE while a couple goons advanced on his fiancée. And sure, she could take care of herself, but...

Nope. Not going there. She loved him and they were partners.

For life.

Which would not end today.

Grey peeked around the Christmas tree. The two gunmen chatted in Spanish. They hadn't noticed them yet.

Christina ducked into the hallway and pressed her back against the wall, out of their line of sight. Great, now his fiancée was on the other side of the room, and here he was, still hiding behind a tree.

No way.

He grabbed the nearest basketball-sized ornament and hefted it off the tree. Surprisingly, the sparkling red orb was made of glass. Good thing Hillspring was a forgiving church. He raised the ornament over his head like when he passed the ball on his wheelchair basketball team. With all his strength, he chucked it across the room. The ornament hit the ground and shattered.

Both gunmen brought their rifles up and ran toward the sound. Grey maneuvered his chair around the tree, out of sight. He stole a glance at Christina. She was running toward him with a—what? A fire extinguisher?

She jogged up and lightly tossed the extinguisher. He caught it and shook his head. The woman never stopped surprising him.

The gunmen realized they'd been played and split up to

investigate. They rounded the tree on opposite sides, rifles at the ready. Grey prayed the men wouldn't radio to anyone else. For some reason, none of them carried comms of any kind. Perhaps they didn't want to risk their communications being picked up by law enforcement.

Christina moved behind Grey, positioning herself back-to-back with him. He didn't bother pulling his gun. One gunshot blast and everyone in the entire church would hear. Their cover would be blown, and the rest of the gunmen would be on them. Grey wasn't sure what the men would do if they thought they were under attack. They could start shooting hostages right in their seats or detonate the explosives.

No, flying under the radar was imperative.

He removed the metal safety pin with a soft *tink* of metal on metal. The first man rounded the tree and saw Grey. A look of shock flashed behind his eyes. Grey aimed the nozzle and depressed the handle. A stream of foam whooshed out and engulfed the man. The pressure of the release blew Grey's wheelchair backward and into Christina. She grunted but held firm.

The gunman dropped his rifle and frantically wiped his eyes with both hands. Grey thrust his chair forward, closing the distance. The man's eyes snapped open, two dark circles in a face of white foam. Grey brought the extinguisher up, but the man caught it and tried to wrestle it away.

Grey yanked the extinguisher to his chest. The gunman, still holding tightly, jerked forward with it. Grey slammed his knuckles into the man's throat and threw an elbow to his ribs.

The gunman released his hold on the fire extinguisher. Eyes bulging, he clutched at his neck with both hands. A high-pitched wheeze escaped.

Grey drove the bottom of the fire extinguisher into the guy's knee. He crumpled with a cry of pain. Balled up, he rolled on the floor in a puddle of agony and white foam.

Drawing his pistol, Grey aimed it at the man. Stole a quick glance at Christina. She was behind the second gunman, working quickly to secure his hands with a zip tie.

Yep, she amazed him all right.

Without a word, she forced her captive to kneel in front of Grey. She moved quickly, securing the hands of the foam-covered gunman. Removed their rifles and handed them to Grey. A quick search turned up a few more zip ties.

Grey tore off two strips of duct tape, and Christina secured it over their mouths. They marched the men to the cry room and forced them to sit in the rocking chairs. He tied them to the chairs while Christina verified the other men were still secure.

Before leaving, Grey glanced at the timer on the screen. It seemed like it was counting down in double time.

Seventeen minutes and forty-four seconds remaining.

NINE

Alana worked her jaw muscle and stared at the countdown timer.

Seventeen minutes left.

Would Tomás really kill the hostage when the clock hit zero? He wouldn't dare do such a thing on a live broadcast. Or would he? Could she stall? Maybe, maybe not. But she could try.

With her hands still on her head, she jumped out of her seat.

The gunmen swarmed.

"Sit down! Back in your seat!" they shouted in Spanish.

She stepped closer to Rocco and stared at Tomás.

"We've had our hands over our heads this whole time. Many of these people are elderly and it's too much. They can't keep this up. Please. Please let us put our hands down," she pleaded in Spanish.

Tomás held his hands behind his back. He stared at her. Impassive.

Movement in her peripheral vision caused her to turn. A masked man came at her with the butt of his rifle. Instinctively,

49

she sidestepped and grabbed the man's hand and wrenched it sideways. Hard, but careful not to break any bones. The man dropped to his knees and howled in pain.

It'd happened before she'd fully processed what she was doing. Second nature from years of studying martial arts katas. Dumb move. Now Tomás had a glimpse of her hand-to-hand combat skills and knew she wasn't an average citizen.

A hairy arm caught her from behind. Looped around her neck in a headlock. The man clasped his hands together and tightened his hold. She dug her nails in. Pried at his fingers. He was too strong.

She dropped her left elbow and pivoted her hips. Twisted to face him and continued the rotation until her head ducked out of his arms. She stepped behind him, put her palm on his forehead, and pulled until he fell flat on his back.

Alana turned in time to see a fist launching at her head and barely leaned back in time to dodge the blow. A gush of wind passed over her face. She widened her stance, bounced on her back heel, and brought her hands up to block.

A deafening blast roared over the microphone.

She froze. Turned.

People screamed and cried, but Alana let the noise fade into static.

On the stage, Tomás held a smoking gun in his outstretched hand. The all-too-familiar metallic smell of gun powder drifted in the still air.

Aaron slumped in the chair. A dark red spot spread across his chest.

TEN

They hadn't moved fast enough.

Hot bile rose in the back of Christina's throat. The concussive gunshot blast had reverberated in the hallway outside the sanctuary and rocked her concentration. They couldn't see what had happened behind the doors, but the screams and cries said it all.

Tomás had killed the first hostage.

Christina flicked her wrist and checked her watch. "He was six minutes early."

Grey dipped his head toward the office door behind her. "Let's call Blake."

They ducked inside a classroom and found a corner where they'd be out of sight if anyone came in. Christina opened her phone to dial Agent Blake and saw she'd missed several calls and texts. She ignored them for now and punched redial. The call connected immediately.

"Where have you been?" he barked. "I've been calling and texting—"

"We can't exactly have a chat when we're trying to fly under the radar here," she said. "We heard a gunshot, and hostages started screaming. What's going on?"

Blake sighed. "He killed the first hostage."

"He was early," Grey said. "What happened?"

"A woman we've identified as Alana Flores stood and asked if they could put their hands down. A gunman made the mistake of trying to force her back in her seat. There was a scuffle, and Tomás used the execution to break things up."

Christina glanced at Grey.

Worry lines creased his forehead, and he scowled at the phone. "No wonder the hostages were screaming. They must be terrified. What a senseless loss."

"Alana Flores is my sister. Sorta," Christina said. "Her son, Rocco, is the young boy on the steps with Boss."

Her stomach clenched at the idea of her young nephew seeing a murder. His innocence destroyed. The lives of the hostages would never be the same again. The dead man surely had family and friends in the crowd or watching the live stream.

"The boy had his back turned, head buried in the dog's neck. I don't think he saw anything."

Grey exhaled. "Small miracle."

Christina didn't respond.

If she dwelled on Rocco's trauma and the emotion it evoked, she'd lose focus. Right now, she had to shut it off. Compartmentalize. Get the job done without another loss of life.

Grey's hand brushed her fingertips. She peered up at him. The temporal vein near his eye bulged as he worked his jaw muscles. They were fighting the same battle. External...and internal.

"What are they doing now?" Christina asked.

"They're moving all the hostages and instructing them to sit on the floor in front of the stage." Blake said. "They've searched them. Confiscated their phones and any concealed weapons. Divided them into groups of fifteen to twenty."

"What's the point of moving them into groups on the floor?" Grey asked.

"We're guessing it's to let the hostages relax a little. Settle in. Looks like they've been allowed to lower their hands, but the men are still keeping a close eye on their movements."

Christina imagined the scene. Groups of people huddled together, filling the altar space normally used for prayer and worship. "Easier for the hostages to communicate, but difficult to stand up without the guards noticing."

"Exactly," Blake said. "But listen. The hostage negotiator isn't getting anywhere. The teams are preparing to, shall we say... take drastic measures to end this."

Christina didn't like the sound of that. If the SWAT team entered the building, things could turn even more violent. Tomás and his men could start killing hostages, or worse— detonate the mines that would destroy the church and everyone in it.

She couldn't let that happen.

"Hold them off a bit longer. We're heading to Wilson's Chapel now. Approaching with caution. How much time do we have?"

"He hasn't started the timer for the next hostage yet, but our teams are organizing now. Forty-five...sixty minutes tops."

Grey locked eyes with Christina in silent communication. She agreed. They needed all the time they could get.

"Buy us some time, Blake. We're doing the best we can," Grey said.

The agent groaned and exhaled. "Fine, I'll see what I can do. Just...make it happen."

Christina disconnected the call and set a silent timer on her watch. Forty-five minutes from now, it would vibrate on her wrist and let her know they were out of time.

Grey caught her hands and kissed her knuckles. "Let's pray."

They bowed their heads, and Christina silently asked God to give them time and favor.

When they finished, there was a shift in the atmosphere between them, and she knew what it was. They'd flipped the switch and stepped into an upgraded type of soldier mode. The kind that trusted in the Almighty to lead them.

"Okay, Wilson's Chapel isn't far. We turn left at the next intersection. The double doors have a thin vertical window above the door handles. It's not privacy glass, so anyone in the room could see us coming."

"Okay, two main doors. What about alternates?" Grey racked his gun to load a bullet into the chamber, then clicked it into his holster.

"Kitchen door. Access in the adjoining hall, but we'd have to go past the main doors and risk being seen. The two exterior doors inside the chapel will be the entrance point for SWAT. Any or all these doors could be rigged with explosives."

"Or not," Grey said. "Think we can peek through the windows on the doors before we breach? See what we're dealing with?"

"Yes, but stealth is still key," she said.

She started across the room, eager to get moving before they wasted any more time. The pressure to get to the south door had doubled. Not only was the FBI ready to break down the doors and come in guns blazing, but Tomás had proved he was willing to kill any hostage at any time. Chaos reigned when dealing with a hostage taker. Tomás wasn't thinking rationally. He was emotionally charged. And in her experience, that was never a good thing.

She poked her head outside the classroom and verified the hall was clear. Maybe the rest of the gunmen were inside the sanctuary, unable to leave the hostages. That would make things easier. They could move faster if they didn't have to secure any more roaming gunmen.

Grey maneuvered his chair to take the lead and stood guard while Christina checked the remaining two classrooms in the hall. When they came to the intersection, Christina gestured to the chapel doors. Pointed to the kitchen entrance.

Grey nodded his understanding.

Ducking low, she followed him down the short hallway to the double doors. At the end, he repositioned his chair. Back to the wall. She did the same on the opposite side.

Christina craned her neck and scanned the room. Three men sat along one wall. Hands tied behind their backs. Legs stretched out and secured with zip ties at the ankles. She immediately recognized the men as the church security guards she'd met during their briefing. Nolan Fry, Mike Harris, and Dean Tyler. All former law enforcement.

Except...where was Bruce?

The door directly ahead led to the commercial kitchen. From this angle, she couldn't see the two doors leading outside. That was the objective. Clear the room so the FBI could enter through the exterior doors and infiltrate the church.

She counted two masked men in the room. Both dressed in the same black clothes as the rest of the gunmen. Neck gaiters over their faces.

A short, stout man sat in a chair in front of the security guards. A pistol in his right hand rested on his meaty thigh. The second, taller gunman paced the room. His rifle slung over his shoulder.

They could do this. Wait until the taller gunman turned his back to walk the length of the room and rush them.

The pacing gunman whirled to face the window. She flattened against the wall. Slowed her breathing. Waited for the moment to move.

The gunman did his about-face, turning to walk away from the door.

She reached for the handle.

Grey's hand caught hers and she flinched. He pointed to a thin silver wire around the base of the door handle. Barely visible.

"We need a new plan," he mouthed.

ELEVEN

Alana stared at the sickening pool of blood seeping into the carpet not ten feet from the prop of baby Jesus's manger.

In her line of work, she'd seen shootings before, but it always left an ugly mark on her soul. And now, her son and all the people who'd witnessed the execution had the same mark. The program meant to bring hope and joy to people had now brought pain and terror.

The thought made her blood boil. The only thing stopping her from tearing Tomás limb from limb was the two men holding her at gun point. One step and the hostages would have another ugly mark to live with.

Her brave son stayed seated on the stage steps and buried his face in Boss's fur. The boy whispered small phrases to the dog as the men removed Aaron's body and disappeared backstage. She couldn't hear Rocco's words over the sound of her own heart hammering, but Boss heard. His ears pricked and twitched at Rocco's words.

She marveled at Boss. The years of training won out over the dog's instinct to attack the bad men. From the way his muscles quivered, she could tell he was eager to hear the attack word come from Rocco's lips. Thankfully Grey had known better than to teach the secret phrase to a child.

Of course, she wouldn't mind knowing it. With her concealed pistol and the bite pressure of the Belgian Malinois, she could take Tomás. Easy.

It was the rest of the gunmen she was worried about.

Boss panted and released a high-pitched whine.

"Shut the dog up before I do," Tomás yelled.

Rocco flinched and wrapped an arm around Boss.

Tomás marched across the stage and waved his gun in her face. "It's your fault that man is dead, mija. You made me kill him early."

"You didn't have to kill him at all." She stared into his black eyes and watched the red creep up his neck.

His hand came up and slapped her across the face. Pain radiated from her jaw. She could've blocked him, but it would only enrage him further.

He got in her face. "You should be ashamed of yourself," he spat in Spanish. "You betray your Latina heritage!"

Typical machismo attitude. What she wouldn't give to give him a taste of his own medicine.

"You should learn to treat women with respect," she said, continuing their exchange in Spanish.

They stood nose to nose, and she smelled the all-too-familiar scent of tequila on his breath. His eyelids twitched. Oh, she'd triggered something, and the knot in her stomach said it wasn't a good thing.

A slow grin spread across his face, and Tomás dipped his head in a slight bow. "Ah, you may be right about that, mija. I should maybe...pick a man to fight with?"

He spun in his fancy shoes and smiled into the camera. "Did

you hear that, ladies and gentlemen?" He switched to English. His demeanor flipped from anger to almost jovial in a matter of seconds.

"This woman thinks I should treat women with respect. I suppose she means I should choose another man for my next example." He threw his head back and laughed. "How is that for your American views on feminism?"

He walked to the edge of the stage and made a show of looking at each hostage on the top step. Alana cringed when he paused in front of Gail. The woman cowered and hid her face under her shawl. Tomás strolled back and forth, making a show out of who he would choose. The air in the church stilled. Every breath held in suspense of who would be next.

Alana's pulse cantered when Tomás stopped in front of Rocco.

No. No. No. Not him. Not Rocco.

Tomás snatched a fistful of Rocco's thick black hair and yanked him to his feet.

"Mom!" Rocco's hands flew to his head and tried to pry Tomás's grip away as the man dragged him across the stage.

Alana's heart thrashed inside her chest. She lunged for Tomás. The guards grabbed her arms and held her back. She could get away, but she couldn't risk Rocco's life.

Boss whipped around and barked at Tomás.

"Boss, hold!" Rocco called.

Boss dropped his head and emitted a low growl. Body rigid and hackles raised, he glared at the man wrestling Rocco into the chair.

"Shhh...shhhh. Settle down." Tomás held a finger to his lips. "Your madre doesn't like the way I treat women, so..." He shrugged. "So, I choose a *man*."

He thumped Rocco on the chest. "Be proud. You're a man now. Hombre, right?"

"Please, please, Tomás. He's just a child," Alana pleaded in

Spanish. "Can't you show mercy on a child? Let him go. Take me instead. I'll go in his place."

He marched to her and stuck a finger in her chest. "This is your fault. You disrespect me. Now you watch your son die!"

"Please, no." Tears rolled down her cheeks. "He's just a boy."

Tomás lifted his chin.

"Take me instead," she whispered, continuing in Spanish. "I'll take his place."

"No, Mom." Rocco's words came out on a sob.

The whimper in Rocco's voice broke her. Her boy. He was everything to her here on earth. Only her relationship with God came before her son. She swallowed hard. The tears streaking his face sent rage coursing through her. Every muscle surged with adrenaline, flushed with fire.

She wasn't going to just sit here and watch him die.

Her fist landed hard into Tomás's mouth. Pain exploded in her knuckles. Then her ribs, as a gunman rammed the butt of a rifle into her side. It was worth it to see the blood trickle from the cut on Tomás's lip.

Tomás wiped the corner of his mouth with the back of his hand and looked at the red smear. He snorted. "Killing your son will be a Christmas gift to myself."

Sixty minutes appeared on the clock.

Tomás gestured to the guard, and the timer began counting down.

TWELVE

If not for Grey's quick thinking, this would all have been over. Christina's heart was still caught in her throat. She could've set off something as simple as a flash-bang grenade, or it could've been far worse. Either way, it had the potential to kill or at the very least, injure them severely. And if the explosion hadn't stopped them, the noise would have alerted the gunmen to finish the job.

The trigger was on the inside, so disarming it wasn't an option. At least, not yet.

Yes, time for a new plan.

Christina followed Grey around the corner to regroup out of earshot. "Now what?"

"We need to draw them out," he said. "Get their attention so at least one of them comes to check it out."

"Okay, but how?"

"Well..." He rocked his wheelchair back and forth, thinking. "We'll talk."

Christina's family, not to mention over a hundred hostages,

had their life on the line. There were explosives on every exit, and SWAT was ready to bust down the doors and accept the loss of life in order to end the standoff. Time was literally ticking down, and he wanted to *talk*?

"You want to talk? *Now*?"

"Okay, argue. Like, a fake argument outside the door. When the men hear us, one will come break it up while the other stays to guard the hostages."

She followed him back to Wilson's Chapel, not really sure they could *fake* an argument convincingly enough to draw attention. Grey paused before they reached the intersection. They were close to the doors but hidden from view if the gunmen inside the room peeked down the hall.

Grey whirled his wheelchair around to face her. "And another thing!"

His shout bounced off the walls. She flinched and shuffled back a few steps. After sneaking around for the last few hours whispering, his volume shattered the silence.

"What kind of woman doesn't have at least ten different Pinterest boards filled with wedding ideas?"

"Pinterest...what?" She blinked.

"I mean, I get down on one knee and propose—not exactly easy for a guy like me, by the way." He gestured to his wheelchair. "And it's five months later and you still haven't set a wedding date!"

"Me?" Her own volume rose to meet his. "*I* haven't set the wedding date? What about *you*? It's your family who has the wedding all planned out at their farm, but *you* haven't set a date!"

"I thought you wanted to get married at my parents'." He clutched the wheels of his chair and leaned forward. "You said they could handle *alllll* the details because you loved how the anniversary party turned out."

Her breaths sped up along with her pulse. What did he

think was supposed to happen? They'd set up the wedding tent, get all dressed up, and stand around waiting for him to show up?

"Frankly, I don't care *where* we get married, Grey. I just want to marry *you!*" Somehow the words came out fierce.

Grey narrowed his eyes. "Are you sure?"

"What...what is this?" She thought this a pretend argument, but...he didn't think she wanted to marry him?

"Admit it, Christina." His voice dropped low and he studied her face. "You were waiting to see if my surgery would work before you committed to life with me."

Christina's hand flew to her mouth. How could he think that? She didn't care about the wheelchair at all. Wheelchair or no wheelchair. Walking or no walking. It didn't matter because she loved Grey for the man he was. What had she done to make him think otherwise?

She dropped her hand and stepped toward him. Implored him with her eyes.

Footsteps thudded on the carpet behind her.

"Hands up! Hands up!" a heavily accented voice yelled.

WELL, THAT'D WORKED.

Sorta.

He hadn't meant to get quite so serious. But for now, mission Liberate the Chapel: Part One was a win. Grey held his gaze over Christina's shoulder. A masked man with his feet spread to shoulder-width apart gripped a pistol in both hands. Every one of these guys looked the same. Black pants. Black shirt. Black mask with a dragon embroidered near the bottom. Their physique was the only variable. This guy was short and stout. Built like a fireplug. It was the man he'd seen sitting in the chair, watching the security guards. The one he'd mentally dubbed "Stubby."

"Whoa! Whoa, man!" Grey said. He showed the stubby man his palms. "Don't shoot. We were just having a little, um... spirited fellowship, if you know what I mean."

Christina rolled her eyes and slowly raised her hands in surrender.

"What are you doing? You shouldn't be—"

"No, it's fine. We're about to leave," Grey said.

Christina took a step backward and shifted her eyes to one side in silent communication. He caught the gist of what she meant. She needed to know if the man was close enough for her to attack. He nodded ever so slightly.

Like some sort of superhero, Christina spun and shot her left leg out in a hook kick. The heel of her boot connected with Stubby's left knee, and he went down with a squawk. Stubby's gun hand wavered, but he didn't drop the weapon. He brought it back toward Christina and aimed.

Grey was there.

Head turned to look at Christina, Stubby left himself defenseless on the right side. Grey cupped his hand and slammed it against the side of Stubby's face. The pop to the ear did the job. It disoriented him long enough for Grey to catch his gun hand, but not before the hard metal thwacked Grey in the head.

The bump to his jaw rattled Grey's teeth, but he ignored the pain and grabbed Stubby's thick wrist. Pressed with his thumb and index finger on the pressure points and twisted. Hard. Heard the crunch of bone as Stubby's trigger finger snapped.

Stubby released the gun with a howl of pain.

Christina caught his hands and secured them behind his back. Grey tore off a strip of duct tape and tossed the roll to Christina. He slapped the tape over the man's mouth while Christina bound his ankles.

When she finished securing Stubby, she glanced up. "That was smooth. You okay?"

They went back to speaking softer. No telling how many gunmen still lurked in the endless hallways. They couldn't let that stop them from reaching the south doors.

Grey rubbed his sore jaw. "I'm good. Time's ticking. We'll have to move faster."

She nodded and grabbed Stubby by his ankles. She walked in a semicircle, dragging the writhing man around with her. "C'mon. Get the door. I'll haul him to the kitchen."

Grey pointed at her wrist. "Your watch is lighting up with a call. We need to let Blake know we're okay."

One of Stubby's legs dropped to the floor as she pulled her phone from her back pocket. She tossed it to him. "Make it quick."

He caught the phone between his palms and answered.

Blake was speaking before Grey even had the phone to his ear. "We're running short on time, guys. I need a sitrep."

Christina kept moving, pulling Stubby along the hallway leading to the kitchen door.

Grey cradled the phone on his shoulder so he could have both hands to push his wheelchair. "We're fine. We'll be at the south doors in less than five. Can't talk—"

"Wait," Blake said. "There was an incident in the sanctuary. The boy..." Blake paused and snapped his fingers.

A faint voice in the background said, "Rocco Flores."

Grey's blood ran cold. Please don't tell him something happened to Rocco. They were minutes from reinforcements and potentially putting an end to this. Don't tell him they were too late.

"I'm sorry to tell you this, but the boy, Rocco Flores. He's in the hot seat—"

"No—"

"—but he's fine. Handling it like a champ, actually," Blake

hurried to add. "Even managed to get the dog to belly crawl across the stage and sit beside the chair. That's one brave kid."

Grey envisioned the scene. The small-framed boy terrified and tied to the chair like the previous hostage. Rocco's nine-year-old legs probably didn't even touch the floor completely. If anything happened to Rocco, Boss might break behavior and attack. The whole scene could turn to chaos in seconds. They had to end this.

Now.

"How—" Grey's voice broke. "How much time?"

Blake hesitated then sighed. "Forty-six minutes."

THIRTEEN

Alana's heart beat a steady pounding rhythm in her chest. She darted her gaze from Tomás to Rocco and prayed he wouldn't do anything drastic before she could act. Behind her, the clock on the LED wall ticked down.

Forty-five minutes.

Her mind raced for a way out of the situation. One that didn't end in Tomás killing her and her son. If she could somehow get the gun away from Tomás...

Tomás called to one of the men holding his rifle on Alana. "Gilberto should have reported back by now. Go see what is taking him so long."

Without a word, the man disappeared backstage.

The backstage doors must be the only safe way in and out of the sanctuary. A glimmer of hope sparked inside Alana. There was a way out.

Because *of course* they had an exit strategy. Tomás wouldn't leave himself trapped without an escape plan.

Now Alana just had to figure it out...and use it to formulate her own plan of escape.

A bead of sweat trickled down her brow, and she caught it with her palm. She rubbed her hands on the front of the ridiculously overpriced jeans she'd purchased for the special night. Her big plan to have a proper family Christmas photo taken with Christina and Grey after the production was out the window. No one wanted a keepsake from this horrific night.

Assuming they survived it.

Tomás answered his cell phone and screamed, "Where is my money!"

The hostage negotiator again. All the communication with the negotiator was in Spanish. It forced the FBI to find a fluent translator and bought him more time while translations happened for the rest of the critical response team.

According to a conversation she'd overheard, money was trickling in from anonymous donors, but not at the rate he needed. Tomás might be a sociopathic terrorist, but he wasn't stupid. Time would run out long before he ran out of hostages. And there wasn't a chance in the world he would get to her son without going through her first.

Tomás paced the stage, phone pressed to his ear. He continued to scream, barking demands to the hostage negotiator. Blue veins bulged and crept up his neck from the edge of his collared shirt. He yanked his tie loose. Unbuttoned the first two buttons and ran his fingers around the collar. He was losing control of the situation, and it infuriated him.

"I don't care how you get my money," Tomás growled. "You get it to me, or I start killing hostages." He punched the screen with his index finger and shoved the phone into his breast pocket.

Boss whined and nuzzled his head into Rocco's lap. Her son remained motionless, head lolling. A blank, unfocused stare behind his droopy eyes.

From her purse on the front row, Rocco's phone blared out an alarm.

Rocco's *insulin* alarm.

The sound shot adrenaline through her, and she didn't think. She simply pushed past the gunman and made a beeline for her purse. The man caught her by the arm. With a quick jerk, she wrenched herself away. Spun and landed a front kick to his ribs. The man doubled over and coughed.

Tomás clutched a clump of her hair and jerked her backward. The back of her head exploded in pain. Teeth clenched, she ducked and twirled to face Tomás.

"Where do you think you're going?" He sneered.

Boss let out three harsh warning barks.

"Boss...st...st...stay." Rocco barely managed the words.

"The alarm on my phone," she panted. "His blood sugar is crashing. The stress, it's too much for him. He needs his emergency insulin."

The alarm continued to blare.

"Tomás, please. It's in my purse. Let me get it!"

He released his grip on her hair, pulled his gun from his waistband, and aimed at Rocco. "I can put the boy out of his misery right now."

"No!" Alana screeched and jumped in front of Rocco. Arms splayed as if they could shield her son from a bullet.

A low rumble came from Boss.

"Tomás, please," she pleaded. "Let me get his medicine."

A primal scream ripped their attention away. Gail clutched her stomach and doubled over. The shawl she'd used to cover her head fell to the floor.

"Are you okay?" Alana realized the stupidity of her question the moment it left her lips.

"Nooooo!" She wailed. Her entire body heaved with rapid breaths. "The baby's coming!"

FOURTEEN

Christina tamped down her fury and funneled all her emotions into their mission. Clearing Wilson's Chapel. Disarming the door. Saving her family and the innocent people of Hillspring Church. And she might have taken a little bit of her frustration out on the gunman who's head she'd accidentally banged on the door while dragging him into the kitchen. She hadn't done it intentionally. But she hadn't exactly been careful either.

Her pulse pounded with a sense of urgency. Time ticked away, and with it, Rocco's life. And if she knew anything about Alana, her life was on the line too. No way could Alana stand by and let Tomás shoot her son. No, Alana would die first. Christina knew it because she would do the same.

She hauled the captured gunman deeper into the commercial-grade kitchen behind the chapel and dropped his feet onto the tile floor. The second gunman was still in the chapel with the security team held hostage, and she headed to the door to check on him.

Before she took two steps, her prisoner rolled from his back to his side and squirmed like an inchworm. She caught him before he crashed into the stainless steel table filled with pots and pans.

Grey's eyes went wide, and he feigned brushing sweat from his forehead.

Close call.

Well, leaving this guy alone in the kitchen wouldn't work. He was clearly trying to notify the other gunman.

Out of the corner of her eye, Christina saw the metal door of a walk-in refrigerator. She grabbed the man by the ankles once again and dragged him with her. Pausing, she held his legs down with her boot to prevent him from rolling again, then opened the door.

A gush of cold mingled with the warm kitchen air and created a temporary fog. She waved it away and peered inside. Her breath caught in her chest. Boxes stacked waist high lined the walls of the refrigerator. In the middle of the floor lay the dead body of Bruce Martin, head of security. Wide vacant eyes stared sightlessly. Skin ashen.

Her stomach roiled.

She glanced at her captive. His black eyes bulged, and he shook his head violently. The duct tape on his mouth muffled his cries. He knew what she meant to do and didn't want to be trapped inside with Bruce's dead body. Christina couldn't blame him. But she was running out of options. And time.

She pulled the man into the cooler behind her. Dropped his legs and squatted by Bruce. She wanted to close his eyes. Adjust his body into a comfortable position. But this was a crime scene, and she was disturbing it enough by leaving the gunman in here.

"Sorry," she whispered to Bruce.

She closed the door, sealing them both inside.

Christina peeked through the kitchen door into the room

where the remaining gunman paced, rifle held on the security officers sitting against the wall.

She turned to Grey. He withdrew a bottle of drain opener from the cabinet under the sink and put it on the counter.

"I need some foil," he whispered.

She pulled the nearest drawers open as quietly as possible. "What are you doing?"

"The tripwire and flash-bangs gave me an idea."

Oh boy.

She found the foil in a drawer behind her and handed it to Grey. He filled a plastic bottle with a small amount of water and carefully tore a piece of foil from the roll. Working quickly, he put the foil inside the plastic bottle.

She watched with curiosity.

"Okay, this is pretty volatile," he whispered. "Once I mix the last ingredient, we'll have only a few seconds to get the lid on and toss the bottle at the gunman inside the room."

She had no idea what Grey had made, but he didn't give her time to question him. He poured drain opener into the bottle and quickly screwed on the cap.

He thrust it in her arms. "Go! Go!"

Christina cracked the kitchen door and saw the gunman had his back to her. She rolled the bottle across the room. It banged into the heel of his boot. The man turned and looked down. Furrowed his brow at the rapidly swelling bottle. A look of confusion on his face. He knelt to inspect it.

Whatever Grey had mixed in the plastic bottle reacted. As the gunman reached for the expanding bottle, it exploded. Bits of plastic and liquid showered his face and clothes. He howled and dropped his rifle. His hands flew to his face, frantically wiping his eyes with his shirt sleeve.

Christina bolted into the room and caught the man by his wrists. Wrenched his hands behind his back and used the zip ties in her back pocket to secure them. He squirmed, shouting in Spanish. Turned his head and rolled his shoulder to rub his face. The pungent odor of the drain opener clung to his clothes.

Grey snagged the man's rifle and cleared it to make it safe. "The chemicals were extremely hot. Good thing he had the face mask and long sleeves to protect his skin."

"He can cool down in the fridge with his friend," she said.

"I'll be glad to take him," Nolan said. "As soon as you untie us."

Grey used his multi-tool gadget to cut the binds of all three men.

Nolan stood and rubbed his wrists. "I'll take it from here."

"There's another gunman secured in the walk-in. So is Bruce." She hesitated and met Nolan's brown eyes. "I'm sorry. He's dead."

Nolan's chest rose and fell with a long, deep breath. The noticeable lump at his throat rolled and he nodded. He shoved the gunman forward, and the man stumbled the first few steps. "I'll detain them both in here. Don't want them near my friend."

Nolan accepted the rifle from Grey and leaned close to the man. Brow furrowed and teeth clenched. "The tables have turned, amigo."

Christina raced to the double doors inside the chapel and studied the tripwire. It stretched across the doorway to a flash-bang grenade mounted near the top of the door. If Grey hadn't stopped her from opening the door earlier, the explosion would have incapacitated them long enough for the gunmen in the room to capture or kill them.

Working double time, she carefully disentangled the tripwire and reset the primary safety pin. She blew out a breath.

"We've restrained six other gunmen," she said. "Mike, Dean? Can you collect them and hold them here?"

They agreed in unison.

Grey supplied both men with the pistols he'd collected and stashed in his bag. "Don't shoot if you can avoid it. We've got stealth on our side for now. You'll find one man in Pastor Leo's office. Four in the cry room," he said.

Christina's watch vibrated. The Forty-five-minute timer she'd set earlier. Now only a few minutes remained. "Call Blake and get the mine off that door. I'll get backstage. We're running out of time."

She rattled off the number, and Grey punched it into his phone but didn't connect the call yet.

"What's going on? Is there a bomb on a timer?" Mike asked.

"Not that we know of, but Tomás Muñoz, the man responsible for this, plans to kill my nephew."

The men mumbled their frustrations.

"Hang on." Grey rolled to a stop in front of her. "Listen, Agent, I'm gonna need you to come back safe. We've got a wedding to plan."

She couldn't stop the slow smile that spread over her face. She cupped Grey's face in her hands and kissed him. "You got it, Captain."

GREY HELD THE PHONE TO HIS EAR AND WATCHED CHRISTINA disappear through the doors of Wilson's Chapel. If he didn't need to neutralize the explosive device and let the SWAT team inside, he'd be by her side. Heading into danger *together*. His lips still tingled from her kiss, and he prayed her gorgeous smile wouldn't be the last one he ever saw.

For now, he had to focus on his task.

"Nolan, I think it's safer if you take that guy into the kitchen and wait there. If this thing goes off..."

Nolan nodded. "I was in the Army. I've had explosive Claymore training. You sure you don't need some help?"

Of course he could use some help, but he wouldn't risk another life. "I'm good."

"At least let me pray over you, man."

Nolan placed a large hand on Grey's shoulder and murmured a short but powerful prayer. When he finished, he patted Grey on the back. "Godspeed."

Grey swallowed hard. The prayer filled him with a sense of peace and determination he hadn't had before. He watched Nolan muscle the gunman out of the room and focused on the mine attached to the lower half of the doors.

The MON-50 was a green plastic rectangle with a slightly concave back. Unlike Christina, he couldn't read Russian, but he knew it read *toward enemy* like most of these mines. It was a joke among soldiers. And they often teased that other military-issued items like guns, tanks, and choppers all needed the same printed on them so soldiers would know which end to point at their enemies.

In the field, Grey wouldn't neutralize incendiary devices by hand. They used a slightly more destructive method. But he'd done it before in cases like this, where stealth was of the utmost importance. And always while wearing Kevlar and a combat helmet. This time he was going in dressed in spiritual armor instead.

He visually followed the wire trailing from the mine's blasting cap to a firing device they called a *clacker*. One squeeze and...

Catastrophic explosion.

Grey heaved a deep breath and removed the wire from the firing device. Both detonator cavities contained fuses. The first came out clean, and he paused before attempting the second. Adrenaline crackled through his veins and ignited a slight tremble in his hands. He took a few seconds to slow his breathing before attempting the second fuse.

With his index finger and thumb, he gently gripped the edge

of the fuse and lifted. It snagged. His heart stopped a full beat. The fuse settled back into the small hole and he tried again. This time it slid out smoothly.

"Thank you, Lord," he breathed.

The mine was disarmed, but still dangerous. Carefully, he unscrewed the mounting bracket and lowered the mine to his lap. He picked up his phone and dialed.

Blake answered almost instantly. "Parker?"

"Yeah, it's me." Grey sighed. "The south doors are clear, but it would be great if your bomb tech could do something with this landmine in my lap."

FIFTEEN

Saturday, 9:42 p.m.

Please, please let her not be making the biggest mistake of her life. Here she was, running into danger without backup. And if she got caught, it might trigger Tomás to kill Rocco on the spot. How could she live with herself if that happened? But her nephew was running out of time, and she wanted him out of that hot seat *now*.

Christina sprinted from Wilson's Chapel to the doors leading backstage. She rounded the corner and stopped dead in her tracks. A gunman pulled the door open and headed backstage, letting it close behind him. Well, at least she knew there wasn't a tripwire.

Before he could get too far, she ran to the door and rapped her knuckles on it. She ducked back and flattened her back to the wall. The man pushed the door open, and she caught it by the edge. Slammed it hard into his face. The door vibrated beneath her hands, and the gunman grunted. He staggered back, clutching his face. She caught the door and held it with her boot.

She pulled her pistol and aimed. "Don't move."

Two bloody hands shot up. Blood trickled from both nostrils.

"Hands behind your back."

He complied and she quickly worked his rifle off his shoulder and slipped it over her head. After using her last remaining zip tie to secure his hands, she patted him down. Found two more plastic zip ties in his pocket and a gun in his waistband.

Now to keep him quiet. She'd left the duct tape with Grey, so she improvised. Bunched up his neck gaiter around his mouth and used a zip tie to secure the gag behind his head. She marched him to the backstage bathroom. Her gut knotted when she remembered Bruce pointing it out during the security walkthrough.

One last pit stop for our more nervous guest speakers, he'd said. *But it's primarily meant as a changing room for our baptismal candidates.*

The baptismal. Yes, perfect!

Her training as a former Army sniper came alive. The oversized fiberglass pool was built into the sanctuary wall several feet over the church stage and had a window to allow church members to view the baptism from their seats. Basically, it was the perfect sniper nest. Too bad she didn't have her rifle.

Using the last zip tie, she looped it through the one on his hands and secured him to the drainpipe. It would hold him, at least for a little while.

Stepping back, she pointed her gun at his head. "You move, you die."

He winced and shook his head. If the zip ties didn't hold him, her threat might. She had no intention of killing a man unless absolutely necessary. But a little fear went a long way.

She switched off the light and closed the bathroom door, then did a quick search of the backstage area. She didn't find any more gunmen, but she found Aaron's body. The waxen expression told her he was dead, but she crouched and felt for a pulse anyway.

Nothing.

She slipped a robe off the clothing rack and covered Alana's friend. Senseless loss.

She spun on her heel and stalked away.

Five steps led up to the baptistry, and she took them two at a time. The pungent smell of chlorine wafted from the clear water in the baptismal. Filled and ready for the baptisms meant to happen after the pageant. Not tonight.

Christina inched across the narrow ledge that supported the handrail and extended around the outer edge of the pool. She halted beside the window and peeked around the curtain. From here she could see the commotion on stage.

Alana crouched beside Rocco and rubbed his chest. The boy's head drooped. Christina couldn't tell if his eyes were open. She didn't see blood or any obvious injury. Was he having a complication with his diabetes?

Boss had his head in Rocco's lap. As if he sensed Christina, the dog lifted his head and tilted it sideways. His dark eyes studied her.

She held up her palm, giving Boss the silent command to hold.

Alana looked at Boss, then followed his gaze to Christina. Her eyes widened with realization. She darted a glance at Tomás, then back to Christina.

Tomás had his gun pointed at Gail, screaming in Spanish. The pregnant woman clutched her stomach. Red-faced and chest heaving, she averted her eyes from Tomás.

It took Christina a moment to interpret what he was saying.

Christina's hand flew to her mouth.

Gail Moore was the abused ex-wife of Tomás. And, of course, she was in labor.

SIXTEEN

The LED wall clock ticked down. Two minutes remained. Christina mentally calculated the risks of moving in without more backup. Any minute, the SWAT team would breach the building, but things inside the sanctuary were deteriorating. Fast.

If Rocco had a diabetic emergency, every second counted. But rushing in could set Tomás off. Even if she reached Rocco in time, what about everyone else?

The faces of terrified hostages impressed themselves upon her heart. A long time ago she'd failed people like these. She couldn't let that happen again.

Tomás left Gail and took up his stance in front of Rocco.

"I want my money," he said to the camera, "or this boy dies in less than two minutes."

Alana was on her feet, blocking her son. "No! He's a sick boy! Leave him alone. Take me instead!"

Tomás gestured with his gun, and a guard stepped forward. Grabbed her by the elbow.

"Stop causing trouble or the boy dies now," Tomás said in Spanish.

The guard wrenched her arms behind her back and secured her wrists with a zip tie. He held her by the shoulder with one hand and pressed a gun into the small of her back. Alana shot Christina a pleading look.

Now.

Christina withdrew the flash-bang from her waistband and showed Alana. Gestured to the baptismal.

Alana lifted her chin in a slight nod. Her black eyes narrowed, but she stayed quiet, glaring now at Tomás despite the tears on her face.

Christina hoped she could be that brave if she and Grey ever had kids. She loved that man, and if she were honest, she was more than ready to marry him and start their own family.

Huh. Guess she was setting that date.

Boss hopped to all fours. Studied Christina with an inquisitive tilt of his head. Training would keep Boss in place. He wouldn't move until released. But if Tomás pulled the trigger...she wasn't so sure.

She pulled the metal safety pin on the flash-bang and gave Alana one final nod. Her sister's features hardened with acknowledgment.

Christina slipped out of the baptismal area. Drew her weapon.

The stage deck had two wings for performers to enter the set. Huge, thick curtains masked both entrances from the audience. She'd enter through the right. Emerge closest to Rocco and Alana. But with only one point five seconds before the grenade exploded, she'd have to book it.

She crept forward. Angled her body perpendicular to the pool of water. Then she tossed the flash-bang in a sweeping motion over her head and bolted.

The hook shot landed in the baptismal with a soft splash as it hit the water and sank. She'd barely made it around the corner and onto the stage when the grenade exploded with a muffled boom.

The blast sent water and debris skyward. Shattered the glass window. Water gushed from the missing window and poured onto the stage. The entire sanctuary erupted into chaos. A thunderous roar of running and screaming vibrated with Christina's thrumming pulse.

Over the shouting, she heard Boss barking his scary deep *I'm going to rip someone's arm off* tone.

Christina zeroed in on Tomás and sprinted through the water raining down around her.

"Boss, get 'em," Christina growled.

At the phrase, Boss lunged at the gunman holding Alana. His teeth sank into the fleshy part of the man's gun hand.

Alana wrenched herself away. Kicked the front of Rocco's chair and knocked him flat on his back as Tomás fired.

Christina barreled forward and hit Tomás in a high tackle worthy of a sanction from World Rugby. The collision snapped his head forward, then back as he ricocheted off Christina's shoulder. The base of his skull bashed against the floor. Christina landed on his chest.

The gun in his hand went off.

Christina cried out as heat seared her shoulder.

She rolled off and snatched his gun away. Panting, she scrambled to her feet. Tossed his gun to Alana, who caught it and pointed it at an unconscious Tomás.

The movement flashed a searing pain through her arm. She sucked air through her teeth.

Shoulder wound, maybe just flesh, but wow, it burned.

Alana's eyes darted between Christina and Tomás. "Christina, you're shot!"

She pressed her hand to her shoulder. "I'm fine, take care of Rocco."

Members of SWAT streamed into the sanctuary from backstage and took over the scene. In all the mayhem, several hostages managed to overtake the terrorists and subdue them. They surrendered without a fight.

"Call your dog off," said a man dressed in tactical body armor.

Boss snarled and tugged on the man's arm. He howled and shouted in pain.

"Boss, out," she said.

Boss released his grip and ran to Christina's side. Pressed his body into her leg. His tongue lolled out, but his focus remained on the writhing gunman.

"Good boy, Boss." Christina patted his side.

Boss followed as she staggered to the edge of the stage and plopped down beside Gail. Maybe it was the adrenaline letdown or maybe the gunshot wound, but her head swam from the movement.

"Gail, are you okay? How far apart are your contractions?"

"Don't worry about me. I've heard labor can last for hours." She balled up her shawl and pressed it to Christina's shoulder.

Christina grimaced. "Ouch."

"Sorry," she apologized. "Thank you for saving us. I don't know what would've happened if you hadn't—"

Christina followed Gail's eyes to Tomás. Officers had him on his feet. They dragged him off stage.

"I'm sorry I didn't get here sooner. Poor Aaron..."

Tears welled in Gail's eyes. "We were...we were just beginning to date."

She wanted to hug Gail, but with her throbbing shoulder, she didn't think she could. Instead, she touched Gail's hand still holding pressure on Christina's wound.

Gail swiped the tears from her face. "But he was so brave."

Brave. Christina searched the sanctuary for Grey but couldn't see him.

Please let him be okay.

Alana sat beside Christina. She held a drowsy Rocco tight against her chest. His dark eyelashes wet from tears. Eyes red-rimmed and swollen. The bullet from Tomás's gun had missed Rocco by inches. The poor kid had been through so much.

"How's he doing?" Christina asked.

"I gave him the emergency insulin. He'll be fine…physically." Alana wrapped an arm around Christina's good shoulder and pulled her close. "Thank you," she whispered.

"I'm so glad you're both alive. I…I thought I was going to lose you both…again." Christina swallowed the sudden sob threatening to escape.

Boss licked Rocco's cheek and neck, and the boy's eyes fluttered open. A smile spread across his face.

A tear slipped down Christina's cheek as the medics arrived.

HE COULDN'T FIND CHRISTINA.

The parking lot of Hillspring Church was bathed in the soft, amber glow of lampposts. Grey scanned the hordes of people talking, sobbing, or clinging to a loved one. So many people. And they all seemed to stand right in front of him, blocking his view and making it impossible to see over their heads from his wheelchair.

The buzz of noise roared in his ears. He strained. Stretched his neck. Searched each face for Christina. Alana. Rocco. Listened for their voices. Nothing.

Grey gritted his teeth in frustration. "Forget this."

He engaged the brakes on his wheelchair. Planted both feet on the asphalt. Inched to the edge of his seat. On wobbly legs, he slowly rose.

A furry tail swished near a dark SUV. The hairs on the back of his neck stood up.

Grey's legs collapsed, and he plopped back into his chair.

Boss.

People lost in their emotional trauma didn't notice him trying to make his way to his dog. They didn't offer the usual polite apology and step aside to make room for his wheelchair.

No problem. Grey kept his focus on the wagging tail and navigated the huddles of people as best he could.

Ten yards away, the dog turned. Through the throng of bystanders, he caught a full glimpse of the dog.

Grey clamped his hands on his wheels and halted. A thick pink tongue dangled in a happy pant. Gray-black fur mingled with a smooth tan coat.

It wasn't Boss.

A wave of nausea washed over him. *The gunshots.*

No...he wouldn't believe it. Someone would have told him. He threw his chair back in a wheelie and pivoted. Spun a one-eighty. Slammed the wheels back down on the asphalt with a clatter and thrust forward.

Less cordial this time, he shouted, "Coming through! Make a hole, please!"

The people took one look at him and scattered.

At the south doors, a uniformed officer stopped him from entering the church.

A lean man in jeans, a blue checkered button-down, and an FBI windbreaker stepped into the doorway. He had the gaunt cheeks and sunken eyes of an overworked, overstressed agent.

"Captain Parker, I'm Special Agent in Charge William Blake. Follow me. I'll take you to your family."

The uniformed officer stepped aside. Nodded an apology as Grey followed Blake into the church.

"Are they okay?" Grey asked.

"The medics are checking them out, but they'll be fine."

They navigated the church halls, this time taking a shorter route to the sanctuary. Grey was grateful Blake didn't try to engage in small talk. His nerves couldn't handle it, stretched so tight they might snap at any moment.

In the hall, they passed the pregnant woman Grey had met backstage earlier, Gail Moore. A paramedic pushed Gail's wheelchair, flanked by two FBI agents. She winced and clutched her stomach.

"Is Gail all right?" Grey asked.

"Ah, so you met Abigail Muñoz?"

"Abigail...Muñoz? As in—"

"Yep. Tomás targeted this church because they were instrumental in helping her escape her abusive husband. He had no idea she was pregnant."

"Wow." Grey couldn't fathom it. "Is the baby okay?"

"The stress sent her into early labor. But they'll get her to the hospital and take good care of her and the baby."

Blake led Grey into the sanctuary through a set of double doors propped open wide. A flurry of activity permeated the room. Agents and SWAT worked to disarm and remove the booby-trap mines attached to the doors. Tomás and his men sat cuffed and detained at gunpoint by SWAT officers.

Grey caught sight of Alana's dark hair. Pushed his way past Blake and made a beeline for Rocco. The small boy lay on a gurney, an IV protruding from his hand. Alana held the clear fluid bag over his head and moved with the paramedic.

"Alana! What's wrong? Rocco...is he...is he okay?"

"He'll be fine," Alana said, briskly moving past Grey to keep pace with the rolling bed. "Insulin crash. Go. Go check on Christina." She pointed with her head to the stage.

His eyes fell on Christina lying on the stage. Her long blonde hair spilled down the steps like a golden waterfall. Grey rushed to where Christina lay.

Boss was on his stomach beside her, his snout nuzzled tight into her neck. Tail flicking.

A paramedic knelt beside her and finished taping a bandage to Christina's shoulder. A red stain besmirched the clean white gauze.

"Christina," he breathed.

Boss lifted his head and whined.

Grey wanted to run to his fiancée. Drop to his knees by her side. Hold her and make sure she was safe. But the blasted stairs...

"Are you—"

"I'm fine," Christina said.

The paramedic helped her sit. Slipped a sling over Christina's head and tucked her arm inside.

"I'll give you a few minutes," the paramedic said, peeling off her gloves. "Then you get a special ride in my rig."

Christina winced. "Gee, thanks."

Boss wagged his whole body and licked Christina's face.

"Good boy, Boss. Yes, you're a good boy. But...move so I can stand up."

"Boss, here," Grey called.

Boss leaped from the stage into Grey's arms. He landed hard against Grey's chest.

"Ooof!" Grey said on a harsh exhale.

Boss swiped Grey's face with his giant tongue.

"Okay, okay..." Grey said, laughing.

"Hey, save some kisses for me," Christina said. She picked her way down each step, moving slowly. One foot at a time.

Grey commanded Boss to get down and the dog obliged.

"Are you okay? What happened?" Grey wanted to pepper her with a thousand questions. But mostly he wanted to hold her and know she was safe.

"I'm fine. Just a flesh wound," she said with a grin.

He smiled and shook his head. He'd told Christina the same thing when he'd been shot in the leg.

When she reached the last step, she fell into his lap with a slight grimace. Flung her arms around his neck and pressed her forehead to his cheek. He rolled backward, out of the harsh lights overhead.

"Christina, I…"

"Shut up and kiss me," she said.

He lifted his mouth and kissed his fiancée. A rush of heat spread throughout his chest. For one perfect moment the world became safe. Perfect.

"Ahem." A man cleared his throat.

Christina broke their kiss.

Grey held his eyes closed a beat. He huffed.

Pastor Leo stood with his hands in his pockets. Rocked back on his heels and studied his shoes.

"Hey, Pastor," Grey said. "You sure know how to throw a party."

The big man chuckled. "I'm sorry to interrupt your reunion. I won't keep you. I've got my own wife waiting outside." He hiked his thumb over his shoulder. "I wanted to thank you both for all your help. Special Agent Blake told me what you did, and I—I can't thank you enough."

"All part of the job," Christina said.

"I'm so sorry about your nephew. The trauma…" He paused and cleared his throat again.

Christina stood with a grimace. "I'm so very sorry about Aaron and Bruce. They were both great men."

Pastor Leo dropped his head and nodded. "We're all devastated by the loss."

Grey never knew what to say to comfort someone who'd lost a loved one. "Will you let their families know we're praying for them?"

"Of course. And Hillspring Church will do everything we

can to help each person deal with the trauma. I'll have counselors and therapists on call twenty-four seven for anyone who needs it."

Grey nodded. "I think that will go a long way to help."

Pastor Leo thrust his hand out. "Thank you again. And if there is anything I can do for you two...anything at all, please say the word."

SEVENTEEN

Christina thanked Pastor Leo for his kindness and watched him walk to Agent Blake. She was impressed the high-profile celebrity pastor thought about the needs of his congregation first. Like a true shepherd, he'd considered the future healing his members would require and planned. It showed his love for the people.

Maybe megachurches weren't so bad after all.

She wrapped her good arm around Grey's shoulder and slid onto his lap. Kissed him with passion that held months of longing and love.

They'd come so close to losing so much tonight. She wouldn't risk another second without Grey knowing how much she wanted to be his wife.

"I'm not sure how we got our wires crossed, but believe me, Grey Parker. I cannot wait to marry you."

"Same." Grey kissed the tip of her nose and tucked a lock of hair behind her ear. "But if you need more time, just know I'll wait as long as you need."

"As long as *I* need?" She drew back. A twinge of pain zipped across her shoulder. "I was waiting for *you* to set the date. I wasn't pushing because I...well, I thought it would put pressure on your recovery."

"How?"

"You said you couldn't wait to stand by my side and dance together on our wedding day."

The corner of his mouth turned up in a grin. "And since when has the wheelchair ever stopped me from doing what I want?"

He was right. The man could do more in a wheelchair than most people could do period. He played basketball, coached children with disabilities, helped Rocco with insane mathematical equations that were, frankly, too advanced for most adults, much less a nine-year-old.

She exhaled. "You're right, but why didn't you say something?"

He shrugged. "I thought...well...I thought you needed more time."

"More time?"

He rubbed the back of his neck. "Those walls you'd erected around your heart. I thought maybe you were still working on letting me in."

"Oh, Grey." She shook her head. "I trust you completely. What do you say we make a pact to always communicate instead of assuming."

"That's a great idea," he said. "Let's set a wedding date. Right here. Right now."

"Well..." She chewed her bottom lip. "Any ideas?"

He looked around. "We're in a church. There's a pastor right there."

"Oh yeah, that would go over well. I'd hate for our friends and family to kill us after we barely survived a hostage crisis."

"All I'm saying is, Mom and Ruby could have the wedding planned like that." He snapped his fingers.

She thought about it for a moment. "Lizzie and Charlie are getting married on Christmas Eve. How do you feel about a New Year's Eve wedding? We'll always have a huge anniversary party ending in fireworks each year."

"I love it," he said. "And I love you, Christina."

She studied his gray eyes. "I love you too, Grey."

He drew her in, careful of her injury. Kissed her strong. Deepened the kiss. Heat flushed her neck, and she slowly, reluctantly, dragged herself away.

"Oh boy, I sure hope we can get the wedding together quickly," she breathed.

"Let me get the ball rolling." Grey snapped his fingers. "Hey, Pastor Leo!"

Agent Blake and Pastor Leo froze and turned to look at Grey.

"Actually...there *is* something you can do for us!"

SILENT NIGHT SEIGE

KELLY UNDERWOOD

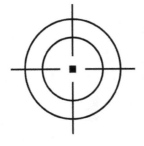

ONE

Dating a billionaire had its advantages. Laila Rabbinowitz whizzed by unending security lines and headed straight to the tarmac to board the private plane.

The second she stepped through the cabin door, she fell into Preston Whittaker's arms. She'd missed everything about this man, from his short dark hair to those chestnut-brown eyes. His high-profile power suit had been replaced with jeans and a long-sleeved gray Henley T-shirt, signifying the beginning of their vacation. "How has it been two weeks since I last saw you?" he murmured into her hair. His tight embrace melted the stress brought on by her job as a bodyguard. She'd just finished a tough assignment—one that had kept her away from her boyfriend for far too long.

"Apparently our jobs get in the way of our lives." She rested her hands on his chest. Two weeks? Try the last three months. Since they'd been seeing each other, the two had only managed a handful of dates filled with camera flashes and paparazzi stalkers. When Preston's life had been in danger, Laila had posed as his wife. They'd gone from pretending to be married to blocking off appointments on busy calendars to ensure they saw each other.

Preston let her go so he could grab her bags, and her skin tingled from the loss of his touch.

She collapsed into the plush leather seat while Preston chatted with the pilot. Traveling in luxury was something new to her. They had the main cabin to themselves. Two seats faced another pair across a table, and each seat came equipped with its own private screen with access to an unending list of movies and entertainment options. She explored the mini-fridge next to her, stocked with all kinds of drinks and snacks. This was definitely the way to travel.

"Laila, I'd like you to meet Phil. He was one of my dad's first pilots. Now he uses his fancy jet to transport dignitaries and other important people. He's nice enough to give us a lift today since he's heading to Colorado for the holidays."

Phil took off his ballcap and gave a dramatic bow. "At your service." The older man ducked into the cockpit.

Laila laughed. "Look at us. Glorified hitchhikers."

Preston shot her a look of mock disdain. "More like I just want a chance to ride on his souped-up jet. I figured you'd like Phil. The man is ex-Army, so we're in expert hands if we crash."

"Let's hope we don't," Laila said. "I think we're over our drama quota for a while."

Their relationship had started with Laila being Preston's bodyguard after his life was threatened. Talk about an intense start to dating. No wonder they seemed to be struggling lately, when life had fallen into a comfortable rhythm instead of throwing them into life-or-death situations.

He sank into the chair next to her and grabbed her hand. "I can't believe this is your first Christmas. Ever."

She shrugged. "With Hanukkah, I always felt like we were

just going through the motions. Even when my mom and I left Israel and moved to the States after the divorce, Christmas became just another day for us. We never got into the gifts and traditions."

"Well, we will have to change that." Preston ran his other hand through her hair, sending shivers down her spine. "I want this to be a Christmas you'll never forget. We have a few days to spend together before we head off to Lizzie and Charlie's Christmas Eve wedding. So I vote we start some of our own traditions."

His words communicated a future. But some days Laila wondered if life would calm down so their relationship had a chance to grow. Because stealing a few minutes here or there wasn't going to cut it long term. Both of their jobs demanded more time and attention than most professions and had them going in different directions ninety-nine percent of the time. They needed to work harder to keep that one percent from shrinking right before their eyes.

She took her eyes off Preston long enough to peek out the window. "So, Colorado? I'm glad you told me to bring a winter coat. I didn't even ask where we were going. All I heard was *get out of town early* and *no paparazzi*. I'm glad my last assignment ended. I need a break."

Preston sat back in his seat, and they buckled up for the takeoff. "I love how you jump on board and don't even know the destination. Since the wedding is in Montana, I figured we could spend a few days at my family's condo in Breckenridge. Don't worry, you don't have to ski."

Another perk of dating a billionaire. His family owned their own ski resort. "Normally I'd relish being outdoors, but skiing sounds cold. Wrapping up in a warm blanket and sitting by a roaring fire sounds divine. Do you have one of those giant fireplaces? That might be more my speed this week." She just wanted to kick back, relax, and reconnect with him.

He laughed. "I called ahead and made sure someone has a fire for us. I even donated some rocking chairs to make sure they have plenty. For the next few days, we are all about chilling in front of a fireplace with nothing scheduled. We both need some time to unwind." He grabbed her hand again and kissed it. "I'm so sorry we haven't seen much of each other lately."

Warmth filled her.

Oh, how she'd missed him.

But how were they ever going to make their relationship work when they lived such different lives? She'd thrown herself into her role as an Elite Guardian bodyguard, and once her assignment of protecting Preston had ended, she'd moved on to another assignment that had consumed all of her attention. Not that he had much time to spare. After the news of his family scandals had simmered down, he'd launched himself full force into his new role as the CEO of Whittaker Enterprises. Job pressures kept them on their toes, but she had to maintain strict focus when people's lives were on the line—which didn't always lend itself to checking on her boyfriend. While he'd had a front row seat to witnessing the intensity of being a bodyguard, she wasn't confident he understood the full magnitude of her role.

"I'll admit that I'm not content with us only catching a few dinners here and there. But what can we do?" Laila shrugged.

"You could quit your job, live like a princess, and fill out an application to be on the next *Real Housewives of Columbia, South Carolina*." His wide smile shot an arrow straight through her heart.

"Can you imagine? I'm bored just thinking about it." Laila would leave that kind of lifestyle to Preston's mother, Sophia, and his sister, Katrina. Between the two, they had enough drama to fill multiple seasons of a reality show. Although Laila's attitude toward Katrina had thawed slightly since the woman was going through an ugly divorce right now.

"You're right," he said, his brown eyes twinkling with

mischief. "I heard they're filming another *Die Hard* movie. That's more your starring role for sure. You can be the new female John McClane."

Their laughter filled the cabin until the speakers crackled to life. "Hi there, folks. I'm Captain Phil Brickell. Just wanted to let you know that we are cleared for takeoff."

Laila took a deep breath, rolling her shoulders to release some of the tension. It was Tuesday, and the wedding was Saturday, meaning she'd have Preston all to herself for the next four days.

"I'm so glad you have Seth to handle things while you are away," she said.

"He's been such an asset to the company. And he's taking my most eligible bachelor title away from me, which I don't mind one bit. But Seth is cautious about dating and is holding out for the right woman."

"Smart. Just like you did."

"Exactly." Preston turned to the laptop on the table. "One last check of emails, and let's say we turn off our phones for the duration of our trip. No work."

Laila rolled her eyes at his command. "Hey, I thought I was the bossy one in this relationship. But a technology-free week sounds amazing."

She checked her phone and noticed an email alert from her former coworker back when she'd worked as an agent for Mossad. Her heartbeat ratcheted up. If Jacob Kohen was emailing her, it wasn't with good news.

The email filled her screen, and she forced herself to read every word and not skim it. "Oh no," she groaned. It wasn't just bad news—it was worse than she could have imagined. Not a great way to start off their getaway.

"What's wrong?" Preston's brown eyes flooded with concern. He dropped his phone onto his lap and fixed his attention on her.

"An old colleague emailed me about my former fiancé, Solomon Mizrahi. He's been in jail ever since he stole classified secrets and sabotaged a mission." Laila swallowed, trying to bite back the sharpness in her voice, but the memories of Solomon made her blood boil. The man had fed her team bad intel and she'd nearly died. Another colleague had gone home in a body bag because of Solomon's evil choices.

She cleared her throat. Her dreams of a stress-free holiday break began to disintegrate. "He escaped prison a few days ago. Mossad tracked him, but they lost his whereabouts. Jacob just wanted to give me a heads-up. They think he's heading to the US."

"Why?" Preston scrubbed a hand over the five-o'clock shadow covering his chin. "Laila, tell me the truth. Would he come for you?"

She frowned. "Not to win me back or anything like that. He blames me for his arrest. I helped Interpol track him down. Maybe he's wanted vengeance all these years." A shudder raced through her. She prayed that she'd never have to face that man again.

"Let's not let this ruin our trip. Phones off, right?" Laila made a show of powering off her phone.

Preston smiled, but it didn't chase away the worry lines etched around his eyes. "Right." He turned off his computer and phone.

She leaned her head back against the seat and closed her eyes, forcing her mind to let go of the past. When she opened them, she blinked back the fog of sleep to find Preston reading a book. "How long was I out?" she asked him.

Preston glanced at his watch. "A little while. We're flying over the Rockies right now and should land in about forty-five minutes."

Laila checked out the view from the window, and her worries about Solomon melted away like the snow on the white-capped mountains. The majesty of the wilderness and the rich red-and-brown colors left her breathless.

A sizzle hissed through the aircraft, and the cabin went dark. Laila's stomach lurched with the plane's sudden downward dip. An oxygen mask fell from the ceiling and dangled in front of her face.

"What was that?" Preston said. He stood up and moved to check on Phil, but the force of the plane's abrupt descent had him clinging to the back of a chair to keep from stumbling.

"Sit down and buckle up." The pilot's voice rang out through the cabin. "We're going to have to make an emergency landing."

Preston complied.

The only sounds Laila heard were the whipping of the wind outside and the thundering of her heartbeat. She willed herself to stay calm while reflexes kicked into warrior mode. She'd trained for all kinds of survival scenarios. The plane had lost power, which made Phil's job to land a challenge. And there was nothing she could do to help except pray and brace herself for the rough landing.

Laila tightened her seatbelt around her waist and gripped Preston's hand. Their relationship had survived some intense ups and downs, but surviving a crash landing might be the ultimate test.

Assuming they survived.

SOMEWHERE OVER THE ROCKY MOUNTAINS
TUESDAY, 2:00 P.M.

PRESTON'S BIG PLANS FOR WHISKING HIS GIRLFRIEND AWAY FOR A memorable weekend fizzled before his eyes. He jammed his free hand into his pocket and grasped the small velvet bag.

Would he get the chance to show Laila how he really felt about her?

Before they died?

He refused to let his mind go there. They had to survive. His pulse jackhammered in his ears. The rushing wind thundered with their rapid descent. His stomach lurched with the plane's rocky movements. He squeezed Laila's hand. Despite her status as a bodyguard, he'd do everything in his power to keep her safe. The fear flashing through her eyes mirrored his own.

"Mayday. Mayday." The pilot continued to communicate to anyone who might hear them, but only silence responded. Metal grated as Phil used the manual controls to try and stop the plane's spiraling descent.

Preston's mind raced faster than the spinning aircraft. If these were his final moments on earth, he didn't have any regrets except one. Why hadn't he fought harder to make Laila a priority? Would they die without her realizing how much he loved her?

"Hang on," Phil shouted. "I'm going to try to land us. It'll be bumpy. We've lost all power."

"I hope we don't crash," Laila yelled over the rumble of the cabin being pummeled by the wind. "I'd like to not die on day one of our vacation."

Preston tried to laugh, but his insides were so twisted he couldn't even muster a smile. He looked over Laila and out the window. Mountain ridges bounced in the distance, and the snow-covered trees loomed closer as the plane dropped in altitude. He prayed that Phil would somehow find a clearing in the wilderness.

They were getting close to the ground but moving too fast for a safe landing.

"At least this time I'm not facing death by myself," Laila said.

"Look, if we don't make it out of this, I just want you to know—"

"Don't say it," Laila yelled, a fierceness in her voice that steadied his nerves. "We'll be fine. I refuse to think otherwise."

Preston clutched Laila's hand. The screeching of tree branches scratching the belly of the plane drowned out his prayers. Steel groaned, and Preston envisioned every bolt holding the aircraft together stretched to its breaking point. He leaned over the arm of the seat and embraced Laila as if to absorb the impact of the crash for her.

"Hang on, everyone!" Phil shouted.

They hit the snow-covered ground and skidded.

Preston's shoulder bore the brunt of the tightened seat belt. Another bump lifted him off the seat, but this time the plane stayed on the ground, careening onward. Preston's insides churned.

Out the window, the world rushed by in a blur of white snow and brown tree branches. Now if the aircraft would only slow down...

Preston squeezed his eyes shut. The crash sounded like a crack of thunder followed by the sound of metal and glass shattering. Smoke burned his nostrils, and Laila coughed near him. At least she was alive.

The plane jerked to a hard stop.

And then everything went quiet.

Preston opened his eyes to find pine needles and twigs filling his vision. Snow-covered limbs swayed from the impact, less than a foot away from where he and Laila sat. They'd hit a tree, which had stopped them. But the tree had taken a chunk out of the side of the airplane and blocked their view of the cockpit.

The only thing Preston could hear was his and Laila's labored breaths.

"We—we made it. Sort of," Laila said, staring at the mess of branches, pine needles, and bark taking up the front of the cabin.

Snow dusted her hair. It must've come in through the fissure in the ceiling. Preston clicked off his seatbelt and tried to stand, but his legs buckled. He held on to the back of the seat to steady himself. "Are you hurt?" Laila had a trickle of blood over her right eyebrow. He reached over to inspect the cut. "It looks like some debris caught you. It's not too deep. Just a scratch." He wiped her forehead with his sleeve, and she flinched.

"I'm concerned about Phil," she said, her voice raspy from the smoke. "We haven't heard him call out, and he took the brunt of that tree we hit."

"Phil?" Preston called out. No answer.

Not good.

Laila unbuckled her seat belt and joined Preston as he pushed tree debris to clear a path to the cockpit door. "Phil?" His head throbbed. Cold seeped into his bones, both from the icy air and Phil's silence. "I can't believe we survived this crash." Preston reached back and gripped Laila's arm, shoving down the images of how close he'd come to losing her forever.

"The tree took out the front side of the plane," Laila whispered. "There's no way Phil survived. He must have taken a direct hit."

Preston entered the cockpit and froze, blocking Laila's view of Phil's lifeless body impaled by a branch.

He turned to look at Laila, gathering his thoughts. Phil had saved their life at the cost of his own. "Phil didn't make it. I can't believe it." He shuddered, the image of his family friend tangled in the mix of tree trunk and twisted metal seared into his brain. Tears burned his eyes.

Laila stared straight ahead through the open door to the shattered windshield, averting her eyes from the deceased pilot. "He intentionally hit that tree and took the brunt of the impact. Because with a few more feet, we'd have tumbled over the side of the mountain. Look."

Preston tore his eyes off Laila's distressed face to follow her gaze. "I see nothing."

"Exactly. It's nothing but sky. Meaning we are perched on the edge of a cliff. The tree stopped us from going over."

Preston moved to the passenger-side window and stared. Dark clouds mixed with blue sky on the horizon, but he looked down and gaped at the massive drop-off that lay beneath them.

TWO

Laila's instincts had morphed from vacation mode to survival the second the power sizzled out. Sure, she'd had plenty of training in her past, but nothing to prepare her for being stranded on a mountain in December. The sun would set in a few hours and temperatures would plummet. And then there was the situation of the plane perched precariously on the edge of a cliff.

"Okay," Preston whispered. "We've got to think. Any suggestions?"

"You said Phil was ex-Army, so he would have had an emergency supply kit on hand." She searched the cockpit and found a small duffel bag with a red cross on it. She threw it over her shoulder and nudged Preston back through the door. "For starters, let's move to the back of the plane," Laila said. "I think the tree lodged into the side will keep us from toppling over, but we shouldn't make any sudden movements or add extra weight to the front."

They headed toward the tail end, which had fared well in the crash. The walls and ceiling were still intact, providing a modicum of shelter from the hole in the ceiling. But they couldn't remain on the plane and not freeze to death.

Laila rummaged through a cabinet and found it stocked with a generous supply of bottled waters and snacks. Nothing that would sustain them for more than a few days, but it was a start.

She searched the bag she'd nabbed from the cockpit. "God bless Phil. His emergency kit has all kinds of things we can use." She dumped the contents on the floor and found a first aid kit, protein bars, a flint for making fire, a multi-tool with a knife, two compact flashlights, and four emergency flares. Preston hadn't been kidding that Phil would be the kind of guy they'd be glad to know in the event of a disaster.

She checked her phone. Dead.

Laila hadn't answered earlier when Preston had asked about what had caused the power outage because she didn't want to validate the nagging storm clouds that had formed in the back of her mind. Could someone have deliberately knocked their plane out of the sky?

They needed to be on the same page if they were to survive. "I don't think this was an accident. The only thing that would kill all of our electronics would be an electromagnetic pulse. It explains why we can't use our phones."

Preston ran his hand through his hair. "An EMP?" He sank into a chair, his face pale with dark circles forming under his eyes. "So that would mean someone wanted us to crash."

"It's a possibility we need to consider." Laila sat next to him. "The only other is a solar flare, and that's highly unlikely. So yes, I'd say this was intentional."

"If someone is out to get us, they might come back to check their handiwork."

His conclusion summed up her biggest concern with this situation. Despite the cold, lack of food, threat of wildlife, and no communications, their chief threat might be a human. "Let's focus on one problem at a time. I think we need to leave this plane and check out our surroundings before we lose daylight. Maybe there's a town nearby, or we find some kind of shelter that isn't about to topple over the side of a mountain. Because the more snow that collects in that hole in the ceiling, the more weight there is on the front. I don't feel safe staying here."

"And you think trekking into the wilderness is safer?" He let out a mirthless laugh. "What if the company that owns the plane sees we crashed and sends help? And we're gone?"

She'd considered this, but the chill racing through her wasn't totally from the cold air. "I've got a bad feeling about this, Preston. My concern is stuck on why we went down in the first place."

He nodded and stood. "You've got the training for this, so I trust your instincts. Let's leave and hike a bit. I'm sure we'll find some doomsday prepper living off the grid that might help us." He emptied his backpack and filled it with essentials like snacks, water, and a blanket.

Laila put on as many layers of clothing as would fit and still allow her to move. Her puffy winter parka helped insulate her somewhat, although it wouldn't stop hypothermia if they were exposed to the elements for too long. But her brain refused to quit nagging her that something wasn't right with their situation. At least her sidearm gave her a minuscule level of comfort that she could protect herself and Preston from bears.

Or predators of the human kind.

They finished filling up Preston's backpack, and he finagled the emergency side door at the back of the plane open. Biting air smacked Laila in the face, chasing the last remnant of warmth from her body.

They shuffled through the snow, knee-deep in some spots, and made their way to the edge of the cliff.

Laila spotted a frozen stream at the bottom of the mountain. She pointed and tried to talk through the multiple layers of fabric covering her face. "Let's stick to the ridgeline of this cliff, following the water below. If there's civilization, it probably would be close to a water source."

"We need to find shelter," Preston said, just his eyes showing through the hood of the jacket and the scarf wrapped around him. "We're not going to last an hour in this weather."

Laila nodded, not wanting to reveal that she was losing feeling in her feet. "I'm praying for a cave." But as soon as she said this, her stomach clenched. Caves meant the possibility of crashing in on the local wildlife, and Laila couldn't shake the image of them waking up a hibernating bear.

They trudged forward, carving out a path in the snow that mirrored the frozen stream below. But everything looked the same around them. Trees, snow, rocks, and the occasional brown shrub were the only sights ahead of them or behind. Laila would swear they were walking in circles if it weren't for the fact that they'd stuck to the edge and had moved in a straight line.

"How long have we been walking?" Preston asked.

Laila pushed aside several layers of clothes around her wrist only to find a dead watch. "EMP. It has to be," she muttered. "My watch is dead. Whatever knocked out the plane electronics fried everything."

Preston stopped and she bumped into him, their puffy coats colliding. He reached out a hand to steady her. "Do you really think someone stalked me, found my itinerary, headed to the mountains, and sat in the middle of nowhere, waiting for our plane to fly over?"

"Well, when you put it that way, it sounds absurd. But if someone's out there, you know I'm going into bodyguard mode. Because if this was intentional, that person went through a lot of trouble."

"The last thing I want you to do is put yourself in danger."

Laila nodded but wanted to argue.

She didn't know whether this was about him or her, but if it came down to it, she'd make sure Preston was safe, whether he liked it or not. When would he realize that being a bodyguard wasn't a nine-to-five job?

She gazed at the view over the cliff's edge. Breathtaking hues of reds and purples backlit the mountain ranges in the distance. They needed to turn around before the darkness chased away the remnants of light. Preston pulled out a bottle of water from his pack and gave her a sip. "Keep the bottle," Laila said. "We can refill it later."

Crack.

A branch snapped, as if something—or someone—had stepped on it.

"We need to move." She grabbed Preston's bulky hand and forced her legs to walk twice as fast back the way they'd come. "Dusk is approaching, and we should head back to the plane. We can leave tomorrow, when daylight is on our side. I haven't seen anything we can use for a shelter. I hate to say it, but we're stuck in the middle of nowhere." She'd kept an eye out for caves or fallen trees, anything that would help them get out of the elements. But the plane was the only enclosure, or at least half of it.

They'd only walked for about fifteen minutes, based on Laila's internal clock. But unseen eyes bored into her back as they retreated.

"Maybe it was an animal, like a bear," Preston said.

"Let's hope it was a bear." Because the latest worst-case-scenario images her mind conjured prompted her to take off her glove and rest her hand on the butt of her sidearm.

TUESDAY, 4:15 P.M.

THE INTENSE GLARE IN LAILA'S EYES MADE PRESTON'S HEART BEAT double time. She'd almost taken off running at the snap of that twig.

In the past, he'd watched Laila morph into bodyguard mode at the first sign of danger, but this was different. Stress radiated off her normal stoic countenance. Her concern for their situation sent his blood pressure through the roof.

Gloved fingers threaded through his, but he noticed her other hand rested on her sidearm. "We're going to get out of this, Laila. It's you and me. We've beat worse odds before. I mean, we survived a plane crash for starters."

"I know." They continued their trek, darkness casting flickering shadows through the trees.

At least he hadn't spotted anything—or anyone—following them.

His feet tingled, a bad sign of just how cold the temperature was getting.

"I...see...the plane." Laila's teeth chattered with each word. She dropped his hand, and he saw the edges of the aircraft glistening in the moonlight. "I can build us a fire. Phil had enough supplies. Maybe someone will see the smoke and send help."

Laila jumped into action with renewed energy, dragging fallen tree branches toward the crash site while Preston fell into step behind her. Yet again, he had become the one she had to protect.

He'd been a Boy Scout in his youth, and he wasn't helpless. Life in the mountains had taught him a thing or two about the outdoors, despite the tabloids painting him as having grown up with a privileged life.

He began to clear the snow in an area near the plane so they could build a fire. His thoughts drifted while he worked. An unseen wedge had been working its way through their relationship, and Preston hadn't wanted to give voice to his concerns.

Was he on the path to losing the woman he loved? It was more than just finding time to connect amid insane schedules. He sensed her pulling away. She talked less about her job, as if he couldn't understand her life as a bodyguard.

But with all the money and stability he could offer her, would he ever be able to keep up with her? Sure, he could run a billion-dollar company, but Laila was an unstoppable force, a one-woman show. Was there enough room in her life for him and her job? At times it seemed like she couldn't separate herself from being a bodyguard. Would she feel the need to protect him the rest of their lives? Because all he wanted to do was provide her a safe space where she didn't have to come to his defense all the time. Where she could just be *Laila*.

But did she want that?

He forced himself to focus on the present and tried to recall his Scouting days. He took some of the branches Laila had collected and added them to the makeshift fire pit he'd created by clearing an area and packing the snow around the empty spot. Inside the plane he found some magazines and paper towels they could use as kindling.

Laila rummaged through his backpack and pulled out Phil's flint. It took her several attempts to get a spark, her huffs revealing her frustration with every strike of the knife.

A tiny spark shone in the dusk, catching the paper products on fire. The wood succumbed to the flames, and within minutes, a fire crackled. It wasn't a blaze, but big enough for them to get warm.

A mischievous grin crept across what little of Laila's face he could see from the layers covering her. She ducked into the plane and emerged with something in her hand.

A French press. "We can make coffee. I saw this earlier in the snack cabinet. Not one crack on the glass." She passed him the pot and some coffee.

"Now that's a woman with her priorities straight."

Gloves made his work difficult, but he packed snow into the glass carafe and held it over the flames. Once it melted, he added the grounds and used the paper cups Laila had found.

After a bit, he handed her a steaming cup. "I'm so grateful for a well-stocked kitchen." The first sip sizzled on his tongue and made his taste buds come alive. At least now one part of his body wasn't frozen solid.

Darkness soon devoured the last flickers of daylight, but the warmth chased away the involuntary trembling that had started on their walk back. He wiggled his toes and counted all ten. They sat by the fire, defrosting and eating protein bars.

"Well, I did promise you a fire," Preston said.

Laila laughed, and he relished the sound amid their bleak surroundings.

"Remember when I told you not to ditch the empty bottles so we could refill them?" Laila asked.

"Sure. I figured you just hated to litter."

She punched his arm, but he couldn't feel anything through the layers. "We need to melt the snow and boil the water to refill the bottles. Then we can sleep in the plane and pack ourselves in with hot water bottles. I found a few more empty ones in the trash inside."

He dumped the grounds from the French press and made several more pots of hot water for the bottles. Snowflakes cascaded around them. The scene might have been romantic if they'd had the shelter of a lodge as a backdrop instead of the inky black wilderness.

A howl in the distance made him jump. "We should hunker down in the plane," Preston said. He'd been watching Laila, who was on high alert with her eyes roaming the black horizon. Her unease was palpable, threading through him as if it were his own.

"I don't see any way out of this," she muttered. "With the winds picking up, I doubt anyone can get a helicopter out here to rescue us. We're on our own."

A shiver overtook him. Her hard bodyguard exterior was showing cracks. For the briefest second, Preston saw raw fear flicker through her eyes. What he wouldn't do to ease her worries about their survival. But he agreed with her assessment.

They were in deep trouble.

"Let's get in the plane and get as warm as we can with the bottles," Laila said, resurrecting her self-imposed take-charge protector role. "We'll keep the fire going. It's far enough from anything that it shouldn't get out of control. And who knows if we'll get another spark from the flint."

The second Preston stepped away from the fire, he missed the heat. But the hot water bottles might carry them through the night. *Might*.

Laila moved into the tail end of the plane, and Preston followed her, shutting the door. Normally she'd have stayed up on guard duty, but they had to get out of the cold. The temperature had less of a bite with the walls shielding them from the elements. Because once the sun had set, the frigid air hit unbearable levels.

With a few blankets and the water bottles sandwiched under their layers of clothing, they built a cocoon between the leather cabin chairs, against the wall of the plane. Anything to block the wind.

Preston sank onto the ground, and Laila dropped next to him. He wrapped his arms around her to absorb the shivers wracking her body.

His thoughts turned reflective again, and he commanded his mind to stop picturing this as the end. He couldn't lose Laila. Not to the cold or to her stubborn refusal to let him be a part of her life. "Laila, I'm so sorry I haven't been there for you lately. I know I promised so much more in our relationship and that I'd make it work." He pushed back the hood of her parka and kissed her temple. "If we find a way back to civilization, I want things to be different."

How had this weekend gone so wrong?

It had started with the hope of reconnecting with the woman he loved, and now they clung to each other to find enough warmth to survive the night.

He sensed her relax in his arms despite the layers of materials between them. He kissed her with a toe-curling kiss that spread warmth throughout him. A kiss that conveyed he'd protect her even if it cost him his life. She didn't have to fight alone anymore, if only she'd let him in. He tried to pull away, but she wrapped her gloved fingers around the back of his neck and tugged him closer.

"Laila Rabbinowitz." A loud voice growled from outside of their shelter, dissolving the ounce of peace they'd just reclaimed.

The ice returned to Preston's veins. Laila's eyes shone a look that he'd never seen on her.

Terror.

"Laila Rabbinowitz. We have you and your new boyfriend surrounded. We'll spare his life. It's you I'm after. But only if you come out of the plane right now."

THREE

S olomon Mizrahi.

She'd recognize that low, lethal baritone anywhere.

Shock waves of adrenaline hit her, and Preston hugged her tighter, as if trying to absorb the tremors wracking her body.

Solomon's scathing last words before he left for prison echoed in her mind.

I will come for you.

The coffee soured in Laila's stomach and threatened to come up. Preston's eyes searched hers.

"It's Solomon," she said, her voice low. "I guess we now know the source of the EMP."

"Do you think he really has us surrounded?"

"He had lots of resources before landing in jail, so he could have hired a crew."

A shot echoed throughout the cabin, and they pressed themselves against the floor of the plane. "Last warning, my precious Laila," Solomon bellowed. "The next bullet goes

116

through Preston Whittaker's temple. I heard you were his bodyguard. Don't you want to spare his life? Come out now."

Laila pulled herself up and shrugged off the blankets.

There had to be a way out of this.

If it came to her life or Preston's, she'd do everything in her power to make sure the man she loved lived. But falling into the hands of the madman outside? Memories of Solomon's trial flickered through her brain. She'd once admired his strength and intelligence, but she'd been played by a master manipulator. Tales of torture and the wake of dead bodies Solomon had left behind had revealed the depths of his evil. The last thing she wanted to do was face off against this beast.

The prickling sensation in her fingers and toes gave her pause. She was in no shape to fight, and her mind taunted her with images of Preston dying. To suppress her rising anxiety, she needed to keep her hands busy.

"How deep are the pockets on your coat?" she asked, examining her own pockets on the interior of her thick parka.

Preston patted down his designer, fleece-lined jacket and nodded. "Pretty deep."

Laila divvied up their supplies. She shoved as much as she could into her pockets and tossed Preston items to take. Protein bars, two mini flashlights, the flares, the flint—anything that might keep them alive, assuming they found a way off the plane. Preston followed her lead, shoving smaller items into his pockets. She even discovered a collapsible tin cup that would come in handy for melting snow to drink. They'd need it later. If they survived.

Think, Laila. Think!

One word screamed through her internal chaos.

Run.

"If he has us surrounded, the only chance we have of escaping is..." She pointed to the front of the plane.

"You want to climb down the side of the cliff?" His face paled as he stared at the cockpit. "That man will kill you immediately and torture me until I beg for death. Either he kills us or the mountain does."

She rummaged around the cabin, locating the parachutes stashed in a cabinet that she'd spotted earlier. Phil took the Army's *Be Prepared* motto to a whole new level. She counted eight chutes.

"Phil must have thought he could land the plane safely, because he never told us to use the chutes to jump," Laila said. They'd have to have a proper funeral for Phil once they got home, because they didn't have time to grieve the man's senseless death or appreciate his sacrifice to save them.

She did some dirty math in her head. Earlier she'd estimated the drop-off to be about forty, maybe fifty feet. Using the knife from Phil's multitool, she sliced the chutes open and pulled out the fabric and cables.

"Here, start tying these together. We should have enough line to make two ropes. We're going to use this to rappel out the missing front window and down the side of the cliff. Let's just hope we have enough rope to get both of us to the bottom." She slowed down to show Preston the basics of how to tie the knot.

"Okay, you're the boss." Even though his eyes communicated the insanity of her plan, he tore open a parachute and copied her knot technique to bind the lines.

"Each chute should have about ten feet of rope. That should get us close to the bottom."

The sound of ripping fabric filled the cabin as she and Preston tied the lines of the parachute. Once they formed the ropes, they dragged them to the cockpit. She tried not to look at Phil's lifeless, snow-covered body as she tied one end of the cord to the control wheel of the plane. The solid aluminum shouldn't budge. Now if only she had that kind of confidence in her ropemaking and knot-tying abilities, not to mention the validity of this half-baked plan.

"Time's up, Laila."

Another shot pinged off the side of the aircraft and forced her to quicken her pace. She threw the other end of the line out the empty front window where a windshield used to be. Looking down, she couldn't see the end in the dark, so she didn't know how close to the bottom the parachute cords would get them.

"This is unbelievable," Preston muttered. "You think this will hold?"

"A parachute is designed to keep a person from falling out of the sky, so the material is pretty strong." He had to know she was bluffing, but they were out of time and options.

A bang sounded at the cabin door, meaning Solomon and his men were seconds from storming the plane. At least the tree blocked him from entering through the hole in the side and slowed the man down.

She showed Preston how to wrap the lines, sliding them between her legs and then around her shoulder to create a makeshift harness. This would give her some control to slow her descent. Good thing she'd taken Preston indoor rock climbing for one of their dates, but what they were about to face didn't even come close to that experience.

He didn't bother to object to her plan but patted his pockets. "I've got everything I need on me. Let's go."

Another gunshot resounded, and Preston and Laila climbed over the dashboard. The windshield hadn't survived the crash, and they stood overlooking the drop-off.

"Stay with me, okay? We've got this." She grabbed the rope with her gloved hand and lowered herself over the edge of the plane. Her feet slipped out from under her, and she stifled a gasp. She swayed in the open air until she connected with the solid granite of the mountainside.

Preston followed her lead and hung beside her. Laila let out some rope with one hand while wrapping the rope below her with the other hand. Sweat trickled down her back despite the wind pelting her face. One false move, and she'd fall to her death. Preston yelled something, but all she heard was her own heartbeat jackhammering in her ears.

Laila looked up and saw Preston just above her, but she counted five forms silhouetted in the moonlight at the top of the cliff. Solomon wasn't taking any chances that she'd survive the crash.

"All he has to do is cut the line, Laila," Preston said, his voice tight.

"Yes, but he won't. Now that he knows we're here, he'll wants us alive to slowly kill us." The figures disappeared, but they weren't gone. Solomon would regroup to figure out how to get down the mountain to intercept them.

She double-timed her descent—one hand grabbing the line, the other reaching down, then changing hands—until she reached the end. In the shadows below, the ground was visible, but it was still a jump.

"No more rope," she called out to Preston, who slowed his descent. Her hands burned.

"Are we close?" Preston stopped next to her, his rope trembling. Neither of them could hold on for much longer.

She looked down. "It's going to be a bit of a jump. It's about fifteen feet." Or more. "It's now or never," she muttered and scooted to the edge of the parachute cord.

She sent up a prayer and let go.

TUESDAY, 9:00 P.M.

"Laila!" She'd let go before he was ready. He'd planned to be the one to—

A thud cut through the quiet of the night, followed by, "I'm okay."

Preston exhaled. He positioned himself at the end of the rope and let go. His feet connected with solid ground. He stumbled but managed to stay upright. Despite the darkness, he could see Laila's silhouette in the moonlight and rushed to her side. Puffy coat colliding with hers, he wrapped his arms around her and lifted her off her feet. Their lips met.

He set her down. "Let's not do that again," he said.

"Let's get a move on. Solomon's men will be rushing down the mountain any moment." A gunshot rang out, followed by an eruption of bark from a nearby tree.

They bolted through the woods, moving as fast as they could through the ankle-deep snow. At some spots, the snow ran deeper, making it harder to maneuver.

Besides an owl hoot, the only sound Preston heard was the crunching of snow under their boots. To the left, the mountain and trees blocked out the moonlight and cast darkness across the ground in front of them. To their right, Preston could only make out shapes of rocks and trees, but he knew the river they'd spotted earlier should be out there.

But Solomon and his men wouldn't be far behind, so they pushed forward.

After a few minutes, they slowed. Preston tried to catch his breath, but his lungs burned from the exertion and the cold. "We're lost," he muttered, shoving branches out of the way as they walked.

"We've been running parallel to the frozen stream, but Solomon will do the same."

"How are we going to outrun these guys?" Preston asked.

"We'll stick close to the rocks. Find a cave to hide out in."

Preston shivered at the thought of being cornered by Solomon in a cave. "Whatever we do, Solomon will match our movements. We have to throw him off our trail." But how?

They trudged on, staying between the frozen water and the rocky terrain. The shelter of the cliff disappeared, exchanged for thick foliage and the occasional boulder. At least their descent wasn't uphill, but his feet were numb again. His calves ached from slogging through the snow. "Any chance we can build a fire again?" Preston whispered, but in the silent night, his voice bounced off the trees.

"I grabbed the flint, plus I have flares, but a fire will make our location known, so we probably shouldn't chance it."

Just as Preston suspected.

They slogged through the snow, the exertion sapping his energy with each step.

"I don't...hear...anything behind us," Laila said. He didn't like the pained effort she'd used to form each word. They needed to stop and rest. But all objects looked the same in the dark. Trees, rocks, and snowbanks gave off the same shadowy appearance.

Then something on the horizon caught his eye. "Let's check out that shadowy object over there." He motioned for Laila to change direction.

They traversed through the wooded area and came to a clearing where a structure jutted out from the ground. Once they got closer, they could see in the moonlight not a man-made structure, but a rock formation with numerous boulders and shards of granite stacked on top of each other, dusted in snow and dirt.

"It looks like the remains of an avalanche," Laila said as she pulled out a flashlight from her pocket. "Stand next to me and use your body to cover the light as much as possible."

"You think it's worth the risk?"

"Yes, because we won't be here by the time they get here."

She flicked the switch for a brief second, and the light illuminated a fissure in the rocks, created by several boulders stacked on top of each other. They climbed over some stones leading up the side of the structure to find that the opening was big enough for them to crawl through.

"I can't see all the way inside. Do you think anything lives in this cave?" Laila asked.

"Which is worse, a bear or Solomon?"

"Getting crushed by these rocks. That's what's worse. But it looks like these have been here for a long time. And we're out of options. Let's check it out." Laila headed to the opening. She belly-crawled through the fissure and disappeared.

"What do you see?" Preston called, not liking her out of his sight.

"The rocks form a small enclosed area. There's enough room for the both of us. Plus, no bears. Bats, but no bears."

Bats? He'd lived his entire life with money and privilege. Bat-infested caves had not been a part of that life. But now he crawled through mystery holes in rocks, hoping to not get shot or eaten by a bear.

He sucked in a breath and wormed his way through the opening. It was a tight fit, but he managed it. He noted the top of their hiding spot, probably ten feet high, leaving plenty of standing room.

Preston put his hand on one of the stones that formed the outer wall. It would make sleeping on the ground cold, but their hideout offered shelter from the wind and elements.

Beams of moonlight filtered through the top of the structure, but not enough for them to see clearly. At least they had the flashlight, which Laila clicked on to inspect their surroundings. But this only served to illuminate the red eyes of the bats that hung overhead, and she immediately switched it off.

"The good news is a bear wouldn't fit through the only opening, and this thing doesn't go deeper than this one enclosed area." Laila's positive spin gave him a sliver of relief. "And anyone walking by would likely miss this spot."

Preston pulled out two squashed protein bars from his pocket and moved to the center of the room to hand one to Laila. She took it and they munched in in silence. These had to sustain them for who knew how long.

"What are we going to do?" Preston asked, knowing neither of them had an answer. "We have no phone, we're off the map, and a madman is chasing us."

She sighed. "I'll keep the flashlight off so we can conserve batteries. And I don't think we want to start a fire in here. So we might have to brave it for tonight. Tomorrow we'll keep moving and hopefully find help."

Preston pulled Laila close to him, wrapping his arms around her. Despite all her training, their predicament was pushing her to the limits. She rarely let her emotions show—except, apparently, when it came to Solomon. Preston had never seen this raw side of Laila before.

"I'm so sorry I got you into this mess," she muttered against him. "If it wasn't for my past—"

He put his gloved finger against her lips. At least, he thought it was her lips. "Not too long ago, you put your life on the line several times because someone wanted to kill me, remember? I'll never hold the actions of someone else against you."

She trembled under his arms. Was it from cold or fear? "I can't believe Solomon came after me. My worst nightmare has come to life. I'd admired Solomon's strength and intellect. It made him a great Mossad agent. But there was another side to the man, one that I didn't recognize until it was too late."

She took a deep breath. "I'm the one who discovered the tortured and battered body of a fellow agent with a note pinned to him saying I'd be next. I knew if Solomon got out of prison, he'd come for me. That man must go back behind bars."

He held her tight. How had she carried this much weight for so long? No wonder she had trouble trusting anyone and opening herself up to even him. But he wanted to be the one that carried these burdens for her, helped her realize she wasn't alone.

"We'll get through this, Laila. I'm not going to let anything happen to you. But for now, we need to rest while we can." Preston let her go and lowered himself to the hard stone floor. He blinked to try and see in the dark. He'd never slept on a rock before—a definite downgrade from the plush beds at the ski resort. He sat on the ground with his back against a rock. "This wasn't what I had in mind for starting Christmas traditions with you," he muttered while Laila dropped next to him.

"What were your traditions growing up?" Laila asked, snuggling close to him.

Preston thought back to his childhood and scoffed, because he struggled to recall a good one. "We acted like the perfect family and did all the typical Christmas fanfare. Parties, decorations, the works. But on the inside, Christmas wasn't always cookies and tinsel. My mom would drink, my dad would retreat to his office, Ethan to his bedroom, and my sister would find a way to sneak out of the house. I always dreamed of someday having a family where we celebrated Christmas, not just put on a show for the world to see."

"Well, so far, my first Christmas experience is one I'd rather forget. At least with Hanukkah there was never a threat of dying of hypothermia."

Preston had planned Laila's first Christmas down to the last detail. Images of the lodge filled his mind, with all the wasted arrangements prepped and waiting for them. There was a horse-drawn carriage that would have taken them through the town and stopped at an Italian restaurant, where he'd planned to propose. He wanted Laila to be a permanent part in his life so they could start their own holiday traditions.

But his life after the plane crash was now broken into fifteen-minute increments. Because that's how long he thought they might withstand this cold.

"Well, I have one fond memory," Preston said. "When we were little, before my dad became a mogul, we were convinced we could wait up for Santa Claus. We laid out the cookies and milk under the tree and hid in the closet to wait. The three of us shoved ourselves in this small closet with the door cracked, never taking our eyes off the Christmas tree. And much to my amusement, Santa showed up. My dad, all dressed in some velvety red Santa suit, burst into the room. We giggled, but Santa didn't bust us. We thought we were so cool, being the only kids to ever see Santa. I still can't believe my dad did that for us."

"I know you miss him a lot," Laila said, her voice betraying her exhaustion. "But what a sweet memory to cherish."

Preston's entire body was numb from the cold, but a warmth grew in his heart.

Despite escaping snow, a plane crash, and gunmen, in the quiet of the cave, Preston had everything he needed. After all, his goal had been a few days away with the woman he loved with no interruptions. No paparazzi, no cell phones or laptops buzzing with urgent messages. He'd wanted life to slow down for a fraction of a second for them to reconnect.

It didn't matter if they were at some swanky resort or stranded in the middle of nowhere. They were together.

They must have fallen asleep, because his next moment of awareness was of a shaft of daylight filtering through the dark cavern. Laila still slept, her face washed with peace for the first time in the last few hours.

His arms ached from the climb down from the plane, his body stiff and numb from the cold ground. But in the stillness of the rock enclosure, he watched her sleep, and all seemed right in the peaceful moment. Because this beautiful woman loved him. And he loved her something fierce.

The few hours of sleep felt good, but he needed much more. He stretched, working the kinks out of his neck from sleeping on rock.

Pebbles pelted the side of their rock enclosure. Heavy footsteps thumped above them and sent him upright. The noise woke up Laila, who was on her feet within seconds.

"What happened?" Laila whispered.

He put a finger to his lips. "We're not alone anymore."

FOUR

In the dark of the cave, Laila held tight to the memories of last night while her mind raced with options for their escape.

She didn't need a fancy resort for the perfect getaway with Preston. Apparently, perfection came in the form of a frigid bat-infested cave as long as she was with the man she loved. The fact that she'd fallen into such a deep sleep said something about how secure she felt wrapped in his arms.

But what would happen if Solomon caught them? She shuddered.

Solomon would kill Preston in the blink of an eye to hurt her.

"What are we going to do?" Preston's whisper bounced off the cave walls.

Laila pushed the images of Solomon's torture from her mind and did a mental count of her frozen fingers and toes. "I don't want to be trapped in a cave with no exit."

She dropped to the ground and shimmied out the entrance.

Two men walked along the edge of the stone formation, just above her head. How had they been tracked? Guns slung over their shoulders and Russian accents told Laila all she needed to know. The rumors were true—she'd heard before his prison stint that Solomon had been in league with Russians.

Laila backtracked into the cavern, and Preston helped her to her feet. "I spotted two armed men, but I know there are more." She kept her voice low. "We've got to get out of here. I'd rather have a chance to run than be cornered."

"Back to my original question. What are we going to do? Cause an avalanche as a distraction and run the other way?"

Laila stilled, then grinned. "Have I ever told you how brilliant you are?" She reached up and kissed him. "I listened to the bats all night long, and they were coming in and out from somewhere above the rocks. There's light in here, so there has to be an opening in the top. What if we can spook the bats into leaving? If we draw attention to the top of the cave, we can crawl out the bottom and make a run for it."

"It's better than being stuck here." Preston turned to pack up what little belongings they had. "How do you propose we spook bats?"

She felt around her jacket pocket. "I have the flares I took from Phil's emergency kit. The light and sparks might just do the trick if we throw it high enough. You watch the goons while I see what I can do."

"I'll handle the bats."

She shook her head. "No, I'm lighter and less likely to dislodge anything that might make noise. You keep an eye out and let me know their location."

"Okay." Preston headed to the entrance, and Laila scaled the rocks stacked up on the side of the cavern until she got as high as she could.

The flare burst to life. The bats stirred in the red glow of the sparks, and their wings beat the air as they headed for the exit just as Laila prayed would happen. It was now or never. She took a deep breath, tossed the flare up to encourage the animals to move faster, then rushed to make her escape. "Go, go!" Laila tried to keep her voice low, but the rush of bat wings drowned her out. But Preston got the message.

They pushed out from the hole in the cave, Preston first. "No sign of the men." He squeezed her hand as he helped her out the opening. Careful not to disturb the gravel, she and Preston scampered down the rocks and onto solid ground. Preston gripped her arm. "There," he whispered and pointed. She tracked where he pointed and spotted two men rushing toward the top. Bats darted out of their safety nest in the cave. It looked like a scene from an Indiana Jones movie, but with a lot more snow.

"It worked," she said, heart thudding. "Preston, it worked."

"Yeah, now let's get out of here."

Once they hit the snow-covered solid ground, they attempted to run, but the snow required maximum exertion for minimal speed. At this rate, they'd be caught for sure, although the snow should serve to slow their opponents. Laila sent up a silent prayer that Solomon's men didn't have snowmobiles or some other way of outmaneuvering the thick snow.

When they rounded the corner of the rock formation, Laila pulled Preston to a quiet stop at the sight of a man with his back turned toward them. She squeezed Preston's hand in the silent signal to not move or breathe or—

She wasn't sure what alerted the guy. A change in the air or maybe one of them made a sound, but he swiveled right, then left.

She and Preston stared at each other. There was nothing they could do if the man spotted them. To one side were rocks, and to the other, more snow-covered forest.

As the man turned their direction, Preston stepped in front of her. But she might be able to hold this guy off long enough for Preston to get away. Making her choice, she shoved Preston into the thick patch of trees and shrubs that hid a small ditch big enough to cover him.

"Run," she said in a hoarse whisper. "You're our only hope. Find help. Go, Preston, please." She wasn't sure he would, but she wasn't lying. She—*they*—needed him to run.

"Looks like it's my lucky day," the man said in Russian. "Solomon will pay me a pretty penny for this." He kept his gun on Laila.

Laila understood enough so far, but she prayed he'd use English with her. She held her hands up.

"Where's your boyfriend?" His English was heavily accented, but she couldn't have been more grateful. That didn't mean she'd answer though.

He took a few steps toward her, eying the area where she'd just sent Preston sprawling. A hood and thick beard covered the man's face, and all her focus was drawn to those hard, dark eyes glaring at her. Unlike Laila, this man moved like he'd stayed warm and not slept on a rock last night. If it came down to a fight, she'd be at a serious disadvantage.

She flexed her fingers and prayed they would cooperate. How could she defeat one man, let alone the other four she'd spotted on the mountain ridge during their escape?

Laila took a few steps to the side, the opposite direction of Preston's hiding spot. "He's well hidden. We separated, so you'll never find him." She glanced around as if she were offering a secret. "Listen, if it's money you want, you obviously know I'm dating a very wealthy man. I can pay you more than Solomon can."

The man grunted. "I know you are dangerous. I will not fall for your tricks. Throw gun to me."

She removed her weapon, placed it on the ground, and kicked it into the undergrowth. If Preston hadn't run, maybe he'd find her gun. She hadn't heard him leave, but she prayed he was long gone.

"If you want my gun, go get it," she said in Russian. She wasn't fluent but could at least make a point that this man would not intimidate her. This guy needed her alive in order to get paid. Solomon wanted to make her suffer before bleeding her dry.

The gunman flicked his gaze to the bushes, and Laila pounced. She kicked the gun from his hand and landed a punch squarely on his jaw. Stunned, he staggered backward. But it didn't take him long to recover. His dark eyes held an evil gleam. She steeled herself.

He counterattacked with a kick aimed at her side, but she managed to sidestep so he didn't connect. The man rounded again.

Her heart raced, partly from exertion but also from the spike of adrenaline.

Her bulky jacket restricted her movements, but she didn't have time to shed it. With each punch she blocked, she took damage. Her body couldn't rally fast enough. Minimal water and food in the past twenty-four hours—along with the freezing cold—showed in her reaction time and weakness. Her A-game was performing at a C-minus and dropping. And this man had clearly been trained by Solomon. The best of the best.

Despite every bone screaming for her to take it easy, she rushed him to catch him off guard. A kick to his side and she swung herself around to land on his back, catching him in a choke hold. He gasped and tried to shake her off, but she held firm—until he took a few steps back and smashed her against the boulders.

Nerve endings exploded in agony when the jagged rocks stabbed her in the back. She gasped and her grip loosened. The man flung her to the side, and she crumpled to the ground. She forced herself to her feet and rounded to kick him before he struck again, but he caught her foot and twisted it.

Fire shot up her leg as the sound of her snapping ankle registered. She stumbled backward and hit the dirt and gravel, the fight draining from her even while she bit her lip against the pain pulsating from the break.

The man whipped out a knife and stood over her. "You'll pay for this. I may just torture you myself before sending you to Solomon for your slow death."

WEDNESDAY, 8:00 A.M.

PRESTON WOULD NEVER FLEE AND LEAVE LAILA TO FEND FOR herself. It wasn't even an *option* for him to run.

And frankly, he could hardly believe her words.

The woman would give up her life to protect him but wouldn't even consider letting him do the same.

And this was their problem, maybe...she never let them be on even ground.

But now wasn't the time. Not with her grappling with a Russian oaf.

He held the gun she'd tossed at him—good thing he'd stuck around to grab it—but he couldn't get a clean shot. Preston had tried to get a shot off when she'd been crushing the man's larynx, but he wouldn't risk hitting Laila.

His heart had nearly exploded when Solomon's hired gunman had slammed Laila into the rocks. Now, he flexed his fingers to wake up his cold-numbed hands and wrapped them around the gun as he crept closer. Sunlight glinted off something in the attacker's hand.

A knife.

He couldn't register the man's words, but Laila wasn't getting up. The goon took one step closer toward her and—

Preston fired.

The man jerked, then dropped like a stone on top of Laila.

Preston raced to Laila and rolled the man's body off her, sparking memories of the night a shot had rung out and Bob Zimmerman's lifeless body had crushed *him*. He checked the Russian's pulse. "Nothing."

Laila blinked and groaned. "We've got to run. Only I can't even stand." Blood speckled her face, but it wasn't hers.

He pointed to her ankle. "I saw what he did. Is it broken?"

"Sure feels like it, but there's no other option. That gunshot is going to bring those other two guys this way."

"Right. Get on my back. No arguing."

All the same, he saw a challenge flicker in her eye. But when he handed her the gun and she tried to stand, she winced. He picked her up without a word.

"Sorry." She slid onto his back.

"Stop. You weigh nothing." Then he took off, using the forest as shelter. They weren't too far from the stream, and if he could find that, they'd at least have a fixed point to follow versus wandering through the woods.

Branches pulled at his jacket sleeves. Laila moaned a few times, but she kept her neck craned behind them, gun patrolling the area.

"I don't see them, but they aren't far away," Laila said. "Preston, I can't walk, let alone fight someone. And I spotted five on that ledge when we rappelled out of the plane. Assuming one is Solomon, that leaves three additional hired guns to contend with."

He pushed forward, but his mind refused to move past her shoving him into the woods at the first sign of trouble. "Don't expect me to duck and run ever again. We're a team. And I've spent my whole life running. I'm not about to start again. Not after I've found you."

But *were* they a team?

He'd seen the warning signs that she'd been drifting away, and he'd chosen to ignore them. And she'd made every single decision since the plane crash. Granted, she was more equipped for this than he was, but...were they heading in different directions? This trip was supposed to be special.

Warmth spread across his chest when she squeezed his shoulders. "I'm sorry," she whispered into his ear as he kept marching forward. "I overreacted in the heat of the moment. They're after me." She sniffed and her voice broke. "I love you, Preston. I don't think I could live with myself if something happened to you."

"Don't you think I feel the same about you?"

A pause. "Yes, of course you do."

"Exactly."

"We have to get out of this," Laila said. "After all we've been through and fought against, it can't end like this."

"It won't."

"I mean, we've managed to finagle our way out of worse situations before," she said as though he'd argued with her. "I was buried alive, and you saved the day. You always show up for me. And we may be outgunned and outnumbered, but God will fight for us. You taught me that."

"I'm with you a hundred percent." They might make it out of this alive, but he wasn't as sure of their relationship.

He brushed some tree branches out of the way, careful not to let them swing back and hit her. The only sound he heard was his heavy breathing and the crunch of snow against his boots. His leg muscles cramped, but he doubled down his efforts to move forward.

"We're both to blame, Preston," Laila said, addressing his unexpressed question. Which could only mean she was thinking along the same lines. "I got distracted with work too," she said. "We live in two different worlds, and we knew that going into this relationship."

"Is that really the reason I feel like I'm losing you? That we can't manage to find time in our busy schedules? Or is the bigger issue that, after what Solomon did to you, the only person you trust to take care of you is...*you*?" Raw, unrealized emotions burned through his chest at the admission. He wanted to stop, to look in her eyes while they had this conversation. But now wasn't the time.

"I keep wondering if we're meant to be together," Laila whispered. "If we're going to make it as a couple. But then here we are, stranded on a mountain after surviving a plane crash. Maybe we're stronger as a couple. If we survive this, I'm sure we can figure out the intricacies of our relationship."

He knew exactly what he wanted.

But did she?

She'd just admitted her doubts about them. "We're not over, Laila. This is just beginning. I love you, and I will fight for us."

"I'm not quitting. And while I will always have trust issues, I know you're the man for me. But time is against us. My job demands a hundred percent of my focus, and so does yours. We lead very different lives." Laila's head swivels back and forth, watching the area for danger. She couldn't let her guard down for a second, despite being carried because of her injury.

His heart broke. She might claim some responsibility, but he shared just as much of the blame. "I'd never make you choose between being a bodyguard and being with me."

The cold air burned his lungs, and he had no idea where he was going but forced his legs to move forward. "We need to find a way to carve out time for just us," he said. "It's not good for either of us to be so focused on work that we neglect each other."

She sighed, a contented sound that communicated hope.

They were in this together, now and in the future. He kept his eyes forward even as his feet stumbled to a stop. They needed to rest a moment.

He shielded his eyes from the sun. In the distance, he saw the outline of a building. Or was it a mirage? "Wait. Do you see that?" He pointed to the horizon.

Laila gasped. "I do. It looks like civilization."

Preston tamped down the urge to run, but renewed hope surged his adrenaline, and he made a beeline for the clearing. As much as he wanted to take another break, the sight of civilization was enough to propel him forward. He readjusted Laila on his back and pushed on.

Ten minutes later, he approached an old, dilapidated sign that read *Welcome to Prospect Hollow*. The building they had spotted came into view. Make that *buildings*. Wooden structures dotted the horizon. He could make out at least four structures with roofs still intact and a few more that had crumbled.

"It's a church." Laila pointed to the far end of the town. Well, it wasn't that far, as Prospect Hollow consisted of one main street with dilapidated buildings lining the sides. "See the cross on the top of what remains of a steeple?"

"It's a sign from God. He's looking out for us."

"It looks like an old mining town," Laila said. "Look, there's a saloon on the right. And up ahead to your left, I think that's a post office." Sure enough, etched in the dirty glass on the window were the words *US Mail*.

"This place seems like the last human left in 1905 and never looked back." Dust, dirt, and snow shellacked every remaining board covering the buildings, but the years and the weather hadn't been kind to these businesses. Most of the store fronts had holes with boards hanging by one rusty nail. One building sat in a heap of crumbling wood. But a few remained intact. Mostly.

And if they'd found this old town, Solomon's men would

likely also discover its existence. They weren't out of danger yet, and he refused to let his guard down for even a second.

Muscles burning, he pointed them toward the saloon, which looked like it had withstood the elements the best out of any of the other structures. Although, he almost rethought that when the door fell off its corroded hinges with one light push. Nevertheless, he used what little strength he had left to step inside.

A splintering bar and a few chairs and tables littered the place.

"At least we'll be out of the cold," Preston said, setting Laila down on the floor on her one good foot, praying it would hold. She inspected an ancient chair before collapsing into it. He dragged another chair over for her to prop her foot up on. "Be right back."

"We'll need to find a better hiding place. Be sure to look for—"

"I've got this. You just rest for a second."

He headed for the door they'd just entered and stepped outside.

So far, so good. No goons in sight. But he and Laila had left a well-marked snow trail to their location. Nothing he could do about that at the moment.

With the coast clear, he scooped up handfuls of snow. Once inside, he removed Laila's boot and packed her foot in snow. The purple-and-blue bruise had crawled up her leg, and the swelling doubled the size of her ankle. There was no way she would walk out of here, much less defend herself in the event Solomon caught up to them.

Laila let out a tense groan. "Definitely sprained. Probably broken."

"Let me scope out this place. I'm sure we can find some old moonshine to keep us warm tonight."

Laila tried to laugh, but it turned into a cough. She might go into shock from her injury, and he was still concerned about both of them developing hypothermia. He moved to the door and propped it up against the opening just in case anyone was watching. No sense in giving this abandoned town any signs of life.

Except fresh footprints in the snow on the street outside the saloon meant they weren't alone.

They had to get out of here. Now.

Preston searched the room. It had that old-timey bar vibe, like in the westerns his dad had loved watching when Preston was a kid. If he closed his eyes, he could picture this place hopping with miners living it up after quitting time. He noted a backroom storage area. As he stepped across the room to investigate their new surroundings, the floorboard let out a loud creak.

But one floorboard had a different sound than the others. He stuck his finger in the side of one and lifted.

"I found where they kept the moonshine," Preston muttered. The small hiding space was filled with bottles of brown and clear liquids, plus an unhealthy amount of dust.

They both froze at a noise outside.

"Laila Rabbinowitz. You are surrounded. Again."

FIVE

P reston's blood ran cold.

A warning shot shattered the dirt-caked windowpane and lodged itself in the wall, sending glass and wood fragments flying. Preston shielded his face and ran to Laila. He scooped her up and scanned the saloon.

Not behind the bar. The storeroom wasn't an option. They'd be spotted the second one of Solomon's men opened the door.

"Just leave me, Preston." Laila tightened her grip around his neck and searched his eyes. "He won't kill me right away. You can find help before he...he—"

"Don't say it. Remember, God's helping us fight. I'm not leaving you behind."

A window shattered in the back corner. He ducked with Laila in his arms, right beside the trap door. "Hide in the floor. There's only enough room for one of us."

"No!" Her panic-laced whisper shattered his heart. "That leaves you with nowhere to go."

"I'll hide in the storage closet."

Laila's eyes held worry and disappointment. He set her into the space and picked up the trapdoor. "I love you," he whispered. "And I will see you soon."

She nodded and offered him the gun. There was no way he'd leave her defenseless. "No, if anyone opens this hatch, you shoot." He lowered her onto the cobweb-covered hole, kissed her head, and closed the hatch.

Bulky footsteps approached the door of the saloon.

He raced to the back storage room. At least the door to the rectangular room stayed on its hinges. The other three walls had rows of built-in shelves, some with cans and bottles still intact. The place was a historical treasure trove that he'd never get to explore because Solomon and his men crashed their way through the front of the saloon. The whole building rattled, knocking dust into the air.

"Laila!" a voice roared. Footsteps headed his way. The closet would be the first place they'd check. Preston surveyed his prison and tried to wedge himself behind the storage rack with no luck. The shelves held firm to the wall.

He touched one of the glass bottles and found it bolted to the wooden rack. Same for the other bottles and cans. Why would they tack supplies down? He felt all around the unit until his fingers ran over some sort of latch. With a click, the shelving unit swung inward, revealing a secret passageway. Preston ducked through the opening and carefully pushed the fake wall closed behind him.

The floor creaked and someone entered the area he'd just left. He peeked through the rotted wood slats of the storage rack lining the back wall, which gave him just enough space to spy a man with a gun scrutinizing the supply closet.

"Nothing here," he called to the others and backed out of the storage closet. Preston let out a breath. He listened and prayed they didn't find Laila.

But his prayers hung in the air unanswered.

A gunshot rang out followed by the thud of a body hitting the floor.

"Pull that trigger again and you die now!"

"Hello, Solomon." Laila's voice sounded strong, confident, even if it was forced.

He held his breath, fighting the urge to rush the man.

But then he'd be dead, and no one would be able to go for help. His gut tightened as he listened to Laila offer a small grunt. Maybe from them tearing her out of her hiding place.

Why had he suggested they separate? She'd have been safe with him in the closet if he'd known about the secret passage.

"I'll be taking that gun from you." Solomon's voice pierced the dusty air. "Someone get that bleeding stopped."

"He's dead, boss," a new voice said.

"Whatever." Feet shuffled like he was turning back to Laila. "I'm surprised you survived the crash, all that poor American influence on you. And taking up with that playboy?" Solomon tsked. "Looks like I'll have to go with plan B. Maybe keeping you alive will benefit me after all."

Laila let out a yelp, and Preston tamped down the desire to burst into the room. What was he going to do? Battle three trained men? And with what? A flashlight and a squashed granola bar?

And again, someone had to find help. He looked behind him. The light filtering through the dirt wall illuminated what looked like a tunnel. At least he had that flashlight.

More dragging and shuffling came from inside. They were moving Laila. It sounded like she'd taken down at least one of the gunmen. Spots clouded his vision. He slumped to the ground and put his head on his knees, trying to calm his racing heart.

Why couldn't he defend the woman he loved?

Relentless. That's how she'd been when she'd been guarding him from Margot Harrington's thugs. He needed some of her resourcefulness and creativity right now—*she* needed him to have it.

He stared into the dark tunnel. "Hang on, Laila. I'm coming for you."

WEDNESDAY, 10:35 A.M.

Laila's worst nightmare had become her reality.

Solomon grabbed Laila, dragged her out the door, and dropped her onto the snow-covered street. She couldn't put any weight on her right foot, so she stayed on the ground. Any attempt at an escape was futile.

Solomon towered over her, and she forced herself not to cower. The hulking man looked like a fire-breathing dragon with his breath swirling around him from the cold. What had happened to the man she'd once admired? His hatred was so tangible she could feel it crawling across her skin.

"You will pay, Laila." With his hand around her arm, he half-carried, half-dragged her down the street.

Between the unforgiving cold and her ankle out of commission, every body part shrieked in agony. Her energy level hovered on empty, but she kept going because Preston had escaped. She'd received a miracle when the men had opened that storage area and not found him.

Her captor came to a stop at one of the buildings on the opposite side of town. He tossed her across the threshold, and she collapsed, panting to catch her breath. The toe of his hard boot nailed her side, and pain exploded. She fought to stay conscious.

Solomon kept coming after her, and she crawled away from his foot using every ounce of energy she had, but he kicked her a few more times. She hit a wall, and a clang rang out as rusty metal bars slammed shut. The entire town was falling apart, but just her luck, the jail cell in the old sheriff's office was the only thing that stood upright. At least the window gave off enough daylight that she could see the one-room police station.

She sat, tasting blood. "What do you want from me, Solomon?" She switched to Hebrew, their native language. "If I hadn't turned you in, any number of your fellow Mossad agents would have. Did you expect me to marry you after you betrayed your country and killed people?"

Solomon opened the jail cell door and pulled her up by her hair. Her ankle gave out, but she shoved the pain from her mind. This man would never have the satisfaction of seeing her break.

The slap came hard and fast, stinging her face. "When will you learn, Laila? You always had to have the last word. But you're not in control anymore. I am."

He threw her to the ground, and she wiped the blood from her mouth with the back of her hand. "Do what you want to me, Solomon. I'm not scared of you. I'll die with honor. But you? You'll just die miserable and alone."

Solomon reared back like he was going to kick the life out of her, but two of his men entered the jail, and he slammed his foot to the floor instead. He retreated, and the prison door clanked shut.

She let herself breathe, at least for the moment. She couldn't let fear take control. With her eyes closed, she laid out all of her options. With Mossad, she'd spent several sleep-deprived days alone in dangerous situations, all to prepare for this very day. She knew how to fight, how to outwit an opponent.

She would not let this madman win. She'd make sure Preston was safe, no matter the cost. But she couldn't wrap her mind around why Solomon was doing this. Vengeance wasn't a great motive. What did he want? Information? To take away everything she'd allegedly taken from him?

She watched as he spoke with the men. His Russian flowed quick, despite his native language being Hebrew. Laila listened, picking out only a few words but able to piece together enough to understand that Solomon was asking about Preston's whereabouts. The man shook his head and Laila exhaled.

Preston was safe for the moment. And this knowledge shot a burst of confidence through her that he just might make it out of this alive.

Solomon locked eyes with her, and she refused to break his stare. The years in prison hadn't been kind to Solomon. His hair had gone gray at the temples, and the fine lines that had dug in the corners of his eyes were deeper, more cruel. His thick beard used to be jet black and neat but was now tangled and littered with white. He was only a few years older than her but looked like time had had its way with him, leaving him gnarled and bitter.

He scowled and stormed to her cell to fling open the iron door. Before she could flinch, he pulled her up by the hair and pinned her against the wall with his arm across her throat. He went nose to nose with her, his rancid breath making her already-queasy stomach churn. "Where. Is. Your. *Boyfriend?*" His staccato words hit her like bullets.

Her good foot dangled, trying to find the ground as her oxygen levels plummeted. She clawed at his arm, but he didn't budge.

"I—I don't know." Her response was true. *God, help Preston survive.*

Spots blotted her field of vision. Her throat throbbed and her eyes grew heavy. Solomon continued to stare her down. "You lie," he hissed but released his arm. She fell to the floor in a heap, gasping for breath. Solomon roared to his two men to continue the hunt for Preston, and they rushed out. "Don't worry. I won't let your death be that easy." He slammed the cell door shut.

She couldn't take much more of this, and Solomon was just getting started.

"What do you want from me?" she rasped, her lungs burning from the exertion. "Solomon, why?"

He entered the cell, rage distorting his face. "You don't talk. You'll soon find out what I want."

Solomon pulled something out of his pocket—a familiar black device with probes on the end—and held it in front of Laila's face. With the press of a button, the air sizzled with a blue electric bolt from the stun gun.

An uncontrollable tremble shook every cell of her body from her toes to the tips of her hair. Whatever reason he had for crashing the plane and chasing her through the mountains almost didn't matter anymore. She prayed Preston found help fast, because if he didn't, she was dead.

And it would hurt a whole lot getting there.

SIX

P reston followed the tunnel, which appeared to link up to the mining shaft running under the entire town. The saloon must have used it for smuggling.

Did anyone know this town existed? Because this place was a gold mine of history. Literally, as evidenced by the overturned mining car and a pile of dynamite sticks stacked on one side of the rock wall. It was a good thing he wasn't claustrophobic, because if he stretched his arms high enough, he could reach the ceiling of the passageway at some points.

The pathway forked. To his right, five rickety steps led to a wood panel similar to the fake wall in the saloon. The left? No idea. He chose the steps, thankful that they held. When he reached the wall, he found the small handle, opened the attached door, and peered around it to find more darkness. All the buildings must connect underground.

The emptiness before him seemed to be another supply closet. He stepped inside and cracked the main door. With the coast clear, he inched his way into the interior of…the post office? A wooden counter lined one wall. The high-tech equipment splayed across the room clashed with the old dusty mining town.

"What do we have here?" Preston muttered. Guns lined one side of the room, laid out on the wooden countertop. He stayed low to the floor, avoiding the picture window in the front, and did a three-sixty to inspect the arsenal of weapons as well as the electronics. The generator-powered place was a cross between an old Western and an aisle at Best Buy. But the most curious item lay in the center of the building, resembling some sort of handheld ray-gun from a bad sci-fi movie.

This had to be the EMP device that had taken down their plane. He shivered at the thought of all they'd come through in the past day and a half. What was this man doing in the middle of nowhere with an arsenal of weapons and a stockpile of technology? This was clearly more than just vengeance for Solomon's stint in jail.

A beam of daylight shone through the dirty post office window, drawing his attention to a box at the back of the room. He crawled, still avoiding any movements that might be seen through the window, in case Solomon's men patrolled the street. A cell phone stood out in the glowing light, as if the beam beckoned him to find it. He picked it up and let relief wash over him for a second. Until he discovered the satellite phone required a passcode. He punched in some random numbers. The phone vibrated and a message indicated two tries remained before the phone permanently locked.

How could he guess the password of a raving lunatic? Frustrated, he resisted chucking the useless thing across the room and gently set it back where he'd found it. His fingers brushed an open laptop on the ground next to him.

When his pinky hit the trackpad, the screen flashed to life. Numbers and letters scrolled across the screen. Preston had plenty of experience with software development, and this program looked like it was running algorithms to hack a password.

Preston minimized the program and navigated to a web browser. Bingo!

Since the laptop connected to a satellite, he had internet access. He logged into a free email account he owned and typed a message to Juliette Montgomery, Laila's coworker and friend from the Elite Guardians. She'd be able to get help, and Juliette was heading to the wedding, so she'd at least be in the same time zone. But how was he going to communicate their location? "Side of the mountain" wasn't a great geographical marker.

He hammered out a brief message.

J, we're stranded on a mountain in Colorado, probably forty-five minutes from Breckenridge. Our plane was brought down with an EMP. Pilot died, but Laila and I survived. Solomon Mizrahi, Laila's ex, is responsible and he's kidnapped her. We are in an old mining town called Prospect Hollow. At least three men, heavily armed. Help us.

He started to type a message to his long-time friend and attorney, Sebastian Coyle, to call in more reinforcements, but footsteps approached the post office door. Every muscle in Preston's body froze. From his vantage point, he watched through the dirt-encrusted window as a man walked by, as if making the rounds on guard duty.

Preston turned off the program the laptop was running. Just to stop whatever progress they were making. Not wanting to push his luck with being out in the open, Preston nabbed one of the backpacks from the table and shoved the computer inside. He grabbed two guns and some ammunition. He'd gone shooting with his dad a few times, though it had been a few years since he'd had any target practice. Once he had the weapons loaded, he headed back into the tunnel.

Time to find Laila.

Preston hurried through the darkness, using the flashlight to guide his path. Voices filtered to him from a distance, and he stopped short, scanning the light over the wall. Another boarded up area that looked similar to the others that had opened. This had to be where they'd taken Laila.

He found a spot to stash the laptop and backpack but kept his fingers wrapped around the grip of one pistol. Moving toward the sound of the voices, he spotted a hole in the rotting wood that allowed him a limited view of the old sheriff's quarters.

Bile rose in his throat. Solomon stood in the center of the room, yelling something in another language. Probably Hebrew. Preston couldn't see Laila, but he could hear her launching a verbal assault against the man.

Two thugs dragged Laila into view, and she struggled against them. Preston clenched his teeth to keep from cheering when she landed a punch to the big guy's jaw. The man was twice her size and had a big scar that ran from his hair line to his eyebrow. He looked like he'd seen the inside of a jail cell or two during his lifetime as a career criminal. The other man, smaller but just as menacing as the first, picked Laila up by the waist and dropped her onto a wooden chair. He pinned both of her wrists behind her back and secured them to the chair with ropes.

The men had stripped off her winter coat and some of her layers of clothing, leaving her in a T-shirt and jeans. Her body trembled, probably from a combination of pain and cold. She stared down her captors with a defiant look that he'd never seen on her.

A crackle hissed through the air, and Solomon approached Laila. Preston saw the spark of light from a stun gun, and everything within him wanted to charge the man and rescue

Laila. But he forced himself to stand down, knowing that the three-against-one odds weren't in his favor.

"You want to know what I want?" Solomon roared at Laila in English. The man shoved his face into hers. "The Israeli government seized my accounts. And you're going to access them for me."

Solomon inched closer to Laila's side with the stun gun. Her head slumped forward as if she was having trouble holding it upright. One touch would be all it took to send those electrical currents pulsing through Laila.

"I'm sure you still know how to access the Mossad system. They kept you on payroll. Tell me the password. If you do, I'll kill you quickly. If you don't comply, I will torture you until you die. The choice is up to you."

Preston stifled a groan. The last thing he was going to do was watch the woman he loved be tortured. There had to be something he could do to rescue her—*Think! Think!*

His entire body shook as he backtracked down the hill and into the tunnel. He had to retreat before he made his presence known. He couldn't help Laila if he were dead.

They'd gotten out of the cave by causing a distraction. What if he could cause a diversion to get these men away from Laila?

A scream pierced the air.

Laila!

The sound of her pain spurred him into action. He ran toward Solomon's electronics lair. If he could take down their systems and rescue Laila, they might have a fighting chance of surviving this ordeal. He grabbed a few bottles of ancient alcohol he found in a crate and stormed into the electronics room.

Preston doused the equipment with the alcohol, eliciting a few sizzles as electricity popped. He pulled one of the two road flares from his coat pocket, took off the cap, and used it to strike the flare. It sparked to life, and he tossed the mini sparkler into the center of the room. The building was crumbling wood, so hopefully the blaze would catch Solomon's attention. Lighting the second flare, he tossed it into the gas generator. If they didn't have power, they couldn't use it against Laila.

Then he raced through the tunnels back to Laila's prison, praying for his distraction to pay off.

WEDNESDAY, 11:30 A.M.

WAS THAT THE WORST SOLOMON COULD DO? SURE, HE'D START small to wear her down and then kick up the torture level. Not that the stun gun hadn't caused unbearable pain as her muscles all spasmed at once, but it wouldn't kill her. Did he really think this would break her? She'd withstood much more in her lifetime.

She sent her captor a challenging smile.

Everything within her screamed at her to stall. To face the pain. Because the longer Solomon dragged out the torture, the more time Preston had to escape. Solomon would eventually kill her, but Preston would live.

Solomon stuck the stun gun inches from her neck. The electrical bolt singed her hair, and heat rippled across her skin. "The password. Now."

She stared at her former fiancé, and with all her warring emotions vying for attention, sadness was the one that won out. She'd found true love in Preston, her happy ending. But this man in front of her? Solomon had traded his soul in favor of greed and money. He'd been a skilled Mossad agent and mentor. She'd genuinely respected him, looked up to him. Even loved him.

Then he'd discarded her and her team, leaving them to die.

Yes, she knew how to access the Mossad system, but even the most trained Mossad agent eventually died.

He wasn't going to win this round.

She hung her head, lacking the energy to keep it upright. An image of Preston popped into her mind. It seemed that every time she faced death—which happened way too frequently these days—her thoughts flew straight to Preston. How would he deal with her loss after still reeling from the death of his father and brother? The tears flowed—partly from her own pain, but also at the thought of Preston's sorrow. She wanted to marry him and have a future with him. But now? She sat strapped to a chair while a madman electrocuted her.

God, why is this happening? Just when I've started living, I'm going to die.

It didn't matter what life threw at them; she was stronger with Preston by her side. How could she have doubted that? He'd taught her what real love was, and she wasn't alone anymore.

Her mind flashed back to the last time she'd stared down death—when she'd been buried alive in a cemetery. She'd survived that ordeal by laying down her weapons and letting God fight for her.

She sent up a prayer that God would not only fight for her but for Preston.

Solomon growled, ready to send thousands of electric volts through her neck.

A loud explosion rocked the building.

"What was that?" Solomon barked orders to his men, who took off.

"The weapons room is on fire," one man yelled back.

Solomon grunted. He backed up, turned off the stun gun, and dashed out the front door.

Laila tried to catch her breath, fighting the rope that secured her hands.

"Laila," a voice whispered from behind her, and she jerked.

"Preston?" she whispered. The exertion of saying his name revealed how much energy Solomon had zapped from her with his stun gun.

Her knight in shining armor stepped into her field of vision.

"What are you—"

Preston pressed his lips to hers and ran a hand through her hair.

"Don't talk. Let's get you out of here. We don't have much time." He unfastened the ropes and rubbed her wrists.

"I thought I'd never see you again!"

Preston grabbed her layers of clothes from the floor and pulled her up, into his arms. "Hey. I'm a man of my word."

How had she ever doubted that they were meant to be together? Preston had come back for her. Like he'd promised.

He carried her to the back of the old sheriff's office. "They built this whole town on a series of tunnels. I'm not sure Solomon knows they exist, but I discovered a fake wall in the saloon supply closet. And I found one here too." He pressed around until he grasped a latch that opened the fake wall.

Preston crept through the tunnel, careful to not bump Laila's leg against the narrow passageway. Smoke from the explosion created a haze, but not enough that they couldn't breathe. "I blew up their command center."

She blinked in surprise.

"And I found a phone. It needed a passcode, but I found a laptop that wasn't locked."

Preston showed her his stash of weapons and the laptop.

"Well," she said. "It looks like you don't need my skills as a bodyguard after all." Preston was more than capable of fending for himself. And he had a knack for showing up at the perfect time to save her.

"You—"

"Ah!" Solomon's bellow cut him off, his displeasure at Laila's disappearance reverberating from the jail. "Find her!"

She shuddered, and Preston set her down to lean against the tunnel wall. When she tried to put weight on her foot, she nearly fell over. "Careful, love, careful," he said and righted her. "I'll carry you on my back, and you can carry the laptop and guns."

She put on her sweatshirt and jacket, the cold already seeping into her bones.

He stooped and Laila climbed onto his back, wrapping her arms and legs around him. She tucked the laptop between them and stuck two guns into the waistband of her jeans. Preston rushed through the passageways like an expert while she tried to not throw up.

Her heart hammered a rapid beat, and sweat rolled down her back. She started to regain feeling in her extremities after being electrocuted and took a deep breath, enjoying the few seconds of peace.

Preston stopped at what looked like the entrance to the mine shaft, and Laila slid down his back, clinging to the wall for support. Wood boards concealed the entrance to the tunnels, but the years hadn't been kind to the barricade. Preston found a hole big enough to make his way outside and check out their surroundings. "I don't see anyone, but if we exit, I think we'll be at the edge of town. Maybe we can make a run for it."

Laila slunk to the ground, her back up against the stone wall. "Run where? We're still stuck on the side of a mountain. What we need to do is capture Solomon. We can't let him get away."

As if she were in any shape to fight with her busted ankle.

But something within her wouldn't let Solomon win. He had to be stopped.

"I'm not letting you fall into that madman's hands again. No way. The first chance we get, we flee." Preston picked up the laptop. "I emailed Juliette, so let's see if she responded. Maybe help is on the way."

He opened the computer while Laila listened for any sign of trouble. She didn't hear Solomon or his henchmen stomping around. But that man wouldn't give up so easily.

"No. Come on." Preston hammered the keyboard and groaned. "It's dead. I didn't think to grab the cord, but it wouldn't have done any good without power. And I blew up the power source."

"I'm sure Juliette got the email and is on her way," Laila said. "But the question is, will she get here in time? If we leave, Juliette will have a harder time finding us."

Preston sank to the ground next to her and wrapped his arms around her shoulders, drawing her to him. "I think we need to move. Head to the mountain. Do our best to put some distance between us and Solomon."

"I'm so sorry, Preston. I can't believe my past put you in the crosshairs of a madman. It's all my fault. I put you in this danger, and I can't even find a way out of this nightmare."

"Just stop." Preston's sharp tone caught her off guard. "I don't need a bodyguard; I need a partner. When are you going to realize that we're equals in this relationship? You've saved my life in the past, and I'm going to be there for you every time you need me. But we'll never have a solid future if we can't share life's burdens. We've got to be a team, but that can't happen unless you stop this one-woman show you've got going on. Laila, I can't keep competing with you."

His words stung, but she realized the truth in them.

God had fulfilled her dreams in this one man. Before Preston, she'd doubted she'd ever fall in love. Not after Solomon's betrayal. But Preston had shown her how genuine love could change a person's heart. Even a heart as self-reliant as hers.

And Preston was, obviously, more than capable of taking care of himself.

"You're right," she whispered. "I've tried to do my own thing for so long that I forget how to let others help me. But you saved my life. Solomon would have killed me."

"We'll find a way out of this, because I'm not leaving you. Ever." Preston wrapped his arms around her and pulled her close.

"How did I get so blessed to find you?" she whispered in his ear.

Preston chuckled. "Apparently it takes killers to bring us closer."

She punched him in the side, but with her energy so sapped, he probably didn't feel it. She gritted her teeth at the thought of standing but knew they needed to go. Solomon was lurking in the shadows.

Preston helped her up. "Let's make our way into the freezing cold and find a place to hide in the mountains," he said. "We'll stay close enough to be able to see if help arrives."

Pain radiated from every inch of her body when Laila attempted to put weight on her foot. Even trying to use Preston like a crutch to keep weight off her swollen ankle made her stumble.

In defeat, she sank back onto the ground. "What are we going to do? I won't make it very far, and it won't be hard for Solomon to track us. I think we need to stay and fight."

SEVEN

L aila tried to form a plan that would get them out of this mess. But she came up empty-handed.

She winced as a flash of pain radiated from her ankle when she stretched out her legs. How would she take down Solomon when she couldn't stand on her own two feet?

But Preston had come to her rescue. Again. She'd have to rely on him if they had any chance of survival. Which put her at odds with protecting him. Still, for once she'd have to trust someone other than herself.

"You really think our best option is to run?" she asked Preston.

"There's only one road in and out of town," Preston whispered as he sat down next to her. "It puts us out in the open, but it's the best way for us to literally get out of dodge."

She wanted to laugh at his joke, but her muscles weren't cooperating. "Solomon is around here somewhere. He wouldn't leave without getting what he wants from me."

"Even if you gave him the password, he'd still kill you."

It didn't require a response because they both knew the truth.

A shiver wracked her. Solomon would never stop hunting her. Even if by some miracle she managed to escape the mountains, she'd be looking over her shoulder for the rest of her life.

"We need to capture him," Laila said. "We can't let him get away from this town. Who knows what danger he'll pose to our country?"

Preston stared at her. "We're outmanned and outgunned. You can't even walk, let alone capture a man."

Laila sighed. "You're right. We should escape while we have the chance. But how are we going to get out of town unnoticed?"

Preston grabbed her hand. "I've been thinking, and it looks like Solomon didn't discover the underground tunnels. What if we create another explosion as a distraction. It might give us the opportunity to get them to one side of the town while we escape into the forest."

His plan would be risky, but if anyone could pull this off, it was Preston. She'd just have to trust God to protect them both.

Preston looked at her, his eyes brightening. "Do you have any more flares?"

She patted her coat pocket. One left. She handed it to him. "What are you thinking?"

"Here. Hold my gun." He passed her the weapon and kissed her. One of those movie kisses that took place right before the hero headed off into battle. Laila didn't want him to go, and wrapped her arms around his neck. Warmth spread from her head to her toes. It didn't matter that they were hiding in a drafty tunnel, cut off from the rest of the world.

She and Preston were better together.

Oh, how she didn't want the kiss to end, but he pulled back and said, "Wait here, and I'll head down into the tunnel and see if I can blow something up. But instead of going after Solomon, we run. I understand national security and all, but right now, all I care about is getting you to safety. I love you, Laila Rabbinowitz. And I'm not letting you go. Got it?"

"Understood, Preston Whittaker."

Preston grabbed the dead laptop and disappeared into the darkness.

She pressed fingers to her lips, still tingling from the kiss. "God, protect that man," she whispered.

What if he didn't make it back? What if Solomon caught Preston? She silenced her thoughts. She could withstand any kind of torture, but losing Preston would shatter her.

The realization hit her like a freight truck. She'd thought they could live their separate lives and somehow make it work. But being with Preston was different. It didn't matter if they were stranded in the middle of nowhere or back home with packed schedules and busy jobs.

They would be together, no matter what.

A gunshot rang out in the distance, but still too close for Laila's comfort.

"I know you're out there." Solomon's voice bounced off the walls of the tunnel. The town wasn't that big, so he had to be close by. He must be standing in the center of town, hurling out his threats because he couldn't find them.

Which meant that Preston was safe, for the moment "Hurry, Preston. Please hurry," she whispered.

As though he had heard her plea, Preston burst from the darkness of the main tunnel that led to the other buildings. "Let's hope this works. I tossed a lit flare onto a pile of old dynamite I spotted earlier. The materials we're working with are a hundred years old. We need them to cause a big explosion. We'll make our way out the opposite side of town."

Laila's ankle throbbed in time to her rising heart rate. "I love you, Preston." She balanced herself with both hands wrapped around his forearm.

"I love you too," he said, "but if this is your way of saying goodbye in case we don't make it, don't. Because we're walking out of this alive. Well, maybe limping, but we're going to do this, right?"

She bit her lip and nodded, then handed Preston his gun. He bent and she climbed onto his back, her gun in one hand and the other wrapped around his chest. "Let's do this," Laila said, tightening her grip.

Preston grabbed a gun and stooped to maneuver them both through the hole in the rotting wood at the entrance to the mining shaft. Laila's eyes scanned the area while her finger hovered over the trigger ready to shoot. Where was Solomon? Where were his goons?

Decades of overgrowth had covered the mine opening. Preston forged on, pushing limbs and other debris out of their way. Remnants of a pathway still existed centuries later, and they emerged from the woods at the opposite end of town from the saloon where they'd first arrived. Now they were closer to the run-down church that framed the edge of town. "Hold it right there," a voice said from behind them. "You're not going anywhere." Laila swiveled her head and saw Solomon's lackey with a gun trained on them. The big guy with the long scar on his forehead. To her left, the gunman stood, watching them with his finger on the trigger. To her right, Solomon stood in the center of the street. Where was the other thug?

She tightened her grip around Preston's chest and wrapped her legs securely around his waist. "Watch out for the third man. I don't see him," she whispered in his ear. He nodded and moved toward the road, facing off with Solomon. Laila kept her eye on the gunman, who covered them from behind. So much for running.

A shiver started in her toes and raced through her whole

body. The missing man stepped out from behind a pile of rubble. He moved toward Solomon.

"We're surrounded," she said.

Preston nodded.

They needed to push Solomon back toward the saloon, to the place where Preston had lit the

dynamite. But the only arrow left in Laila's quiver was to somehow negotiate with a madman.

Here goes nothing.

Before she could hurl idle threats Solomon's way, Preston took over.

"I have something you need, Solomon," Preston yelled and took a few steps closer to Solomon. "You won't want to shoot us just yet."

Was Preston bluffing? If so, her admiration swelled a thousand percent for her boyfriend, because that took some serious guts. Did he have a plan to push Solomon toward the saloon? Maybe the dynamite might take out Solomon. If it would just ignite.

She took a mental inventory of everyone's position. One gunman behind them. The other to their left. Solomon straight ahead. If any of them so much as flinched…

"You have that right," Solomon said. "I'll be taking your girl. If you're lucky, I'll let you escape long enough for the bears or mountain lions to kill you."

Preston took another bold step closer to Solomon, and Laila tried to keep visual contact with the other two gunmen. She had to cover Preston's back. Whatever plan he had, she needed to make sure someone didn't shoot them first.

"You won't be taking anyone, Solomon." Preston moved another two steps forward. "Because I have your laptop. It wasn't incinerated in the explosion."

Solomon sucked in an audible breath as Preston's verbal punch landed. The man double-fisted the barrel of his gun and growled. "You are in no position to negotiate with me." He nodded, and the two gunmen closed in on Preston and Laila. She ping-ponged the sight of her gun between the men while hanging on to Preston.

Come on, dynamite. Do your thing.

At least everyone was accounted for, despite her and Preston's being outnumbered. Now only one question screamed through Laila's mind.

Who would be the first to shoot?

WEDNESDAY, HIGH NOON

PRESTON'S PULSE THUMPED IN HIS EARS, AND HE WILLED HIS hands to steady. A few more steps and he'd have to stop moving forward to keep a safe distance away from the location of the underground dynamite.

"I saw the program, Solomon. And I have it."

Snow dusted Solomon's shaggy hair. Why hadn't the dynamite ignited? Preston was close enough to see the plumes of steam swirling from the man's breath.

Standing eight feet from Solomon, Preston maneuvered another two steps. Solomon hadn't expected another bold move forward, and his eyes danced wildly toward his hired guns.

"Take them," Solomon commanded, but retreated a few steps backward.

Preston felt Laila's arm swivel her gun between the other two gunmen.

Preston claimed the minor victory at Solomon's retreat. But what was the point of this plan now that the dynamite didn't seem to work? Maybe it was time to put all his cards on the table. Because they had nothing to lose at this point.

They were outnumbered, and Solomon's men were drawing close.

"If you let us walk away, I'll tell you where I stashed the laptop. I know it's important to you."

Everyone froze. Preston and Solomon stared at each other over the sights of their guns.

Solomon snorted. "You don't call the shots around here." But he snapped his fingers, and the man on the left lowered his weapon.

"Okay, I'll play your game, Preston. I give you my word that I'll let you and Laila leave town if you give me the laptop." Solomon held his hands up in mock surrender, the gun hanging limply in his hand.

Of course, it was all for show. Like Preston would take the word of this lunatic. Solomon would shoot them in the back in a heartbeat once he got what he wanted. But Preston needed this standoff to end, so he'd play along. "It's in the saloon, Solomon. Why don't you go check for yourself? I left it on the bar."

A flicker of confusion crossed Solomon's face as Preston revealed his one and only bargaining chip. But would Solomon be greedy enough to fall into Preston's trap to retrieve the laptop? If only the old dynamite would ignite before spring thawed the winter chill and the police found their frozen, bullet-ridden bodies.

The man on their left moved toward the saloon while Solomon backed up until he was even with the entrance of the building. Solomon kept one eye on the door and the other on Preston and Laila.

Perfect.

Laila kept her gun aimed over her shoulder at the gunman to their back, who hadn't wavered his stance. Solomon's other man headed inside and returned with the prized item.

"Looks like I have two things I want, Preston. The laptop and now the girl."

Game over. The dynamite wasn't going to ignite, and Preston was out of moves.

"My plan failed. I'm so sorry, Laila."

"It's not over, Preston," Laila responded. "I trust you. Have faith. We're getting out of this alive." And right then, the earth convulsed. As if it hiccupped, the ground belched, then shuddered.

And with it, so did Solomon's balance.

It was the distraction Laila needed to take a shot at the man behind them. Preston heard the thump as the guy hit the ground.

Solomon stumbled but refused to fall.

Until the ground convulsed again, as if God was helping. Solomon tripped, buckling to his knees. He let out a shout as he caught himself, but his gun bounced away.

The man that had entered the saloon tucked the laptop under his arm, turned, and ran away from the shaking road.

And now the explosion hit the street. The blast shot dirt, snow, wood fragments, and pebbles sky-high like a dust geyser.

A crevice broke open the road, a gulf widening fast between them and Solomon, but Preston bolted. Then he stopped, breathing hard to Laila's shout.

"He's getting away!"

He turned to see Solomon crawling away from the expanding hole in the ground.

Another explosion shook the town. Laila sucked in a breath. "The saloon is shaking. It's going to collapse. We might have sunk the entire town."

No sooner had she predicted it than the wooden saloon groaned and creaked as the earth opened and swallowed the old building.

And then, the crater opened up and swallowed Solomon whole.

Just like that, their captor disappeared.

Even Laila gasped.

A dust plume billowed across the center of town, raining debris all around the crater. Laila doubled down on her grip around Preston's chest.

"If Solomon's guy knew what was good for him, he'd bolt," Laila said.

As if on cue, the roar of a snow mobile in the distance echoed through the remaining buildings of the town.

"Aw, man. They had snowmobiles?" Preston grumbled. "Let's go find them."

"If Juliette is on her way, the best thing we can do is stay here." Laila slipped off Preston's back and leaned against a tree for support, her eyes searching for any signs of life.

With the dropping temperatures and the setting sun, another chilly night awaited them. "I'm going to check on Solomon to see if he survived," Preston said. "Then I'll check on a safe place for us to camp out tonight. Someplace preferably without bats. Are you okay by yourself for a minute?" Preston needed to check the crater for any signs of life. Because as much as he didn't wish death on anyone, he wanted that hole to be Solomon's permanent resting place.

She nodded, and now that the danger had passed, he saw the toll Solomon and the cold had inflicted on her. Her eyes were rimmed in dark circles and devoid of their usual gleam. Her pale face concerned him the most, her skin almost translucent. He hated to leave her but headed to the edge of the crater. He needed visual confirmation that their nightmare ended here. Now.

Snow and dust filtered through the air, and Preston used his scarf as a mask. He spotted Solomon, who lay sprawled across the debris with his leg bent behind him, the bone sticking out.

There was no way Solomon had survived with the amount of blood flowing from a head wound. Preston looked away.

Laila was safe from this evil man's clutches. Forever.

The one building that had remained relatively untouched—a far, safe distance from the crater—was the lonely, small church. Despite the age of the building, most of it remained intact. Hints of the white façade still clung to the walls, and the steeple still towered over the town like a beacon. He made his way to the church, keeping one eye on Laila, who managed to stay upright under the tree. The roof had some holes in it, but all four walls were still standing.

He ducked through the entrance. The years had weathered the place, but it would give them some shelter from the snow. In the corner of the room sat a wood burning stove. A second miracle, one he hadn't thought possible. They might be able to stay warm until Juliette found them.

If Juliette found them. He'd start a fire and send up a smoke signal.

Not wanting to leave Laila unattended for long, he rushed back outside. As he approached, he watched her sway.

"Laila!" He raced toward her and caught her in his arms just as she passed out.

EIGHT

Preston!

Laila struggled to chase the fog from her mind, but the images refused to budge. They flickered behind her eyes like a movie reel.

The ground opened its hungry mouth and swallowed Solomon in one bite.

Preston raced toward the hole, but Laila lost sight of him. Why couldn't she see him? She tried to shout his name, but her vocal cords were frozen. The ground groaned again. If Preston wasn't careful, the ground would take him from her.

"Preston!"

Laila forced her eyes open and tried to focus them. Where was he? Wooden beams filled her view, with a few snowflakes wafting through the holes in a dilapidated roof. She moved her hands and felt the cool stone floor beneath her.

"I'm right here." Preston's voice instantly killed the visions of him falling into the black abyss. Her heart stuttered when her eyes landed on his face.

168

Preston had survived.

"Solomon?" She forced out the name that she never wanted to have cross her lips again.

"He's not going to bother you ever again."

She winced.

Solomon had made his choices, and in the end, his bad choices had buried him. The man had taken so much from her over the years, but he couldn't destroy her future.

Her future was Preston.

"Where...where are we?" Pain reminded her of their ordeal, and Preston helped her sit up. She rested her back against a wooden wall and caught her first glimpse of the inside of the one-room building. The church?

Pews lined the interior—some barely standing, but most were crumpled fragments of wood and dirt. Wait, why was she warm in the crumbling sanctuary? She was covered in a blanket. Or was that Preston's jacket? Still, the sun was about to set, and the snow continued to fall through the cracks in the ceiling. Yet a familiar scent tickled her nose. It reminded her of a campfire mixed with something else.

Coffee?

"Here, drink this." Preston handed her a tin cup.

Preston had turned one corner of the run-down church into a cozy shelter complete with a wood-burning stove. He'd removed a few of their outer layers and created a thin cushion by the fire. Snow formed small piles around the room, but their quaint spot of the church stayed fairly warm and dry.

She took the cup and drank, reveling in the warmth of the hot liquid. "Coffee? Where did you get this?"

Preston laughed. "Apparently, in our panic to leave the airplane, you shoved the package of coffee into the bottom of your jacket pocket. Smart."

"Well, I grabbed the essentials." She smiled, unwinding now that no one was chasing them.

Laila stretched out on the floor in front of the stove, but the throbbing in her ankle limited her movements. Preston sank next to her on the stone floor, and she leaned her head against his shoulder.

"You've worked wonders with this place. How long was I out?"

Preston shrugged. "I lost track of time. But you probably slept a few hours."

"Still no Juliette?" Laila asked, already assuming the answer.

"I keep listening for any signs of life, whether it's the good guys arriving for a rescue or the bad guy returning. But so far, all has been quiet."

"Well, you did promise me a cozy fire." Some overpriced resort in the mountains couldn't compete with this ambiance. "I think I passed out from the pain. My ankle is still screaming." A beat passed between them.

She looked up at Preston. He'd chiseled away some of the walls she'd built around her heart, but he'd also shown her how to depend on God. No longer was her first course of action to rely on herself. And she'd found the love of her life in the process of letting go of her past.

With her fingers laced through his, Laila snuggled deeper against Preston's chest.

"I'm so sorry that I put my job ahead of you," Preston said. "It took a plane crash and being stranded for me to realize that you felt like I was pushing you away."

She sighed. "Preston, I want more than time. I don't want us to go back to the same. Earlier, what you said in the tunnel before you set the explosion—you were right. I want us to be a team. I don't want to go back to carving out a few minutes here or there. I'm all in. I'm willing to do whatever it takes to make our relationship work. Even if it means my priorities change. Even if it means I'm not a bodyguard anymore."

Preston chuckled. "You will always be a bodyguard. Just not

my bodyguard." He squeezed her hand, a gesture to communicate that things would change. That they'd make it as a couple, no matter what obstacles they faced.

Laila looked around their shelter and realized that there wasn't any place she'd rather be than right here. "While this is a far cry from a fancy resort, this is the most perfect Christmas tradition I could have asked for."

Preston snorted. "Tradition? A maniac tried to kill you. And don't forget about surviving the plane crash. What about this adventure makes you want to repeat this?"

She looked up and met his eyes. "I don't care where I am, as long as I'm with you. You promised me a lodge with a fireplace. We've got that, sort of. And what better Christmas decor is there than actual snow falling on us? I think it's quite romantic."

Despite the freezing cold, almost being electrocuted to death, surviving after falling out of the sky, and blowing up a mining town, she wanted to live in this moment. "I'm serious. I don't want to go home," she whispered.

"Hmm? Are you suggesting that we stay here, in an abandoned church where it's quite possible we'll freeze to death?"

She looked around the room. Moonlight filtered through the cracks in the ceiling, and a light dusting of snow shimmered in the flicker of the fire. The stove gave off enough heat to make the frigid temperature bearable. Only a few days until Christmas, and she finally had a sense of peace. "In this moment, I have you. I don't want to lose this connection again." She sighed. "I don't want to lose you."

WEDNESDAY, 5:00 P.M.

Laila's words stabbed Preston in the gut. Was the only way for them to have a shot at a relationship to completely remove themselves from their current lives?

Words lodged in his throat. What could he say to make Laila believe that they'd make it?

This wasn't how he'd planned their getaway, but now was the time to speak from his heart.

"When I saw you, tied to that chair and Solomon standing over you, I—I wanted to die. I didn't know what to do, so I left. I refused to watch him torture you, and I thought the best thing I could do was create a distraction."

"That may have saved my life."

He shrugged. "Maybe. I was out of options. But as I raced to their electronics room—I swear this is going to sound crazy—I felt your pain. My skin burned at the thought of him touching you with that stun gun. Your scream echoed in my mind long after I'd left the area. I've never been that connected to anyone before. If I lost you, I'd lose myself."

Preston shifted to face Laila. Even in the flickering light of the fire, he saw a bruise forming around her eye. Her hair had matted spots with dried blood. But she'd never looked more beautiful.

"Do you think that when all of this drama dies down and we make our way back home, that somehow things will be different? It seems like we find our rhythm when danger stares us in the face."

She shifted to look him in the eyes. "You always come for me. Whether I'm trapped under water, in a grave, or on a snow-covered mountainside, you find me. But I want you there for the day-to-day mundane routines of life too."

Their lives weren't some action movie where, once the reel ended, the credits would roll and they'd go back to their normal lives. Preston didn't need a plane crash and a Western shootout to know that he wanted Laila by his side through the boring days and the perilous ones.

"Well, then, we just don't go home," Preston announced. "Because my home is wherever you are, not some location on the map. It's with you."

He ran a hand through Laila's hair. "I don't want to go back to our normal lives either," he whispered. "I will not lose you again, and we now know that we can survive any situation. Which means we can make it through the day-to-day drudgery or being chased by a homicidal maniac on the side of a mountain. I won't wait for life to slow down or the right time or anything else. This is the moment we've been given. This is the moment I want to live in. Forever."

"Forever sounds perfect."

She leaned in and kissed him with the kind of passion that ignited a fire strong enough to melt all the snow around them. The past twenty-four hours dissipated as if a distant memory, and all Preston wanted was a future with Laila.

It didn't matter what happened to them, someway he'd always find his way back to her.

When she broke the kiss, he rested his forehead on hers and heaved a sigh of contentment. "I feel like we are over the lifetime quota of being chased by lunatics threatening to kill us."

She giggled, the rare sound lifting a weight off his chest. Her bruises would get bigger and darker, but her feisty spirit set his heart beating double time.

Laila's eyelids drooped, and while she needed to rest, he couldn't wait another second.

He shifted on the ground until he was on one knee. From inside his pocket, he pulled out a small velvet bag. "I need to make forever official. I bought a ring the day after our first date. I knew I wanted to marry you; I just was never sure of the timing. A spur-of-the-moment retreat to a private ski lodge seemed like the perfect setting for a proposal. And while this seems more like a nightmare than a dream, I can't think of a better time or place." He sucked in a deep breath and smiled. "Laila Rabbinowitz, will you marry me? I don't care where we live or work. All I care about is that I'm with you."

Laila's eyes glistened with unshed tears in the moonlight that flickered through the cracks in the ceiling. She wasn't much of a crier, so he took it as a compliment for his fantastic proposal—complete with a snow-filled chapel, frigid temperatures, and a million injuries. But he wouldn't have it any other way.

"Yes. Of course I'll marry you. I'd marry you right now if we had a minister. I mean, we're in a quaint church. And there's no paparazzi stalking us."

He laughed. "True. I definitely want to elope. But I'm thinking Maui might make a great wedding and honeymoon spot all rolled into one. Who knows, maybe we don't come back."

Another toe-curling kiss, and Preston was done. Done with being separated from the woman he loved by life and busyness. As long as he had Laila in his life, all of the other details would fit like puzzle pieces locking into place.

The whooshing sound of a distant motor thrummed through the chapel. "Juliette! She found us." Preston stood. "Wait here. I'll go flag her down. I'm sure they can't miss the smoking crater in the side of the mountain, but just in case, I'll make sure she doesn't pass us by."

Laila nodded and he rushed out the front door of the chapel, which fell off its hinge with his eager push. The sound of the helicopter rotor grew louder, and a spotlight lit up the trees. Preston ran toward the light on the horizon. Because, despite the darkness and danger they'd just endured, Laila and Preston's future lit up like the brightest spotlight the world had ever seen.

NINE

What was taking her fiancé so long?

Preston had probably only been gone a few minutes, but it felt like an eternity. She didn't want to let the man out of her sight. But oh, how she loved to call him her fiancé.

She sat against the wall in the quiet chapel and held her hand closer to the fire in the stove. Yes, this sanctuary with its dilapidated exterior and weather-beaten interior would beat anything some stuffy upscale resort had to offer. The flickering light hit her ring and splashed a sparkling display of twinkling lights across the room.

The snow continued to drift through the cracks in the church, but it seemed like God had placed each flake in the sky just for Laila to enjoy the magic of this night. The coziness of the snow-covered pews and the warmth of the fire stove chased away the bad memories of the last twenty-four hours. If only Preston would hurry up and return, the moment would be complete.

"Thank You, God," she whispered into the silent sanctuary. "Thank You for saving my life yet again and bringing me a man that loves me. Something I never thought possible." Her heart overflowed from joy. She was loved by the Creator of the universe.

And by Preston Whittaker.

Voices gave her a burst of energy. The cavalry had arrived. She grabbed the wall to steady herself and tried to rise on her one good foot.

"Wow, Preston said you were in bad shape." Juliette Montgomery rushed to her side, and Laila looped an arm around her friend's neck for support. Juliette brushed the snow flurries from her short blonde hair. While she may have a few inches on Laila's five-foot-two frame, Juliet could match Laila's combat skills any time.

"It seems to me that you're doing pretty good, stranded with that hunk of a boyfriend of yours. Or shall I call him your fiancé?" Of course Juliette hadn't missed the rock on Laila's finger.

"Guilty." She let a chuckle escape her lips. "We're engaged."

"I'll save my girlie-girl squeal for once we get you to safety. Another storm is brewing just in time for Charlie and Lizzie's wedding, and we've got to get going before we're all snowed in here."

She could hear Preston laugh as he came into the chapel with another man. Juliette introduced the chopper pilot. Preston put out the fire. He got on the other side of Laila, and he and Juliette carried her out the door of the church, past the sign that announced they were leaving Prospect Hollow. What seemed like a thousand miles was probably not even a mile, but they trudged through snow and tree branches until Laila saw a clearing big enough for the helicopter to land in. Barely.

The pilot had some medical training and gave Laila something that knocked her out. She didn't remember the helicopter ride or arriving at the hospital. Her dreams were filled with visions of Preston and their future.

She awoke and squinted in the fluorescent-tube lighting from the hospital room. Preston sat on one side of the bed with Juliette dozing in a chair on her other side. The room was tight with three of them in there, plus the myriad of beeping machines lined against the wall. But she'd take this sterile ambiance over being stuck on a frigid mountain any day.

She and Preston were safe.

Preston handed her some water, and she sipped slowly, the cool liquid soothing her burning throat. "What...what's the prognosis?"

His smile lit up the room. "We made it, Laila. We're in a town with an actual hospital and not on that mountain anymore. You're safe, and more importantly, warm."

Juliette woke up and stretched. "I'm going to find some coffee. I'll bring you some back."

"You speak my love language, Juliette," Preston said. Juliette tossed Laila a smile over her shoulder and sauntered off in search of liquid sustenance.

"But you've been checked out by the doctor?" Laila asked.

Preston nodded. "I'm okay. They were concerned about some frostbite, and once I got warm, my toes hurt as they thawed out, but I'm in good shape."

"What about me? I feel like a thousand angry bees stung me." She wiggled her fingers and toes, and they seemed to be all accounted for.

Preston pressed her hand lightly between his. "The doctor said it's normal for there to be pain as you warm up. But you don't have any major damage other than a bad sprain. We lucked out. To have survived the crash was a miracle in and of itself. Not to mention all the other stuff that happened after."

"I've never rappelled down a mountain with a parachute as a rope before. That one's a record for me."

Preston laughed, the sound a balm to her. She checked out her glistening ring finger. "I can't believe you've been carrying around this ring for months."

He shot her a sheepish look. "I think I've loved you since the first time we met. Well, maybe second time, since our first encounter you tackled me."

"How could I forget?" Images flooded her mind from their whirlwind meeting and romance. There wasn't anyone else in the world that she wanted to spend the rest of her life with.

"How are we going to get to Lizzie and Charlie's wedding?" Laila asked, realizing that their plans had derailed a long time ago. The analog clock on the wall showed one a.m.

Preston shrugged. "Last time I checked, the doctor didn't want to release you until tomorrow. Something about dehydration. I think you need to rest for now. We'll figure things out in the morning."

She dozed off, and when she woke, she saw Preston and Juliette drinking coffee.

"Are we getting out of here anytime soon?" Laila asked.

Preston exchanged a look with Juliette, then moved to the edge of Laila's bed. "There's a bad storm heading toward the lodge in Montana. We had to send the chopper pilot home before the storm hits. I'm not sure we'll be able to get anyone to fly us in this weather."

Laila shook her head. "I'm not too keen on getting into a small airplane, especially with the storm." She shuddered at the flashbacks of the plane crash and sent up a silent prayer for Phil's family. The pilot had died to save them during the crash, and she'd never forget his sacrifice. "Maybe we can drive?"

"It might be just as treacherous on the roads, not to mention the time crunch," Juliette said. "We've got less than two days to figure out a way to get to Montana."

Laila's thoughts drifted. Two days. My, how things could

change. Look at *her* last forty-eight hours. The man she loved and who loved her in return.

Yes, life sure moved fast. Who knew what the next two days had in store for her? But at least one thing was certain.

She and Preston Whittaker would be side by side.

CHRISTMAS SNOWSTORM STANDOFF

SAMI A. ABRAMS

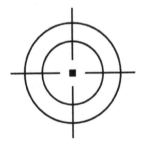

ONE

Two days before Christmas Eve, Lizzie Tremaine's dream of a winter wonderland wedding surrounded by friends and family at Wild Sapphire Ranch in Montana was slowly vanishing. The unexpected snowstorm had her once again questioning God's plan for her life—which was odd since He'd been so faithful in showing her what to do and how to do it. But right now, she held her breath and prayed.

She'd slipped outside a few minutes ago when the gravity of the situation had become too much.

God, am I not supposed to get married? Okay, yes, I know I'm being ridiculous, but can You blame me? I mean, You know my past as well as I do.

A past where she'd loved and lost so many times that forgetting became hard.

Hooded parka on and insulated-gloved hands shoved in her pockets, Lizzie peered into the distance at the vast yard in front of her. To her left, the guest lodge and cabins that created a C shape were mere shadows in the falling snow. The never-ending falling snow. *Seriously, Lord? You calmed the waves of the storm, but You can't hold back the snow?*

Of course He could, but for whatever reason, He'd chosen not to, and she should probably stop whining about it.

The wraparound porch of the main house at the Montana ranch protected her from the worst of the storm, but the frigid temperatures nipped at her exposed cheeks. At least it hadn't dropped into the single digits.

The front door creaked, and a blanket dropped around her shoulders. "I wanted to thank you for helping me prep the barn for the storm. The horses are grateful." Her hostess, Mary Price, eased next to her and wrapped the edges of her wool shawl across her body.

"My pleasure." Lizzie tugged the fleece blanket tighter around her. "But I've got to ask. How do you do it, Mary?" Not only had Wild Sapphire Ranch stolen her heart, but so had Harold and Mary Price, the sixty-something couple who owned the ranch and treated her and Charlie like family.

"Do what?"

"Live here in the middle of nowhere—in the cold."

Mary shrugged. "You get used to it. But I'll admit, things aren't as easy as they used to be. Harold struggles when the fences are damaged or the horses get sick. We aren't exactly young anymore, you know?"

"Does that happen a lot? The fences and the horses?"

"Seems like more than it should."

"Ever consider moving?"

"We've talked about it. Even had an offer to buy the place. But the land has been passed down through generations. Although, living in Florida near our daughter sounds pretty good right now." Mary chuckled.

Lizzie returned her gaze to the open land and the falling snow. The heavy weight of depression crept in. "Our friends and family, not to mention my mom, who's bringing Addy, won't arrive in time for the Christmas Eve wedding."

"Don't give up hope. Your friends will make it."

"But the weather…"

"Sweetie, this storm will pass. Besides, it's not a big one. Just enough to shut down a few airports and roads for a bit. More of an annoyance than anything else. According to the weatherman, we're only supposed to get about twenty inches of snow. It's not like we're getting six feet of the stuff. And yes, the wind will wreak havoc and cause drifting, but that's minor in these parts."

"Our wedding is only two days away. The timing is horrible." What was with her and the whining?

"Have a little faith, Lizzie."

Faith. She sighed. That's what scared her the most. Trusting and being disappointed. Frustration zipped through her. She'd thought she'd conquered this issue, and here it was staring her in the face again.

Mary placed a hand on her shoulder. "What's really bothering you?"

She shifted to face the older woman who reminded her of her mother except for the gray streaks in her otherwise-brown hair. "What if this is God's way of saying I'm not supposed to marry Charlie?"

"Hogwash. It only takes a minute being around the two of you to see you're meant to be together."

"I *do* love him." And that's where the problem lay. She loved Charlie so much that it scared her.

"Then stop fretting. Things will work out the way God planned them."

"I'm sure you're right." She *was* right. Lizzie just had to believe it and claim it. So why was that so hard again?

"Of course I'm right," Mary said. "Now, come in out of the cold before you catch pneumonia. Can't have a bride sick on her wedding day."

Lizzie loved this lady. She was still worried about the effects of the snowstorm, but Mary had a point about the weather and her concerns. "I'll come inside in a few minutes. I promise not to become a popsicle."

"Good enough. I think I'll skedaddle. That man of yours is heading this way. And might I say, he's a handsome one." Mary patted her on the back and slipped inside.

Charlie, decked out in his boots and fleece-lined parka, strode the length of the porch from the side of the house. His long legs ate up the distance, and soon he wrapped his arms around her from behind. "Hey, gorgeous."

Lizzie tilted her head and peered up at him. "Hi."

He spun her to face him. "What's wrong?"

"Nothing, really."

"Nope, I don't believe it." He kissed her forehead and pulled her close. "They'll make it."

Her jaw dropped. "How'd you know?"

"Because I'm thinking the same thing."

"Oh."

He leaned back and raised an eyebrow. "What? You think since I'm a man that I don't want to have a nice wedding with my family and friends?"

"No—not exactly." She pivoted in his arms to face the front yard and long lane meandering to the house, and snuggled into his hold. Being in Charlie's arms always chased away her doubts. "Whose bright idea was it, anyway, to have a winter wonderland wedding?"

"That would have been your precocious daughter." Charlie chuckled. "And we couldn't say no."

"You mean *you* couldn't say no. And as of Saturday, she'll be *our* daughter. You can't give into Addy's every want."

"There is that." He rested his chin on the top of her head and sighed. "I'll learn."

It seemed as though Charlie could read her mind. But it had

always been that way between the two of them. "You'll have to, or we won't be able to live with her."

He chuckled.

Enjoying the warmth of his embrace, she stood in silence and watched the storm. The mix of the powerful dump of snow and angry night sky fascinated Lizzie. If only the storm had happened three days from now, after her friends and family had arrived and her wedding had taken place.

"Did you and Harold get the cabins ready for the storm?" she asked.

"Sure did."

"Mary and I took care of the horses..." A shadow bobbed part way down the lane. Lizzie squinted, unsure if she'd actually seen someone or not. She waited. There it was again.

"Lizzie?"

"Charlie, look." She pointed to a spot on the road that led to the house. If not for the sliver of moonlight peeking through the dark clouds, she would have missed it.

He leaned over her shoulder. "That's a person. Who in their right mind is out in this mess?"

The person stumbled and fell, then staggered to their feet.

"I don't know, but whoever it is looks like they're in trouble."

Charlie tugged on her hand. "Come on."

They hurried down the porch steps and trod through the yard in the foot-deep snow.

Lizzie plodded alongside Charlie, head down, fighting against the wind. The cold stung her face and bit at the skin beneath her sweatpants. The frigid air seemed to find every gap in her clothing and every bit of exposed skin.

The person struggling wobbled in their direction.

Whoever it was needed help—fast.

CHARLIE WANTED NOTHING MORE THAN TO GET HIS FUTURE WIFE out of the freezing temperatures and figure out what had Lizzie tied in knots. Had she changed her mind about marrying him and was afraid to tell him?

His chest tightened, remembering how Susan, his ex-fiancée, had thrown him away like a piece of trash. He loved Lizzie with the very fiber of his being and refused to let her give up on him. Of course, he might be overreacting—then again, maybe not.

He wiped at the snow that splatted on his cheeks and matted his eyelashes, making it difficult to see the person stumbling down the lane. Who in their right mind was out in this stuff?

Even through his heavy winter clothes, his legs stung from the cold. What he wouldn't give for a good pair of snow pants right now.

Lizzie stumbled, and he caught her arm in time to keep her from falling face-first into the shin-deep snow.

"Are you okay?"

She nodded. "Fine. Keep going."

The low temperatures and lack of shelter hadn't taken long to affect him and Lizzie. If the person plodding down the lane had been out in the open for any length of time, he or she was in trouble.

The wind whistled through the massive front yard, and the snow continued to fall. He caught glimpses of the individual staggering, then, a moment later, the person fell. A blue ski jacket stood out against the white of the snow.

"Hurry." Lizzie pushed forward, her boots crunching in the drifts.

After what seemed like hours but had only been minutes, he and Lizzie reached the person. Charlie crouched and jolted at the long brown hair coated with ice. A petite woman.

He rolled her over, and Lizzie wiped the snow from the woman's face. He sucked in a ragged breath, searing his lungs with the frigid air. "Susan?"

Lizzie's gaze met his. "What do you mean Susan? As in your ex-fiancée Susan?"

Charlie nodded, struck mute. What was Susan doing on a ranch—*this* ranch in Montana—in the middle of a snowstorm? "We have to get her out of the cold before hypothermia sets in." If it hadn't already. Charlie scooped her into his arms.

Susan muttered something incoherent, then her head drooped against his shoulder.

"Let's get out of this storm before we all freeze to death." Lizzie placed her hand on his back.

A loud crack echoed through the air, and snow sprayed next to his foot.

Lizzie flinched. "What in the—is someone *shooting* at us?"

"Not a clue, but I don't like it. Hurry."

Lizzie tucked her head and held on to the back of his coat.

A gunshot rang through the air, and a bullet sliced across his coat sleeve. "Definitely shooting at us! Go!" No doubt about it now. Someone had them in their crosshairs, and the open area offered no options for cover.

"The cabins! Over there!" Lizzie pointed to the right and placed herself between him and the gunman as they ran for cover.

With a quick switch in direction, Charlie aimed for one of the small cabins. The shooting had stopped, but he refused to take any chances. Once at the structure, they tucked around the back, out of the line of fire. He hoped.

The building blocked the bulk of the wind. He rested against the side of the cabin with Susan in his arms. Trembles vibrated through him—either from the cold or the adrenaline coursing through him.

He shifted his attention to Susan. She was unconscious, but her breathing appeared normal. "We need to get her inside."

Lizzie slipped to the corner of the cabin, peeked around, then spun to face him. "This side of the cabin has a straight shot to the front of the house. The lack of visibility should work in our favor as well." She motioned him over to join her.

He inhaled and tucked Susan tighter into his arms. "Let's do it."

They ducked their heads and hurried to the house, struggling against the snow. He had to admit he was surprised when they made it up the porch with no more bullets winging their way.

Lizzie grabbed the handle to the front door of the main house and flung it open.

Charlie stumbled inside and headed straight for the living room.

"Mary! Harold!" Lizzie shut the door and flipped the deadbolt.

Mary hurried in with her husband on her heels. "Oh my. What happened out there?"

"Not exactly sure, but we have to get her warmed up, and fast." He moved to the fireplace and sat on the raised hearth with Susan in his arms.

The older couple had insisted he and Lizzie join them in the main house during the snowstorm. And right now, Charlie breathed a sigh of relief that they'd agreed.

Harold's gaze darted between them, no doubt waiting for an explanation.

"Someone shot at us—or her. Who knows at this point?" Lizzie shrugged and strode to Charlie's side and pointed at his torn sleeve. "What I *do* know is that those bullets were too close for comfort."

"I'll second that. We have to get Suz warmed up." Charlie shifted Susan to the hearth and tightened his grip.

Lizzie removed her boots and coat. "Since you two are taking care of Susan, I'll get our guns, check the doors and windows, and call the sheriff."

Harold nodded. "I'll check the locks on the doors and

windows. Be back in a minute." He strode from the room with Lizzie right behind him.

"Let's get that girl warm and dry." Mary worked on peeling off Charlie's ex-fiancée's wet outerwear.

Charlie glanced at the trail they'd left from the front door. "Sorry about the mess, Mary."

"Pssh. We live on a ranch. We're used to messes. Don't give it another thought. As soon as we get this girl out of those wet clothes, I'll grab a few towels and sop it up."

"Thank you." He shifted Susan closer to the warmth of the blaze, careful not to expose any one area too long.

Mary finished and rushed out of the room as Harold returned. "The house is secure. How is she?" He pointed to Susan.

Until now, Charlie had been focused on getting Suz out of the snow and getting her next to the fire. He took a good look at her for the first time. "The good news is her skin is pink and not translucent. Her breathing seems to be okay." He lifted her fingers, examined the tips, and then placed his against her pulse point. "No frostbite, and her heart rate appears normal."

"Doesn't sound like she's in danger of hypothermia."

Charlie frowned. "Then why isn't she awake?"

"That, I can't answer, but trudging through the snow with the winds whipping around you can be exhausting. She might be just plum wore out," Harold said.

The nugget of wisdom had Charlie playing out different scenarios. "Anything is possible at this point."

"What can I do to help?" Harold asked.

"How about getting the couch ready so I can lay her down."

"That I can do." Harold busied himself prepping the cushions with a thick blanket and laying an electric one at the end to use as a cover. "By the way, I appreciate the help preparing the cabins for the storm."

"It wasn't a problem, Harold. I was happy to help."

Harold straightened and waved a hand. "You're our guests and shouldn't be working, but I'm grateful nonetheless." The older man looked around the room. "Anything else I can do?"

"Keep an eye out for whoever shot at us."

"Guaranteed. I'll go see if Mary needs help and start the kettle for hot tea." Harold strode away.

Lizzie returned with her weapon on her hip, laid his Glock on the coffee table, and joined him at the fireplace. "It's a no go on the phone call. All I got was an odd busy signal. I'll try again later." She arranged Susan's coat, outer sweater, and boots on the other side of the hearth. "How is she?"

"Medically speaking, I don't think she's in any danger."

Lizzie examined Susan. "You're right. She's not struggling to breathe, her skin color is normal, and she's not as cold to the touch as I expected."

"Her love of skiing saved her from the freezing temperatures."

Lizzie arched a brow. "Excuse me?"

He motioned to Susan's coat, boots, hat, and gloves. "Top-of-the-line ski gear. Maybe not made for below-zero temps, but since it's in the teens outside, it worked. Her outerwear might be wet, but her pants and sweatshirt are dry."

"Hopefully, she'll wake up soon and tell us what's going on." Lizzie stared at Susan for a moment, then shifted her gaze to him. "Ready to get her onto the couch?"

"Sure." He pushed to his feet, transferred Susan to the couch, and cocooned her in the electric blanket while Lizzie stoked the fire. He brushed the strands of brown hair from her face and stared at the petite woman who'd ripped his heart out years ago.

The inability to call for backup concerned Charlie, but they'd stand guard until they reached the authorities. Until then, he'd get Susan warm and pray she had answers to all the questions swirling in his brain. Everything from why she was here to who shot at them.

"What's going on in that mind of yours?" Lizzie rubbed her hand up and down his arm.

"Nothing."

"Come on, Hotshot. I know better than that."

He thought for a moment. How did he put it into words? "She's not what I remember."

"You mean the fact she doesn't have gnarly teeth and a pointy nose?" Lizzie raised an eyebrow.

"Lizzie. That's not funny."

She smirked. "Are you sure about that?"

"Okay, maybe it is a little." He pursed his lips to hide his smile. "Seriously, though. I don't know, she looks vulnerable. I don't think I've ever seen her like that."

"Collapsing face down in the snow might do that to a person."

He turned to Lizzie and eyed her. His soon-to-be wife had a protective streak that rivaled a momma bear. "Are you going to play nice?"

"Come on. You know me better than that. She needs our help, and I plan to give it to her." Lizzie glanced over his shoulder at the unconscious Susan. "I hate what she did to you, so yes, I'm a little peeved she hurt you, but I'm more intrigued as to why she's here and who shot at us."

Charlie placed his finger under her chin. "I love you. You know that, right?"

"Absolutely." Lizzie winked. Her smile appeared forced.

Why did he get the feeling that something was bothering her? "Watch over Susan. I want to check the windows."

Lizzie placed her hand on his arm. "I'll do it. You stay and take care of her. She might need to see a familiar face if she wakes up." She squeezed his shoulder and headed out of the room.

Charlie's stomach churned. Why had Susan shown up at this ranch—at this time? It couldn't be a coincidence. The woman thought he was reckless and wanted nothing to do with him. So why come find him? Not that he had feelings for her anymore—far from it. He loved Lizzie with everything in him. But Susan's declaration all those years ago that he wasn't husband material echoed in his head. He'd dealt with her hurtful words and moved past his self-doubt—hadn't he?

He glanced at Susan. *God, why am I doubting myself again? I thought I was over the damage she'd done.*

Funny how the past could tug you back in without warning and turn everything upside down again.

TWO

When Lizzie had awoken that morning, her worst fear had been her friends not making it to the wedding. She'd never imagined Charlie's former fiancée landing on her doorstep, bringing gunfire in her wake.

Sweat beaded on Lizzie's upper lip, and she struggled to slow her breathing. The panic attacks that used to come at regular intervals had faded since Charlie's proposal, but she couldn't deny the familiar feelings twisting within her. Thankful for coping skills, she kept going, breathing in through her nose and out through her mouth. It would pass. It always did.

She hurried from the living room into the kitchen while the sound of the gunshots rang in her head along with visions of the spray of snow beside Charlie's foot and the slice in his sleeve. She wanted to throw up.

Mary emerged from the laundry room next to the mudroom with extra blankets in her arms. She pulled to a stop. "Sweetie, are you okay? You look a little green."

All those times that the men in her life had died came rolling back at Lizzie like a tsunami. She placed her hands on the table and hung her head, sucking in several deep breaths. "I had finally given my fears over to God and accepted a future with Charlie. But the past has a way of sneaking up on you when you least expect it."

"Care to explain?" Mary moved to her side and set the laundry on the table.

Lizzie peered into the older woman's eyes. "It's kind of complicated, but all the men I've ever loved, including my father and Addy's dad, have died. I struggled with God for years until Charlie. I still had issues, but I learned to trust God again." At least, she thought she had.

"So now you've given it all to God, and you're marrying the man you love. I guess I don't see the problem."

"When those bullets came close to hitting Charlie, those past losses spun on repeat in my mind." She shrugged. "That's to be expected, I guess. Normal." She paused. How did she convey what was troubling her so? "But this time is different."

"How so?"

"As we ran to the house for cover, I was terrified that he'd be shot. But...we're bodyguards. We're put in dangerous situations more times than I care to admit. But what if I lose focus or make a poor choice because I'm too concerned that he'll get hurt? What if we can't be partners anymore due to my fears? What if he's not supposed to be my husband?" There. She'd said it. And desperately wanted to take the words back. Because they sounded silly. And yet, she'd voiced them for a reason.

Mary fell silent a moment, then reached for Lizzie's hand. "Lizzie, do you truly trust God and believe that He knows best? Not just knows best, but *wants* the best for His children?"

Unlike before, she did trust Him with the man she loved. She nodded. "Of course. But what if He makes a decision about Charlie—like it's his time to die? How do I deal with that? How do I let that go?" It was so weird how this was the absolute one area of her life that she had trouble just handing over to God. Even when it came to Addy, she didn't stress like she did with Charlie.

"Sweetie." Mary squeezed her shoulder. "I think you're letting your anxiety control you. Give yourself a minute to breathe. And go talk to that man of yours. I have a feeling he'd be happy to reassure you. I've seen a lot of couples come through this place—a few I thought shouldn't marry. But the two of you are perfect for each other."

She and Charlie had clicked as partners and then as a couple. But after the bullet had almost hit him, she questioned whether she could handle the panic that would consume her if and when danger struck again. Because in their line of work, danger was a given.

Unable to stop her mind from all the what-if situations, Lizzie had to escape Mary's discerning gaze. "I'm going to see if I have some clothes for Susan to sleep in. And she's going to need something for tomorrow."

The older woman hugged the blankets to her chest. "Okay, sweetie. I'll take these to Charlie."

Without another word, Lizzie jogged up the stairs, entered her room, and tossed her bag on the bed.

She placed her hand on the Glock at her hip. The cool metal against her palm calmed her nerves. Protecting Charlie had become her life's mission. Not from physical danger—okay, who was she kidding? That too—but more than anything, she intended to make sure no one ever dismissed him again. Like his father and Susan had.

Right now, her Susan nightmare lay downstairs. Why was the woman here? To stop her and Charlie from getting married? Or for another reason? And who had fired at them?

Lizzie changed out of her damp clothes and added layers to her new outfit in case they encountered the person who shot at them earlier. This time she'd be prepared for a trip outside if needed.

Her mind drifted to Susan's sudden appearance as she tucked a change of clothes for the woman under her arm and zipped the bag.

Why had Susan ended up at Wild Sapphire Ranch?

The look on Charlie's face when he'd recognized Susan had gutted Lizzie, but at the same time, she knew where his heart lay—with her. She had no doubt about that. She knew the depths of his love for her, so jealousy really hadn't been the emotion to spear her. It was the pain Susan had caused him that made her want to go all ninja on the woman. But the bullets that had followed the woman...Susan must be scared out of her mind to come find him. And for that reason, Lizzie planned to defend Susan against whatever had brought her here.

Funny, Lizzie actually felt sorry for the woman who'd *thrown* Charlie away. And even the anger had cooled toward Susan. She moved to Charlie's room and retrieved the extra ammo from his bag, because what ex-cop/bodyguard went anywhere unprepared? Not a good one.

After adding dry clothes for Charlie to her collection, she went to the window and peered out into the night, searching the darkness for any signs of the person who'd shot at them. She came up empty, but the lack of visibility might have something to do with that.

Her cop senses hummed. She knew the shooter hadn't given up. Was he out there watching? Or had he found shelter and planned to wait out the storm? Not likely. More than probable, he'd come prepared for the bad weather—and had the patience to wait for another chance to strike.

With her arms full, she made her way downstairs, placed the clothing on the coffee table, then handed the extra clip to Charlie. "Here."

"Thanks."

He tucked the second clip in his pants pocket as she did with hers. She sat the extra ammo boxes on the end table next to the couch. "Just in case."

"I don't want you to be right, but after what happened outside…"

Yeah, she understood exactly what he hadn't said.

"How's she doing?" Lizzie stood next to him and studied Susan.

Charlie took Lizzie's hand. "She woke up for a bit and mumbled something. But that's it." He pointed to the mug on the coffee table. "I did get a little bit of hot tea down her."

"That's good. Warming her from the inside out will help."

Charlie's gaze focused on Susan, and he dropped onto the recliner. A deep crease marked his forehead. "Lizzie, why did she come here? I'm the last person she'd want to see, but I've no doubt her appearance is not an accident."

The torment in his eyes broke Lizzie's heart. She knelt beside him. "I think it's just the opposite. I have no idea why she said all the hurtful things to you years ago. Only she can answer that. But I believe deep down Susan knew you're the man she could turn to—someone she could trust."

"Maybe. I just wish she'd wake up and tell us what's going on."

"I can't help you there. What I do know is that until we can figure it out, you and I will keep her safe." She cupped his face and ran her thumb over his cheek. "I'm here for you. Remember that."

Mary rushed into the living room. "Have either of you seen Harold?"

"No, ma'am. Why?" Charlie stood and guided Lizzie to their worried hostess.

"He went out to search for our ranch foreman, Phil, a little while ago, and neither has come back."

With a shooter on the loose, Lizzie had a bad feeling about the missing men.

The tension flowing off Charlie told her he shared her concerns. "I'll go search for them."

Lizzie followed Charlie through the kitchen to the mudroom, her belly tight, but she stayed silent while he shoved his feet in his boots. When he finished donning the rest of his winter gear, he looked at her. "You stay with Mary and Susan. Confirm all the blinds are closed and doors are locked. You know the drill."

Nausea churned in Lizzie's stomach, and tears pricked her eyes, but she nodded. "Be careful. Please."

"Of course." He checked his weapon, gave her a quick kiss, then slipped out the back door.

Lizzie rested her forehead on it for a brief moment. *God, I'm leaving this in Your hands. Please keep Charlie safe and help him find those men.*

Susan's sudden appearance, Lizzie's odd reactions that Charlie was certain only he had noticed, along with a shooter and two missing men had his gut tied in knots. The cold wind slapped his face as he tromped through the snow to the barn, Glock at his side, ready if he needed it.

Had Harold and Phil run into troubles of the human kind, or had something else delayed them? It was a ranch, so anything was possible, but after getting shot at, he was slightly paranoid.

Charlie debated whether or not to shout out to the men but ruled it out. Too risky.

His foot sank into a snow drift. The cold penetrated his pant leg above the edge of his boot, sending a shiver down his back.

He headed to the barn door and slowed. The sixth sense he'd honed on the job had him scanning the area.

The howling winds and the minimal moonlight filtering through the clouds added to his unease. The eerie vibe had Charlie's nerves on edge.

A few feet from the entrance, the door flung open.

Charlie raised his Glock.

Harold stepped out, his cap pulled low, not noticing Charlie yet. With his arm around Phil's waist and the man's arm draped over his shoulder, Harold staggered under the weight of his ranch foreman.

Charlie holstered his weapon and hurried to Phil's other side to assist Harold. "What happened?"

"I rode out to the creek and found him lying in the snow, bleeding," Harold said. "Got him as far as the barn when we heard shots, so I ducked in here."

From the small bulb over the barn entrance that gave off a dim glow, Charlie noticed blood dripping from Phil's head, but the faint light and the surrounding darkness made it impossible to get a good look. "What did he hit? A rock?"

"A bullet grazed the side of his head. Enough to take him down." Harold's heavy breathing betrayed his fatigue.

What was going on around this place? Someone had shot at them when they'd rescued Susan, and now a bullet hit the ranch foreman? Who was the guy after? "Is there any reason someone would want to shoot Phil?"

Before Harold answered, shots erupted from behind the hay barn.

Charlie's foot struck something under the snow, and he stumbled to his knees, taking Harold and Phil with him as one of the bullets whizzed past his head. He'd never been so grateful to trip. Moving fast, he hefted Phil over his shoulder in a fireman's carry. "I've got him, go!" They hurried toward the house.

Gunshots rang in the air and, with every step, he expected to feel the hot fire of a bullet hitting him in the back, but he kept moving.

Return fire came from the porch.

He lifted his gaze to the house and spotted a familiar figure, gun in hand.

Lizzie. Always his heroine. Knowing she had his back, he focused on the back door of the main house and pushed himself faster through the snow.

Lizzie stepped aside. "Get in here!"

Harold, ten feet ahead of him, dashed through the door.

Lizzie squeezed off six more shots, laying down cover.

Charlie used the moment to his advantage and darted through the entrance. A second later, Lizzie dove in behind him and slammed the door shut. He knelt and Lizzie help him lay Phil on the floor. Then he sat back and struggled to catch his breath while she moved in.

Her hands started at his face and ran down his arms. "No holes," she whispered. Her ragged breaths came hard and fast. She smacked him on the chest. "Don't ever do that again!"

He scrambled to make sense of her words. "Lizzie, it's in our job description."

"You're right. Just don't do it two days before we're supposed to get married."

An underlying worry in her tone concerned him, but he brushed it aside for the moment. "Your timing was perfect, as always." If she hadn't saved his hide, he'd be talking with Jesus right now. And while that sounded pretty good, he'd like to spend a little more time on this earth with the woman he loved.

Trepidation flashed across Lizzie's face, then vanished. "The shooter is getting closer to the house. I want to know what this guy wants." Without further discussion, she turned off the lights near the back door. "I don't want him able to see in. I'll go try to call 911 and the sheriff again for help, then take care of the rest of the lights." Lizzie strode out of the small room.

Mary hurried in from the kitchen, wiping her hand on a towel. When she spotted Harold, she threw her arms around him. "What happened?"

Harold hugged his wife. "Phil was shot."

"Oh my." She rushed to Phil's side.

"It only a graze, honey, but left a groove that bled a lot."

"Let's get him to the bedroom. I'll clean it up and take a look." Mary glanced at Charlie. "Can you manage him?"

Charlie shed his coat and boots, placing them where they belonged. "Yes. Which room?"

"The main bedroom. I'll grab the first aid kit from the laundry room and meet you there." Mary left to get the supplies.

Phil was too heavy for Charlie to carry in his arms like he had Susan earlier, so he lifted the man over his shoulder and followed Harold to the bedroom. He lowered the ranch foreman onto the mattress.

"Hang in there, Phil. You're going to be okay." Charlie helped Harold remove Phil's wet top layer of clothes and covered the man with a blanket.

Mary came in carrying a first aid kit that looked like a tackle box. "We've got him. You go help that girl of yours. She's a little tiger, but everyone can use assistance."

He chuckled. Tiger. Yeah, that fit. "If you need anything, let me know."

The older woman shooed him out the door.

Charlie strode to the living room, ready to defend and protect, and found Lizzie standing to the side of the living room window next to the Christmas tree, her fingers splitting the blinds to peek outside.

"Anything?"

She jumped. "Would you quit sneaking up on me?"

"Not my intention." He crossed his arms. "Well?"

"Nothing. And it was a no go on the sheriff and 911. The line still has that busy signal." She pivoted to face him. "I know he's out there."

"We're assuming it's a man. It could be a woman." He'd made that mistake before and refused to do it again.

"I don't care if it's bigfoot." Lizzie moved away from the window. She gestured toward Susan. "Who do you think he was after? Her or Phil?"

"Beats me. After she left me, I never heard from her again. And I certainly didn't search her out. But if the guy is targeting Susan, why shoot the ranch foreman?"

"Maybe Phil witnessed the attempt on Susan? Saw the guy— or gal—who pulled the trigger?" Lizzie rubbed her eyes. "We have to figure out what we're up against."

As if on cue, Susan groaned.

Charlie rushed to her side. "Susan, can you hear me?"

Her eyes fluttered open. "Charlie?"

He tugged another blanket over and tucked it around her. "Yes, it's me. How do you feel?"

"Tired. Exhausted, really, but other than that, okay." The crease between her eyes deepened. "Where am I?"

"Wild Sapphire Ranch in Montana."

She blinked, then closed her eyes. "I made it."

"Well, if your goal was here, then yes, you made it. But why?" Charlie sat on the edge of the coffee table.

"To find you."

Had his ex-fiancée heard about his wedding and come to warn Lizzie not to marry him? "Susan, there's—"

"No. No, Charlie. I came for help. I want to hire you."

"Me? As in for a bodyguard?"

Lizzie had eased next to him, no doubt wanting to hear every word.

"My life is in danger," Susan said. "I didn't know who else to trust."

"Did you go to the police?" Lizzie asked.

Susan shook her head. "I can't."

"Why not?" Charlie clasped his hands between his knees.

Tears shimmered in Susan's eyes.

To Charlie's surprise, Lizzie knelt beside Susan and held her hand. "We have to know what's going on. There's someone outside shooting at anything that moves."

"I'm sorry." Susan's mouth quivered.

"Don't be. Just start from the beginning. And Susan"—Lizzie held her gaze—"the details are important. We need to know fast, before anyone else gets hurt."

She nodded and exhaled. "About a week ago, I witnessed a murder. A guy named Chris Snyder robbed a clothing store. Apparently, he thought the place was empty, minus the worker. I was in the dressing room when it happened and peeked out. I witnessed him shooting the clerk. The police arrested Snyder, and while the man waited for arraignment, the District Attorney asked me to testify at the trial. Then the detective on the case called and informed me that the judge had released Chris on bail. I don't know how he found out about me—or tracked me—but I left Seattle as soon as I heard."

"How'd you end up here?" Charlie refrained from rushing Susan, but his gut told him they had to know—and quick.

"Once I left Seattle, I called the Elite Guardians Agency. I'd heard Olivia had recruited you as a bodyguard, and I'd planned to hire you. Olivia told me where you were, so I came straight here. Unfortunately, I got scared when I saw a set of headlights behind me, and lost control of my car about a mile from the ranch."

"That explains why we found you walking in the snow. But why come find *me*?" Charlie asked, unsure he wanted to hear the answer.

"Because you're the only man I can trust." The tears swimming in Susan's eyes fell down her cheeks.

He jolted like someone had slapped him. Trust? Him? Wow, what had happened to the woman who'd hated him?

Before he'd wrapped his mind around Susan's words, Lizzie rubbed Susan's back to comfort her. "So you think the person whose car you saw is the same man you saw kill someone?"

"With the threat and the fact he already shot another person..." Susan shrugged. "Yes."

He understood why Susan thought that. It made sense. But he had to cover all the possibilities. "Do you have any other enemies?"

The crease in her forehead deepened. "Not that I can think of."

"Anyone that might be angry with you? Even if it sounds silly," Lizzie prodded.

Susan looked away. "I have an ex who refuses to take no for an answer, and my boss is a jerk. But I can't see either one of them wanting me dead."

"You never know what someone is capable of," Lizzie said.

"That is so true." Susan's words sent Charlie's curiosity into overdrive.

The simple phrase hid a secret, and Charlie intended to find out what. "Do you really think Snyder followed you to Montana?"

"I honestly don't know. Maybe I'm just paranoid." Susan twisted the blanket in her hands.

He had more questions, but Lizzie spoke up before he could ask.

"I know it isn't easy, but thank you for your help." Lizzie stood and shifted her attention to Charlie. "Why don't you and Susan work on specifics of the murder she witnessed. I'll go do a thorough check of the house again. If he's as determined as he appears, locked doors and windows won't stop him for long. And while I'm at it, I'll try placing a call to the sheriff again and see if we can get help out here." She squeezed Charlie's shoulder, checked her Glock, then headed to the kitchen to the landline.

A murderer on the loose in Montana. He pursed his lips and exhaled. His gaze landed on Susan. The woman was terrified. He had questions. Lots of them. He'd ask, but Susan needed reassuring. "You'll be fine."

"How can you be sure?" Her wide eyes chipped at the ice around his heart.

"Because it's our job. Not only that, this guy tweaked a tiger's tail." He pointed in the direction Lizzie had gone. "We won't let him get close enough to hurt you."

He and Lizzie often placed their lives on the line while guarding clients, but today, two days before his wedding, that reality bothered him more than he cared to admit.

LIZZIE COULDN'T GET AHOLD OF THE SHERIFF AND HAD NO IDEA what the shooter had planned or why. True, she and Charlie had faced tougher situations, but the dread pooling in her belly made her pulse race.

She entered the kitchen and spotted Mary at the counter, opening teabags and placing them in mugs. The only lights in the kitchen were the clock on the microwave and the flame under the teapot.

Lizzie slipped to the window and pulled the curtain aside an inch to peek out. "How's Phil?"

"In and out. He woke up long enough to say he saw a rifle and dove for the ground, then he fell back asleep."

"Did he say who?"

"Nah, I don't think he's with it enough to give detailed information."

Frustration tugged at Lizzie. Nothing specific to go on, just speculation. And that could get them all killed.

Mary poured two cups of tea and added a bit of honey to each. "I figured Phil and your friend in there could use a warm drink."

Her friend. Hmm. She didn't exactly consider Susan a friend, but the woman did need their help.

"I'll take these to our patients." Mary gathered the two mugs and disappeared into the living room.

Lizzie rolled her neck to relieve the building tension. So much for the relaxing downtime before the wedding. She lifted the phone from the wall and held it to her ear, praying she got through this time. When the call rang through, she let out a long breath. *Thank You, God.*

"Sheriff's office. Sheriff Raymond Harper."

"Sheriff, this is Lizzie Tremaine with the Elite Guardians Agency."

"Tremaine...Tremaine. Oh yes, the wedding at Wild Sapphire Ranch this weekend."

"Um...yes. Exactly. But how did you know?"

Harper chuckled. "Small town. Everyone knows everything about everybody."

Lizzie couldn't help but smile. "I guess so. Anyway, I tried to call earlier but got a weird busy tone."

"Sorry about that. It happens when the system is overloaded. But now you've got me. What can I do for you?"

"We found a woman walking through the storm toward the ranch. When we went out to help her, someone shot at us. Then the Prices' ranch foreman was shot at and injured."

"Are Phil and the woman okay?" Sheriff Harper shifted to all business.

"For now, yes. But the shooter is still out there. He tried again not too long ago." Lizzie explained Susan's situation and relayed what little Phil had told Mary and Harold.

"Are you armed?"

"Yes, sir." Her hand instinctively went to her Glock.

"Good. Because I can't get out there. The roads aren't passable at the moment. However, as soon as I can get through, I'll try to find the spot where this Susan left her car. If I find evidence that someone followed her, I'll let you know."

"Thanks. One more favor?"

"Sure."

"Can you look into the murder she witnessed in Seattle and ask about Chris Snyder's whereabouts?"

"Can do." The sheriff sighed. She envisioned him tipping his cowboy hat back and scratching his head. "I'll confess, I did a little digging into your agency when I heard about the wedding. I wanted to make sure y'all were on the up and up. Y'all are impressive. I'd appreciate it if you and that beau of yours would protect my friends out there."

"That's a promise." One she intended to keep.

"Much obliged, ma'am." The sheriff hung up.

Lizzie replaced the handpiece and double-checked the lock on the back door.

A crash sounded from down the hall.

Lizzie sprinted from the kitchen and jerked her Glock from the holster at her hip. She almost ran into Charlie in the hallway.

"Charlie, stay here and cover Susan. I've got this."

He yanked his gun from the holster and held it at his side. "Be safe!"

"Always." She threw the word over her shoulder. Harold peered out of the main bedroom. "Stay inside and lock the door."

He ducked out of sight, and she heard the lock snick.

Lizzie rushed into the bathroom near the rear side of the house, where she thought the sound had come from. Cold air rushed through a small section of broken glass. She halted and did a visual search of the small room. No way the gunman had entered from the hole in the window. Why break the glass?

The answer hit her like a roundhouse kick to the chest. "Oh no you don't." She took off running toward the office, where she'd seen a sliding glass door that led to the porch, and prayed the distraction hadn't slowed her too much.

A dark figure stood on the wraparound porch near the adjacent bedroom, lifting the window open.

"Gotcha," she whispered. Gun at the ready, Lizzie eased open the slider and slipped out. The howl of the wind hid her movement, but with each step toward the intruder, she held her breath. One wrong move and—

The wooden deck creaked under her feet.

She froze.

The man spun and rushed her, throwing a punch at her head.

Lizzie ducked, but his fist raked across her cheek. She grunted at the glancing blow but didn't go down.

Lunging, she grabbed his hand and yanked his arm behind his back.

He stepped back and flipped her over his body.

She landed with a thud. Air still whooshed from her lungs despite the thick layer of snow that helped cushion her fall. She swept her leg out and took her assailant to the ground, then scrambled through the snow to her gun that lay five feet away. The cold seeped into her pants legs, and her hands had lost most feeling.

With a growl, the man rose to his full height and towered above her. He stomped toward her. "You're going to pay for that."

Her numb fingers struggled to grip the weapon.

The guy stood over her and laughed. "Nice try, but I win."

"I don't think so." She wrapped her arm around his leg and yanked him off balance.

His arms flailed, but he tumbled to the deck. His meaty hand swiped for her, but she rolled out of reach. He rose to his feet and lunged.

She grabbed her Glock, ignoring the snow and the cold of the grip, flipped to her back, and pulled the trigger.

The attacker staggered backward and fell over the edge of the porch.

Breathing heavily, Lizzie hauled herself to her feet with her gun aimed in the direction of the assailant and stumbled to the low rail in time to see the man dart off into the night toward the barns.

She'd shot him. She knew that. But between the cold and the quickness of her reaction, she had no idea where the bullet had hit.

Lizzie wiped her cheek with the back of her hand where his fist had made contact. The mistake of losing focus and letting the goon surprise her had left a mark. Rookie mistake. How embarrassing. Then again, the man had skills and a hundred pounds on her, so she figured she'd done okay, all things considered. Even though Laila had trained her well in the Israeli martial art Krav Maga, the man had gotten away. Which stunk.

Mental note to self: *Up your workouts with Laila.*

With a sigh, she slipped back through the sliding door and secured the lock. She'd tell Harold about the break in the window so he could temporarily cover it with a piece of wood or something.

"Lizzie!" Charlie's panicked voice had never sounded so wonderful.

The darkness outside and the minimal light inside made it difficult to see her way to the office door. Plus, her cheek stung, and her back ached from where she'd hit the deck. But her pride hurt the most. Lizzie had to step up her game. She refused to let the guy best her again. Although, he was the one sporting a gunshot wound—not her.

When she entered the living room where she'd left Mary, Susan, and Charlie, Charlie stood with his gun drawn, aiming it at her. "Whoa there, Hotshot."

He exhaled and lowered his weapon. "Are you okay?"

"Fine." Or she would be when the adrenaline crash disappeared. She shoved her shaking hands into her pockets to hide the unwanted reaction.

"We heard the struggle and the gunshot. I thought..." Charlie's Adam's apple bobbed.

"I'm good. Really. I hate to admit it, but I underestimated this guy. Let's just say I'm glad Laila and I have trained together over the past month. And the gunshot was mine, not his."

Charlie holstered his weapon. "You hit him?"

She nodded. "He took off toward the barns. He's wounded, but I doubt that'll stop him from trying again."

"He's going to kill me," Susan whimpered.

Mary rushed to Susan's side and brushed the hair from her forehead. "Shh, honey, it'll be okay."

"We're going to make sure that doesn't happen." Lizzie's gaze met Charlie's. "I want him caught."

Charlie rubbed the back of his neck. "Then we better come up with a plan. I'm sick of being on the defensive."

Without a word, Mary hurried down the hall. More than likely to check on Harold and Phil after the attempted break-in.

Lizzie strode to the kitchen, retrieved a bag of frozen peas from the freezer, laid it against her aching cheek, and returned to the living room.

"You're hurt." Charlie came over and placed his hands on her upper arms, studying the side of her face.

"My pride—mostly. He got in a lucky blow." She lifted the bag from her cheek for him to get a better look. "See, it's not so bad."

Charlie narrowed his eyes. "Lizzie."

"Let it be," she whispered and stepped from his hold. She

shifted her attention to Susan. "Tell me about Chris, the man you witnessed murdering someone. Height, weight, anything you can think of."

As Susan described the killer, Lizzie compared the attributes to the man she'd struggled with, looking for identifying features and any weaknesses they could exploit. Because Lizzie knew the fight the attacker had started was far from over. No matter who the man had come after, he wanted his target dead and had no intention of stopping until he'd completed the job.

"Do you think it's the same guy?" Charlie asked.

"Basic description is right, but in the darkness..." Lizzie closed her eyes and pictured the creep she'd fought. She wanted to confirm the assumption, but her skirmish hadn't allowed her to get a good look at him. Lizzie opened her eyes and shook her head. "I can't say for sure."

"Which means," Charlie said quietly, "we're no closer to figuring out who is hunting down Susan. Or even *if* it is Susan that he's after."

He'd allowed himself to get shot. How could he have been so stupid?

The exertion from trudging to the barn in the deepening snow had the shirtsleeve inside his coat sticking to his skin. The warmth of the blood trailed down his arm and dripped from his fingertips.

He stumbled and caught himself before he face-planted in the snow. He had to get to the barn and patch up the bullet wound that should never have happened.

He'd underestimated the woman. Not something he planned to repeat.

Next time he'd shoot first. Two targets were better than one. A smile tugged on his lips. Soon he'd accomplish his mission.

He gripped the handle to the barn, eased the door open, and slipped inside.

The pungent aroma of hay and horses assaulted him. He fought back a sneeze that tickled his nose, and made his way through the barn, searching for a first aid kit. At the end, to the right, he found a small office and sought-after medical supplies.

He eased onto the chair, peeled his sleeve from the wound, and grimaced as the material pulled on the open flesh. The gash widened and bled more heavily. "When I get my hands on that…" He sucked in a breath at the final pull.

He grabbed a water bottle from the mini-fridge in the corner and poured it over the wound. The bullet had cut a groove in his upper arm, and it hurt like a thousand bee stings, but he'd live. He placed a thick square of gauze on the injury and wrapped it tightly with an ace bandage. Using his teeth to hold one end, he tightened the knot.

Two Tylenol later, he put his coat on and leaned back in the chair with a long exhale. A few minutes of rest to let the meds take effect, then he'd plan his final attack that would get him to his goal.

As far as he was concerned, they all could die as long as he got what he wanted.

THREE

The twinge in Charlie's head that he'd attempted to ignore threatened to explode into a full-blown migraine. Not what he needed right now. He had to think straight before someone died. He paced the living room, wondering how hard to push Susan for information.

Mind made up, he moved to her side. "I'm sorry to do this, but I'd like you to go over everything again. I don't want to miss a detail that could cause a fatal mistake."

She tugged at a thread on the blanket lying over her lap, then lifted her brown eyes to meet his. "Whatever you need."

Her willingness surprised him. Such a different Susan than he remembered. But they'd both changed. He honestly prayed she'd found what she wanted in life.

Lizzie ambled to the recliner and lowered herself onto the seat, slow and easy. "We appreciate that, Susan."

The hesitations in Lizzie's movements bothered Charlie. She'd taken a harder fall than she let on. He'd like to surround the woman in bubble wrap, but that might cause marital strife before they walked down the aisle. He stuffed his response away before his mouth got him in trouble.

Lizzie shifted in her seat. "You said earlier your boyfriend won't take no for an answer and that your boss is a jerk. Tell us about them."

Susan jolted at the request. "Ex."

"Okay, *ex*-boyfriend," Lizzie said.

Charlie glanced at the clock. Whatever Susan was hiding, it would take time to nudge her to give up the information, but they didn't have all night. The attacker had already stayed quiet a long time. Charlie was braced for what came next, but until then, he'd continue gathering information and praying for safety.

Susan ducked her head, refusing to make eye contact. "My ex-boyfriend's a loser."

Lizzie moved to the couch and scooted closer to her. "What did he do to you?"

Charlie studied Susan's demeanor, and his blood pressure skyrocketed. "He hit you, didn't he?"

"Charlie," Lizzie cautioned.

He didn't care what Susan had done or said to him. No one, man or woman, should live in fear of abuse. "Susan?"

She refused to make eye contact but nodded.

If he got his hands on that man… "Please tell me you left him and didn't stay."

Susan swallowed hard. Tears pooled on her lashes. "Not after the first time, but when it happened again, I grabbed my things and got out."

At least she'd escaped before she'd ended up in the hospital—or dead. He'd seen too much domestic violence as an officer not to understand the results. Women afraid to leave or believing they deserved the beatings. The whole idea churned his stomach. "Good."

Susan huffed out a laugh. "Right. I wish it had ended there."

Charlie now understood her cryptic words from earlier. "That's what you meant by he wouldn't take no for an answer. He keeps trying to get you to come back, doesn't he?"

Tears now streamed down Susan's cheeks. "Yes."

"What's his name?" Charlie planned to do a little digging into the scumbag once the storm quit wreaking havoc on his cell phone.

"Michael Ulrich," Susan whispered, as if saying his name aloud would conjure up the man.

Suspect number two. Charlie hated to continue with the questions, but they had to have all the information. "And what about your jerk of a boss?"

Susan sighed. "At first, Joe was nice. Then I discovered an accounting mistake and mentioned it to him. He blamed me, and he's looked over my shoulder ever since. I didn't do anything wrong, but he won't believe me."

"Is something fishy going on at the company?" Charlie asked.

"I don't think so. The mistake looked like someone simply typed the numbers in wrong. All the errors were within acceptable amounts in a business that big. But the way he responded...who knows? Bottom line is...he thinks I did it." She covered her face with her hands. "Why is everything bad happening to me?"

Charlie had no words for the woman he'd once cared for. It did seem like the world hadn't been kind to her recently.

Lizzie slid closer to Susan and held her while she cried.

Harold walked in with his arm wrapped around Mary. "Can we help with anything?"

"I'm not sure." Charlie rubbed his temples, wishing his headache would disappear. "We have a few possible suspects, but nothing concrete."

"What about us?" Lizzie asked.

"What do you mean?" He wasn't following his fiancée's question.

"Because of what we do as bodyguards, we've made people mad. What if it's not Susan, but us, the person is after?"

He supposed it was a possibility. "Then why wait until now? We've been here several days."

"It could be that whoever it is just learned how to find us."

"Well, add another hundred people to our suspect list." He sighed, then turned to Harold. "If we go along the same path of thinking, what about the two of you and this ranch? Anything we should know?"

The creases deepened in Harold's forehead. "I don't think so. We've had a few more issues with the fences lately. And a couple of horses got sick, but they're okay now."

"Do you think someone caused those problems?"

"Honestly, I'd have to say no. We've gone so far as to put security cameras up around the barns a while back, but nothing has ever appeared out of the ordinary." Harold shrugged. "It is a ranch, and things like that happen. And one of those times, our neighbor backed into the fence line on accident. Not exactly nefarious intentions."

"That's true." Charlie considered what the man had said. He'd put the incidents into the solid "maybe" column with the exception of the accident, only because he'd learned to be skeptical during his police department days. "That makes sense. However, I'd really like to see that video footage. It might be exactly what we need to solve this."

Harold nodded. "It'll take me a little bit since it's on the cloud and the internet isn't stable, but I'll do my best to get that for you as quickly as possible."

But why go after Susan, Lizzie, or me? More confused than ever, Charlie strode to the window and peered out. Where had the gunman gone?

Charlie knew deep down the man hadn't given up. It was only a matter of time before he made another attempt.

He ran a hand across the back of his neck. Three suspects, plus the never-ending list from his and Lizzie's past.

What had started as simple—a single suspect—had become a mess of confusion.

This weekend was no longer about getting married.

It was about staying alive.

Of all the things Lizzie had thought she'd be doing this week, holding Charlie's ex while the woman cried hadn't even made the list. Then again, neither had fighting off a shooter a couple days before her wedding.

She joined Charlie at the window. "What's going on?"

He pivoted to face her. "I don't like the fact our creep with a gun hasn't made an appearance."

"Do you know how that sounds?" She chuckled.

He rolled his eyes. "You know what I mean."

"Yeah, I do. But don't borrow trouble. We have a moment of peace. Let's use it to our benefit." She mentally flipped through the events of the evening. There had to be a clue in there somewhere.

"You're right. Like always."

"Ooooh, can I quote you on that?"

Charlie tweaked her nose. "Not a chance, sweetheart."

"I was afraid you'd say that." She wrapped her arms around him and laid her head on his chest. "Not the wedding prep I thought we'd have."

"No, but it's somehow fitting for us."

She peered up at him, confused.

He smiled. "We never do anything normal."

"This is true." Lizzie's mind tumbled back to their three-year partnership, then to the weird events involving Charlie's amnesia, an undercover drug sting, guns, and bombs that had led them to a relationship and quick engagement. "'Normal' isn't in our vocabulary."

Her heart ached like someone had reached in and squeezed it. As Charlie's partner, she'd endured the worry and pain during their assignments. Could she face those same occurrences as his wife without losing her mind or making a wrong move that got one of them killed?

He stiffened in her arms as if the same reality had hit him too.

After a moment, he tightened his embrace and rested his cheek on her head. "Who do you think is our shooter?"

She sighed. "Any of the three is possible. But I'm still leaning toward Chris, the killer Susan plans to testify against."

It made the most sense. What were the chances of Michael or Joe following Susan out here? Either would have to be desperate to go to those lengths. Still… "I have to agree, but I don't want to guess wrong either."

"Why don't you stay here and continue talking with Susan while I try to call the sheriff again and see if he's heard anything useful."

Charlie kissed the top of her head. "Sounds like a plan."

Lizzie excused herself from the group and went to the kitchen to place the call from the landline, assuming the storm hadn't taken out the service for that too.

She lifted the receiver and got a dial tone. *Hallelujah.*

"Sheriff Harper here."

"Hi, Sheriff. This is Lizzie Tremaine."

"Oh, yes. Hello, Lizzie. I was just about to call the ranch."

"You have news?"

"I do. I called the Seattle Police Department. They filled me in on the details of the case."

"And?"

"It's just as your friend told you. I also checked…where…

of...suspect."

"Come again, Sheriff. You're breaking up."

"He...until...but...attorney..."

"Sheriff?"

The phone went dead.

Great. Now what? Temptation to throw the handset across the room warred with common sense. In the end, she replaced the receiver and rested her forehead on the wall.

"Lizzie?"

She eased back and shifted to face Charlie.

"What did the sheriff say?"

"He tried to tell me something, but we got cut off."

"Did you get any of it?"

"Just that he contacted Seattle PD. He tried to say something about Chris Snyder's whereabouts and then mentioned the attorney, but the call broke up and completely dropped."

Charlie rubbed his forehead. "That leaves us with assuming every one of our suspects is still in play."

"Looks that way." Lizzie moved to the counter, popped a K-Cup in the Keurig, and hit start. "Does anyone come to mind who'd come after us?"

"I've racked my brain and can't think of anyone that desperate." He shrugged. "But I guess you never know. Susan did expound upon her ex-boyfriend and her boss. The ex, Michael, is a bit obsessive, but would he go as far as killing her? I'm not sure. As for the boss, I think Susan stumbled upon something hinky in the books. Whether he's guilty or truly suspects her is anyone's guess."

The coffee maker gurgled and beeped. She extracted the mug and sat at the kitchen table. "Let's run it down."

Charlie sat next to her and clasped her hand. "Go on."

"Someone shot at Susan and, by default, us. Phil Edwards, our ranch foreman, has a gash on his head from a bullet, according to him during his moments of consciousness. And when you helped Harold bring Phil to the house, the guy outside shot at the three of you." She sipped the bold brew and offered it to Charlie.

"Sounds about right." He accepted the cup, took a drink, then handed it back.

Lizzie tapped her lip with her finger. "Who was the gunman shooting at? Phil? Harold? You? Describe what happened when the three of you ran to the house."

Charlie released her, leaned back, and folded his hands over his chest. "I had Phil on one side, and Harold took the other. Thankfully, I tripped and fell, taking the two men down with me. The bullet whizzed over my head."

"Which side were you on?"

"If that's the farmhouse, I was on this side." He indicated the left side with a tap on the table. "And Harold was here." He pointed to the right.

"And the shot was fired from here?" Lizzie reached across and put her finger where the hay barn sat.

"Yes."

"Then why aim for you when Harold and Phil were the easier targets?"

Charlie's eyes widened. "He shot at me?"

Acid swirled in her belly. "Sounds like it." She paused. "You're the common denominator in both shootings."

He frowned. "True, but it makes no sense." Charlie stood and paced the kitchen.

"No, it doesn't. But we can't ignore the facts."

He ran his fingers through his hair. "Lizzie, do you think this is somehow about me? I mean, except for Phil, I'm the one whose sleeve was sliced by a bullet, and I appear to have been the target when we brought Phil in. But why?"

"That, I can't answer." She lifted the mug and paused. "Let's keep thinking on it."

She watched as Charlie's nervous energy got the best of him.

He strode to the window, lifted a single slat on the blinds, and peered out. He leaned in closer to the glass.

"What are you doing?" she asked.

Charlie straightened, then rushed to the mudroom, shoved his feet into his boots, and grabbed his coat from the hook at the back door. "This ends now."

"What?" Lizzie went to the window to see what had caused Charlie's reaction.

The motion sensor lights over the storage barn had clicked on, and the door stood wide open, but she didn't see anyone or anything.

"Charlie?"

"Someone went into the smaller barn."

Before she could respond, Charlie flung open the back door and took the few steps off the porch as fast as the snow-ladened ground allowed.

"Charlie, wait!" She slipped her feet into her boots and shoved her arms into the sleeves of her coat. If that man got himself killed, she was going to…

And there was the problem. Could she be his wife and be on the front line, watching him face danger every day? Pushing the heart-aching thought to the back of her mind, she grabbed the door knob and shouted over her shoulder, "Harold! Guard the house!" then took off outside.

Her mind had barely registered that the winds had died down and the snow had quit falling when she saw fire flicker in the storage barn.

She stood helpless as the building burst into flames. Tears burned behind her eyes at the sight before her. Shaking off the paralyzing terror, she quickened her pace toward the barn.

A loud crack filled the air, and beams fell from the ceiling, blocking the entrance.

The sight stole the air from her lungs.

She had to help Charlie before he burned alive.

FOUR

Charlie had done it again. He'd put himself at risk, just like Susan had accused him of in the past. He watched in horror as flames surrounded him. Maybe Suz was right and he'd never learn. So where did that leave him and Lizzie?

He shook off the depressing thought. He didn't have time for a pity party if he wanted to live.

When the suspect had stood at the back door and lit the accelerant, the mini-explosion had knocked Charlie to the ground. In the short time it'd taken for him to regain his equilibrium, the flames had spread through the paths of fuel and caught the other parts of the barn on fire.

And flames now blocked the rear door, cutting off the back exit. The heat of the blaze whooshed in his direction. He moved toward the front entrance, where the fire hadn't taken hold, only to find several heavy beams blocking his path.

Thick smoke rolled along the ceiling. Fire licked the walls of the building and spread toward him at a rapid pace. Heat filled the interior.

If he stayed too long, the fire would bake him alive. The smoke had grown heavy, and the inside of the barn now resembled an inferno. He wrapped his scarf around his nose and mouth and dropped onto all fours. His eyes watered, and his lungs protested.

His mind flashed back to the apartment fire he and Lizzie had barely escaped. This time Lizzie wasn't there to save him. On the plus side, he didn't have to worry about her getting hurt.

The fire roared around him, and the heat from the blaze had him fighting the urge to remove his coat—the little protection he had from the soaring temperature in the building.

He owed Lizzie an apology for his reckless behavior. He should have trusted their partnership and not gone off on his own. *Lord, let me live to apologize, please.*

He examined the beams and quickly weighed his options. With his arms around the hunk of wood, he pulled.

The more he struggled with the huge piece of wood, the faster he breathed and the more smoke he inhaled, causing him to cough hard enough to hurt his ribs. His vision tunneled, threatening to snuff out the light and drag him into unconsciousness.

He fought to stay in the moment. He wanted to marry Lizzie and have a life with her and Addy. The realization that he might lose his dream stole what little air he had left. He had to get out of there.

Waves of flames undulated across the floor, and columns of red and orange tentacles twisted together to slither up the walls.

With more determination, he readjusted his grip and tried again. Inch by inch, it moved until he had enough room to crawl around it. Fresh air filtered through the gaps of the other beams, and he sucked it in. The way the two remaining beams crisscrossed over the exit was still a problem. He had no idea how he'd get through, but he had to try.

He wanted to live. He wanted Lizzie.

FLAMES SHOT FROM THE ROOF, AND THE SIDES OF THE BUILDING glowed in red and orange. The entry door stood wide open, but heavy wood beams blocked the passageway, trapping Charlie inside. Lizzie had no way to get to him. Her worst nightmare had come to life.

"Charlie!"

Lizzie lowered herself to the ground and lifted the neck of her coat around her nose and mouth. She peered between the beams, scanning the interior for her fiancé. But the visibility was awful.

God, please help me find him before it's too late.

"Lizzie?"

"Charlie, where are you?" Tears streamed down her cheeks. Whether from the smoke or fear, she wasn't sure. Probably both.

"Right here." His hand stuck through the gap, and she grabbed ahold of it. "Help me."

The same words Charlie had left her on her voicemail four months ago when someone had almost killed him sucked the air from her lungs.

This time she wouldn't fail him. Because losing him—not an option.

"Hang on!" The blaze roared inside. "I've got you."

"I can't get through." He coughed so hard she ached for him.

"Give me a second." She let go and studied the problem. The space between the floor and the first beam encouraged her. Charlie only needed a little more room. "If I lift the bottom piece about six inches, can you wiggle through?"

"That should do it. But Lizzie, they're heavy. I can't help and crawl through at the same time."

"I have to try." Hands under the beam, she lifted. Nothing

226

happened. She needed a better grip. She tried again. It rose a few inches, but she had to let it down.

"Lizzie, whatever you do, don't risk your life. If it comes to it, leave me before the building collapses. Promise me."

Would Charlie lose his life days before their wedding? And what about Addy? Lizzie couldn't leave her daughter an orphan. But walking away from Charlie... Tears welled in her eyes at the thought, but she wasn't giving up. Not yet. "Just be ready to move."

"If I don't make it, tell Addy I love her."

"Stop it."

"Promise me!"

"Fine. I promise! But you can tell her yourself. Now, for the love of everything, let me focus." She glanced to her right, then to her left, searching for anything that could help her move the beam. There, next to the barn, lay a two-by-four she could use for leverage. She scurried to grab it and placed it under the massive piece of wood she'd tried to move moments ago.

"Okay, Hotshot, when I say go, you have to hurry and get through. I don't know how long I can hold it up."

"I'm ready when you are."

Lizzie took a deep breath of smoke and coughed it out. With the board stuck under the beam at an angle, she placed her hands on top and pushed. The large beam lifted, but not enough. She added her body weight to her efforts. "Go!"

She glanced down and saw Charlie's head and shoulders come through.

Her muscles quivered, and her hands started to slip. "Hurry!" Bile rose in her throat at the thought of dropping the wood and crushing him.

Charlie pulled with his arms and wiggled his hips back and forth until he was free.

Lizzie dropped the heavy wood and fell onto her rear. She

wanted to sit and catch her breath, but the fire crept closer with each passing minute.

She rose and bent over him. "Let's get out of here."

The two rushed from the barn and headed to a large stack of tarped hay to shield them from whoever had started the fire.

Once away from the immediate danger, they dropped to the snow and leaned against the plastic cover.

Lizzie inhaled the clean air and threw up a prayer of thanks. She'd have a longer conversation with the Almighty later. For now, a thank-you would have to do. She had no energy for more.

Charlie sat beside her, alternating between breathing hard and coughing to clear his lungs. He rolled his head to face her. "What is it with us and burning buildings?"

Lizzie stared at him. She wanted to laugh and cry at the same time, but the truth slammed into her. She didn't have the strength to be his wife and keep her sanity every time Charlie faced danger.

"Charlie, I can't do this."

FIVE

Flames danced in the air, and sparks crackled like fireworks on the Fourth of July. Charlie had tasted death once again. His pulse raced at how close he'd come to losing his life. Thanks to Lizzie, they'd both survived. But it wasn't the fire that threatened to stop his heart. It was her words.

Charlie stared at Lizzie. "What do you mean you can't do this?"

"I thought I could, but I can't. I can't watch you put yourself in harm's way and wonder if this is the day you'll die. I've been kidding myself that I have a future that includes a husband."

"Lizzie, take a minute. Don't let the emotions of the moment dictate our future."

When she stayed quiet, he thought about what she'd said. His risk-taking behavior had been the catalyst for her fears. He wanted to scream at his careless actions.

For the first time since he'd escaped the inferno, his mind focused on the danger. With the stop of the snowfall, there wasn't anything to obstruct the view, giving the shooter an open target.

The threat came first, but there was no way he'd let her go without a fight. "We'll talk about this later. Right now, we need to get inside."

A dull clunk came from his left.

Lizzie held her finger to her lips and removed her Glock from the holster at her hip.

He reached for his, then remembered removing it and placing it on the end table in the living room when he'd changed clothes earlier.

Lizzie scooted to the end of the stacked hay pile and peered around the corner on her side. A shot rang out. She whipped back behind the stack of logs. "He's running our way on your side. I don't have a clear shot. Here take it." She tossed him her weapon.

He caught, moved to his right, and dropped to his belly. The man ducked behind a tree, then popped out and took aim.

Charlie fired, and the shooter fell.

"Pocket knife," he said, "front pants pocket. Cut off some of the rope holding down the tarp."

He shifted so Lizzie could retrieve his knife and follow his instructions.

"Come on. I'll cover you while you secure him."

They walked toward the man who lay in the snow, bleeding.

Lizzie yanked the guy's arms behind his back, tied them together like a pro, and then flipped him over. Blood oozed from his shoulder where the bullet had hit him. "You're going to pay for this."

"I don't think so. Now, be quiet. I'll get to you in a minute, but I need to have a chat with my fiancée." Charlie relaxed for the first time in hours. "See, Lizzie. We make a great team."

She stepped back to his side. "I know that. We always have. But what if I hesitate and you get hurt?"

He wanted to laugh but knew better than to give her any more reasons to doubt. "Let me ask you this. Do you love me any less today than you will after we get married?"

"Well, no."

"Then how will it be different?"

He could see the confusion on her face as she pondered his question.

"I'm not saying I don't have my share of worries. Especially after Suz arrived. But Lizzie, once we get married, we'll have something a lot of couples don't have."

Her gaze met his. "What's that?"

"We'll have God in our marriage."

"True, but the fear is still here." She tapped at the place over her heart.

"I get it. I do. You don't think you scare the life out of me when you study new things?"

"Yeah, I suppose learning how to disarm a bomb might worry you a little." Her lopsided smile warmed his heart.

"Yeah, you think?" He chuckled. "How about we agree to share those fears and not let them control us."

She simply nodded. But when he saw her shoulders relax, he breathed a bit easier.

"I'm sorry for my freak-out moment. I do love you."

"As long as you still want to marry me, we're good." He itched to pull her into a hug but kept his attention on the gunman. "By the way, I don't think I've thanked you for saving my hide back there."

"Hmm...I think I'll take a kiss as payment." Lizzie smirked. His fiancée enjoyed teasing him a little too much.

"Ah, another *Charlie kiss*. That I can do." He smiled.

She gestured toward the gunman lying on the ground. "First, I suppose we should take him inside. That bullet hole in his shoulder must hurt, and he's probably freezing." Lizzie didn't sound a bit upset about those facts.

Charlie pursed his lips to hide a smile. *Oh, Lizzie girl, you are something else.* "Then come on, let's get him in the house." Charlie handed Lizzie back her weapon and crouched beside the lame excuse for a human. "I guess we should patch you up and see if we can raise the sheriff."

Lizzie aimed the gun at the attacker in custody while Charlie helped the man to his feet.

"Besides, I have a few million questions that need to be answered." He grabbed the man's uninjured arm. "Time to put the pieces together."

Charlie marched the guy to the house, hoping someone inside could identify him so they could put this whole mess behind them.

HER HEART LIGHTER AFTER TALKING WITH CHARLIE, LIZZIE followed behind her future husband with her gun ready to defend. She refused to let the killer escape. The game of cat and mouse had gotten old. She, too, wanted answers. But more than anything, she wanted a future with Charlie.

When she'd gotten a good look at the man, she hadn't recognized him, and neither had Charlie, so she'd mentally crossed off anyone from their past. At least, anyone obvious.

Charlie ushered their prisoner into the house, where they got rid of their boots and coats and continued into the living room.

He jerked to a stop.

Lizzie joined him by his side and halted. She stared down the barrel of a shotgun.

Harold had his weapon trained on them. "You caught him."

"Sure did. Now, could you please point that thing

somewhere else?" Charlie's calm demeanor almost made her laugh.

"Sorry." Harold lowered the weapon.

Charlie pulled off the man's hat and lifted his chin for everyone to get a good look. "Time to get this over with. Harold, would you flip on the lights?"

"Sure thing."

The lights came on, and it took a moment for everyone's eyes to adjust.

Mary gasped. "You?"

Lizzie's gaze flew to the man in cuffs. "Who?"

"Our neighbor, Simon Elliott." Mary's voice quivered.

Of all the possibilities, Lizzie hadn't expected that to be the right one.

Charlie maneuvered Simon to a chair and not-so-gently made him sit, then pulled back the man's coat to examine the wound. "Why come after Susan and me?" He poked at the bullet hole, and the guy winced.

Simon gritted his teeth. "I wasn't shooting at her. I planned to kill you, and when your bride attacked me outside, I figured I'd take her out too."

Harold's eyes widened. "What did they ever do to you?"

The man scoffed. "I've tried to run you off this property with the broken fences and sick horses. I thought maybe you'd realize you're too old to run a ranch, but nothing worked. What better way to force you to sell than have one of your precious couples die? No one would want to get married here after that. You'd go bankrupt."

Harold closed his eyes and shook his head. "And what? Phil got in your way?"

"Bingo."

"I'll get the first aid kit and take care of that wound." Mary patted her husband on the back and left the room.

"So it was never about the crime I witnessed?" Susan sat on the couch and gripped the blanket on her lap like a lifeline.

Lizzie moved to her side. "That's the way it appears. But I want to talk with the sheriff and Seattle PD before we consider you out of harm's way. And I have a friend out there who can help you with your ex-boyfriend."

"Thank you." Susan glanced at Charlie, then back to Lizzie. "I don't deserve your kindness."

"Sure you do. Everyone makes mistakes." Lizzie knew that firsthand. She'd almost made the biggest one of all by walking away from marrying Charlie out of fear. "It's what we do about them that counts."

Only the crackle of the fire in the fireplace broke the silence.

Mary returned with the first aid kit and tended to Simon's injuries while everyone else pondered the turn of events.

Determined to see Simon behind bars for a good long time, Lizzie planned to have everything the sheriff needed to make that happen. "Harold, do you have that video ready for us?"

"What does it matter now?"

"I want airtight proof. Yes, we have eyewitness accounts, but a picture—or video—will go a long way."

The older man gave her a quick nod. "My laptop is on the kitchen table, cued up and ready to go."

"Would you watch over Simon while we take a look?"

"Sure thing, missy." Harold retrieved his shotgun and held it, ready to defend.

Lizzie bit her lip to keep from laughing at his serious stance, although she knew Harold had Simon under control. "Come on, Charlie."

With a quick glance at Simon and a long one at Susan, Charlie sighed and joined Lizzie in the kitchen.

"She'll be all right."

"What?" He blinked, confusion stamped across his features.

"Susan. She's shaken, but she's okay."

"I just...she's so..." He huffed and dropped onto the chair at the table.

"Well, that's a first."

He frowned. "What is?"

"You at a loss for words. Never thought I'd see the day." Lizzie grinned.

"Very funny."

She rested her hand on his arm. "She's stronger than she looks."

"You're probably right."

"I know I am."

He smiled. "Even as much as she hurt me, it's still hard not to worry about her."

"Trust me, I understand. You can't wipe away your past. You learn from it and move on. And with how it ended, I can only imagine the things whirling in that brain of yours." She paused and faced him. "Know this, Charlie Lee. You are a good man. A man with a big heart. Don't let yourself ever doubt that."

He slid his hand behind her neck and tugged her close. "I don't know what I did to deserve you, but whatever it was, I'm glad you agreed to marry me." With that, he lowered his lips to hers and gave her one of his *Charlie kisses* that she loved so much.

After her brain settled from his mind-blowing kiss, she pulled up the video. "Here we go."

Charlie peered over her shoulder and watched with her as a figure snuck into the small barn with a gas can. The clip showed Charlie go inside, and a few moments later, the building burst into flames.

She captured several screenshots of the man exiting out the back of the barn and enhanced the pictures, the man's face visible in each one. "Got it."

Lizzie and Charlie made their way back to the living room.

"We have video and stills proving that Simon burned down

your barn plus our accounts of what happened, and when Phil wakes up, he can add his too. With all that, you'll have more than enough evidence to convict him," Lizzie said.

Mary sniffed. "That's wonderful. It's been a worry for me that my Harold or one of the boys working the ranch would get hurt, but I had no idea Simon had caused the problems."

Harold wrapped Mary in his arms and kissed her head. "It's over."

"The photo and the video are now saved in a separate file," Charlie added.

"I can't thank you enough for your help." Harold released Mary and sank into the recliner.

"I'm sorry about your barn. I'd have saved it if I could have." Charlie joined Lizzie.

"It's only a building."

The phone in the kitchen rang.

Mary waved everyone off. "I've got it."

A few moments later, she returned to the living room. "The sheriff's on the phone and asked to speak with one of you." Her finger toggled between Lizzie and Charlie.

"I'll go." Lizzie walked to the kitchen and picked up the receiver from the counter. "This is Lizzie."

"I'm glad phone lines are up again. It's a good thing it was only a limb across the wires and our telephone guys are on it. I had news when the line went dead."

"It's okay, Sheriff Harper. We got the—"

"I don't know who's after you, but I can say without a doubt that Chris Snyder is not the killer. His attorney confirmed SPD arrested him again after killing a man during a bar fight. There were tons of witnesses. The guy won't see the outside of a jail cell for a long time. So I'm not sure who—"

"Sheriff," Lizzie interrupted. "We caught the attacker. It's Simon Elliott, the Prices' neighbor. He wanted their land and was willing to kill to get it."

"Simon Elliot!" Lizzie winced at the shout. "Well, I'll be…he alive or dead?"

"Alive. But with a bullet hole in his shoulder." Lizzie exhaled. Might as well admit the truth now. "Compliments of Charlie."

"The guy got off easy if you ask me," the sheriff muttered. "Don't worry, ma'am. I'll take your statements once the county clears the roads and I can get to the ranch. Then we can put it all behind you and get you hitched tomorrow."

Lizzie bit back a laugh. Harper really was a good ol' boy sheriff. "I appreciate that. One more thing."

"Go on."

"We have photographic evidence of Simon burning down the Prices' small barn. And I have a feeling that once Phil wakes up, he'll add to the charges against him."

"I can't thank you and that man of yours enough."

"No need, Sheriff. I'm just glad it's over." With a final goodbye, she hung up and joined the others in the living room.

After she filled them in on her conversation, Mary and Harold excused themselves to go check on Phil, and Susan took the Prices up on their offer of the extra bedroom, leaving Lizzie and Charlie alone with Simon.

"Lie down, Simon. The sheriff will send an ambulance when the county plows the roads." She pointed to the couch.

Simon moved without argument.

"All that for nothing." Lizzie shook her head. "I had asked Mary before the storm hit about the land and their business. She told me they use it as a wedding venue for the joy of it, not the income. The property is paid for in full. And even if it wasn't, they could use the sapphires to pay the bills. You never had a chance at making them go bankrupt."

The man opened his mouth to say something, then changed his mind.

Charlie stood across from the couch and folded his arms over his chest.

Lizzie checked the time. Two in the morning. Her body ached, and exhaustion poured over her. But Charlie had spent more time in the cold and had taken the brunt of the smoke. The man appeared ready to fold. Lizzie strolled over and placed her hand on his bicep. "Go get some sleep."

"I can watch him."

"I know you can. But I'd like my fiancé functional to walk down the aisle on our wedding day."

Charlie's brow arched. "I look that bad?"

"I'm pleading the fifth."

"Good call." Charlie kissed the top of her head. "I love you."

"I love you too." She smiled. "Now scram."

"Scramming. But I'll be back in a couple of hours to relieve you."

"Deal."

She watched Charlie climb the stairs to the room Mary had given him before the storm.

Her gaze moved to Simon. The guy who'd almost caused her to lose the man she loved.

Since she'd started trusting God a few months ago with the people she cared about, days like today didn't have the same smothering effect.

SIX

The day before Charlie's wedding, and here he sat in a house with his former fiancée and the love of his life, Lizzie. The concept was so remote that he had no idea what to think. He knew one thing for sure: he still struggled against letting Susan's accusations take hold. And for his and Lizzie's sakes, he had to find a way to let it go.

Charlie carried two cups of coffee to the kitchen table and sat one in front of Lizzie. "There ya go."

"Thanks." She wrapped her hands around the mug.

They both had caught a couple hours of sleep but required large amounts of caffeine to face the morning.

Mary stood at the sink, washing dishes from the huge breakfast spread that had once filled the table, while Susan dried. The two had hit it off and chattered nonstop since Susan joined them this morning.

Everyone had eaten except Lizzie, who'd recently emerged from her bedroom.

With Harold guarding Simon, he and Lizzie had a moment together, albeit with extra ears.

"Tomorrow's the day." He pulled out a chair and lowered himself onto it. "Are you ready?"

Lizzie smiled, giving him hope that she wouldn't cancel due to lack of family and friends. After the events over the last twelve hours, he wanted more than anything to make her his wife. "Most definitely."

He hated having the conversation in front of Mary and Susan, but he had to know. "Any hesitation?" If she had her heart set on waiting, he'd agree just to see her happy.

She thought a moment. "No. I only need you and God with me."

He swallowed the unexpected emotion building in his throat. "I love you, Lizzie."

"I love you too, Charlie." She took a sip and sighed. "Cell service has been restored. I wish someone would answer their phone."

Yeah, he didn't understand why every person on their guest list refused to pick up.

When the sun rose, Harold had informed Charlie that the county plows would be out in full force now that the snow had stopped, and they'd better be prepared. So he and Harold had left Mary in charge of Simon while Lizzie slept. The two men had plowed the driveway and around the cabins and main lodge, allowing help to arrive.

Engines rumbled outside, then shut off. Charlie ambled to the front window and peeked out. He spotted the sheriff's SUV and an ambulance.

Sheriff Harper and one of his deputies stepped from their vehicle along with two paramedics from the ambulance.

The foursome strode with care to the house, avoiding slick spots the shovel might have missed.

Charlie opened the front door. "Morning, Sheriff."

The man offered his hand, and Charlie shook it. "Glad to make it. I hear you have a prisoner for us. And some evidence that will help me put him behind bars."

"The USB with evidence is waiting in an envelope on the end table, and Simon Elliott, who we'll gladly turn over into your custody, is right there." He motioned toward the couch.

The paramedics, along with a deputy, stomped the snow from their boots and followed the sheriff inside. They scooted past him to tend to Simon's injury.

Sheriff Harper paused beside Charlie. "I'll need your statements. Then once the boys get our suspect into the ambulance and take a look at Phil, we'll be out of your hair."

Charlie appreciated the man's efficiency. "Thank you for that."

"No need to spoil any more of your wedding plans. Now, if you'll point me to Ms. Welch, I'd like to give her the news about Chris Snyder in person."

Charlie gestured toward the kitchen. "She's in there with Mary."

"Thank you, son." Sheriff Harper hooked his thumbs in his utility belt and sauntered away.

Charlie chuckled at the classic Old-West-sheriff vibe that oozed from the lawman.

Not long after their arrival, the paramedics and the deputy had Simon loaded in the ambulance and headed to town. Phil had woken and identified Simon as his assailant. The sheriff had taken his statement, but Phil refused the ambulance ride. He said he'd contact his doctor, but Harold insisted that he go to the hospital, so Sheriff Harper promised to drop him off at the emergency room on his way to the office.

Thirty minutes later, the sheriff had everyone's statements. He'd promised to review the video and make sure Simon stayed behind bars for a very long time.

"I'll get Phil here loaded in the car." Harper turned to Susan.

"I had your vehicle towed to the station. Whenever you're ready, I'll take you to it."

"I appreciate that." Susan turned to Lizzie. "I can't thank you enough."

"You're welcome." Lizzie's warm smile melted Charlie's heart. "Take care of yourself."

Susan nodded, then shifted to face him and scraped her teeth over her bottom lip. "Can I speak with you for a minute—in private?"

"Sure." Charlie's imagination ran wild wondering what she planned to say. He'd gotten over her hateful words when she left him—mostly. And for Pete's sake, he and Lizzie had saved her life.

"Oh, would you relax." She rolled her eyes. "I'm not going say anything bad."

So maybe he had nothing to worry about. He motioned her toward a quiet corner in the front room near the Christmas tree. "Okay, you have my attention."

"Charlie, I…" Susan blew out a breath. "Wow, this isn't easy."

He furrowed his brow. "Just spit it out. I can take it."

She threw her head back and laughed.

"What's so funny?" How could a woman he hadn't seen in years and no longer had feelings for twist him in knots?

"Sorry." Susan turned serious. "Charlie Lee, you're a good man. I was wrong to break up with you the way I did."

Not what he'd expected to hear. "I'd like to say it was okay, but to be honest, it really hurt."

"I know, and for that, I'm sorry." She took his hand. "I never should have said those things."

"I appreciate that." He peered into her eyes and found honesty behind her words. "Although, it was a good thing you did."

Susan nodded. "We were never meant to be together."

"I didn't see it at the time, but I do now." His gaze drifted to

Lizzie, who stood across the room like a momma bear ready to defend a cub. That was his Lizzie. Protective to a fault.

Susan's gaze followed his. "She's good for you."

"Yeah, she is." He couldn't imagine life without Lizzie. She made him a better person.

"Charlie."

He returned his attention back to Susan.

"You have your perfect match in Lizzie. She's the woman God made for you. I'm happy for you."

"Thanks, Suz."

"You'll make an awesome husband and father."

His eyebrows rose to his hairline. He'd longed to hear those words for years. Susan's opinion shouldn't matter, but at the core of his doubt, it did. "Really?"

She chuckled. "Like I said. I was wrong telling you otherwise."

The sheriff strode over. "You ready, miss? I'd like to get back to the station."

"I'll be with you in just a minute, thank you."

The man nodded and walked away.

"I'm sorry all this happened to you." Charlie meant every word.

Susan shrugged a shoulder. "It gave me the chance to apologize."

A smile tugged at his lips. "You could have just picked up the phone."

"There is that." She rose on her tiptoes and placed a kiss on his cheek. "Goodbye, Charlie." She motioned toward Lizzie. "Take care of her."

"I plan to."

Susan squeezed his shoulder and joined the sheriff.

Wow, he hadn't expected that. But it felt nice to clear the air. And even nicer that the remaining self-doubt vanished with Susan's words. He'd needed them more than he'd ever imagined.

Hands slipped around his waist from behind, and Lizzie rested her cheek on his back. "Are you doing okay?"

He shifted and pulled her to his side. "Better than."

"You mean I don't need to go all momma bear on her?"

Charlie laughed. "No, honey. You can relax. She actually apologized."

Lizzie leaned back and blinked.

He tucked her in close. "Not what you expected, was it?"

"Not at all. However, I guess it shouldn't surprise me. She did come looking for you because she trusted you."

He hadn't thought of that. Her presence and the attacks had blindsided him, leaving him no time to consider her motives. "You know what else she told me?" he whispered in her ear.

"What?"

"That you are my perfect match."

"Hmm. I think I'm beginning to like her."

He chuckled. "She's right, you know. You and I are meant to be together."

"I won't argue with that." She nestled in his arms and watched the sheriff's car leave with Susan and Phil.

He led Lizzie into the house, and they helped Mr. and Mrs. Price tidy up from everyone stomping in and out.

Once finished, Harold sank into the recliner. "That was quite a night."

"It sure was." Charlie stood beside Harold. "Sorry about all the trouble."

"Not your fault. And partially ours." Harold motioned toward Lizzie. "Ready for tomorrow?"

Charlie glanced at Lizzie and Mary, who hugged and exchanged a quiet word. "More than you'll ever know."

Harold's gaze drifted to his wife, and he smiled. "Oh, I think I can guess."

Yeah, the older man probably could.

When all was quiet, they left the main house and moved into

the six-bedroom lodge. The place should have been filled with laughter and their friends' shenanigans, but instead, deafening silence greeted them.

Charlie built a roaring fire and snuggled with Lizzie on the couch. A Christmas tree sat off to the side of the large rock wall fireplace. Its multicolored lights reflected off the glass ornaments, giving a twinkling effect on the walls and ceiling. The gifts they'd brought for the others lay nestled under the tree, waiting for Christmas Day.

Their wedding was tomorrow, on Christmas Eve, and Charlie doubted their friends and family would make it. The airports had reopened, but the probability of the others securing flights was slim to none. But he didn't care. All he wanted was for the woman next to him to finally become his wife.

He closed his eyes and rested his cheek on her hair. "I'm sorry it won't be the wedding we had planned."

Lizzie placed her palm on his chest. "I'm actually okay with it. After last night, I don't want to wait for the perfect moment. Being married to you is all I need."

He smiled and tugged her closer. "Honestly? No regrets if it's only us?"

"No regrets."

Her words filled him with a contentment he hadn't felt in a long time. Last night had put a new perspective on life for him and apparently for Lizzie as well. As long as they had God and each other, life would turn out okay.

The exhaustion from the little rest last night and the warmth from the fire had them drifting off to sleep in each other's arms.

Charlie jerked awake and scanned the room. What had pulled him from his nap? Nothing appeared out of place.

Lizzie stirred and glanced up at him. "Something wrong?"

"I'm not sure."

Car doors slammed, and voices rose in the air.

"What in the world?" Lizzie untangled herself from him and stood.

He joined her and laced their fingers together. "Not a clue."

They hurried to the front window and peered out.

"Momma!"

"Addy?" Lizzie glanced at him, and they rushed to the door together.

Several SUVs lined the driveway. Their friends and family poured from the vehicles laughing, talking, and taking a moment for an impromptu snowball fight.

Lizzie burst through the door and hurried down the steps. She threw her arms around her daughter. "My Addy girl!"

Charlie strolled over and hugged his sister. "You guys made it."

"Thanks to Preston and his private plane. As soon as we had the all-clear, we were in the air. There was no way we were missing this." Olivia grinned at him. A mischievous glint sparkled in her eyes.

He studied her a moment. "I have a feeling there's a story or two there."

She slapped him on the back. "Oh, dear brother, you have no idea."

"Well, we might have one of our own to tell." And boy, did they, but it could wait.

Unrestrained laughter erupted from the group.

Charlie's gaze roamed the scene playing out in front of him.

Grey sat in his wheelchair on the concrete drive that Charlie had helped Mr. Price clear earlier that day, and he scooped a handful of snow. Christina's face when he pegged her in the ear was priceless.

"Grey Parker, you did not just do that." Christina narrowed her eyes at her man and marched to stand in front of him, hands planted on her hips.

A grin spread across Grey's face. "Oh, but I did." He tugged her into his lap, and Christina's laughter rang out.

Laila hobbled along next to Preston. Even with an injured ankle or foot—Charlie didn't know which—and what appeared to be a broken finger, she refused to be left out of the fun.

Heart full, Charlie sighed. His friends had arrived, and they were happy.

Olivia cleared her throat and eyed him. "You're spilling it later. For now, let's join in."

"You're on." Charlie bent, scooped up snow, and tossed it at his sister.

"Hey!" She wiped the moisture from her face. "This means war."

Lizzie caught his gaze and smiled.

Without another thought, he jogged to his soon-to-be wife and tackled her and his new daughter to the snow.

Lizzie's stomach hurt from laughing so hard. Her family was here, and she planned to enjoy her last evening as a single woman. Not that married life sounded bad—on the contrary. The thought of marrying Charlie did funny things to her insides. Excitement, anticipation, and a little nervousness, all rolled into one amazing future with the man she loved.

After a warm shower to relieve her aching body from her battle the night before and to chase away the cold from the snowball fight, she towel-dried her hair, dressed, and headed downstairs. Her family and friends spilled from one room into another, chatting and having fun.

"There you are." Charlie swept her off her feet and carried her to the middle of the room.

She swatted his arm. "You're not supposed to carry me until tomorrow night."

"Honey, I plan to do it then too." He winked.

Lizzie felt her cheeks warm at the thought of their first night together.

Charlie grinned. The brat knew what he had done. He placed her on her feet. "Time to party."

"You just like to have fun."

"Guilty."

"Go. Enjoy your friends."

He dipped his chin and got serious. "Are you sure? Because I have no problem staying by your side all evening."

"As tempting as that sounds..." She smiled and cupped his cheek, enjoying the scruff on his face. "Yes, I'm sure. I have information to pry out of Christina and Laila. Something is going on, and I want to know what."

Charlie shook his head. "Women."

"Listen here, mister—" He swooped in for a kiss, halting her admonishment. The mere action scrambled her thoughts.

"Bye." He took off to the kitchen. No doubt for food.

Once her brain engaged, she called after him. "Brat!" Tomorrow couldn't come fast enough.

She made a beeline for her friends. Christina's arm in a sling and Laila's two broken fingers and sprained ankle concerned Lizzie. She'd heard the basics of their stories but wanted to know what else was up with Laila.

Her friend stood with the rest of the Elite Guardians—Maddy and Quinn, Olivia and Wade, and Katie and Daniel—drinking a cup of hot chocolate and remaining suspiciously quiet, even for her.

"Hey, y'all, can I steal Laila for a second?"

"Sure. Just make sure to bring her back." Maddy grinned.

"Will do." Lizzie turned to Laila. "Come on. Let's go over there." She gestured to a spot next to the Christmas tree, where it was semi-quiet. Once they were out of earshot, Lizzie turned to face her. "What is going on with you?"

"What do you mean?"

Oh, Laila was good at acting all innocent, but Lizzie didn't buy it. She snorted. "Right. Miss Never Comfortable in a Crowd suddenly doesn't seem to mind the chaos happening around her. And the way you looked at Preston earlier...give it up, girl. Something's going on."

Laila chewed on her lower lip, reluctant to share, then shrugged. "Fine." She explained in more detail the plane crash and being hunted. "Then, when it was all over, Preston asked me to marry him."

Her eyes shot open wide. "And you said..."

Her friend reached into her pocket and pulled out a beautiful diamond ring. "I said yes."

Lizzie squealed. "That's fantastic!"

The room grew quiet, and all eyes turned to them.

Lizzie leaned in and whispered, "Sorry."

"That's okay. We just thought people would think it's too fast."

She shook her head. "No way. When God's behind it, it's perfect, no matter the timing."

"You think?" The hope in Laila's eyes tugged at Lizzie's heart.

Lizzie searched the faces in the room until she found Charlie and smiled. "I know so." She squeezed Laila's hand. "Are you going to announce it, or am I?"

Laila laughed and slid the ring onto her finger. "I hate attention."

"I understand, but this is too good not to share."

"I suppose." Laila's excited expression belied her nonchalant tone. That was Laila. Former Mossad and one all-around fierce chick. Laila motioned Preston over. "Everyone, we have something to tell you."

Lizzie wound her way through the crowd to Charlie's side.

Preston joined Laila. The man looked as though he might burst from pride and love.

"As you know, Preston and I had a couple of crazy days."

The group laughed at the downplay of the events.

"I thought maybe it was too soon to say anything, but Lizzie convinced me otherwise." She laced her fingers with Preston's and held up their hands. Her diamond ring sparkled in the light. "Preston asked me to marry him, and I said yes."

Cheers went up around the room.

The couple received hugs and slaps on the back as each member of the Elite Guardians and their families congratulated them.

Charlie wrapped his arm around Lizzie's shoulder and handed her a glass of punch. "I'm glad you encouraged them to announce it. It makes tonight even more special."

"I couldn't agree more." She snuggled in closer and enjoyed the excitement.

A clinking sound broke through the merriment, and everyone's attention turned to Grey, who lowered the knife he'd tapped on the side of his glass. "Laila, Preston, congratulations. We're all very happy for you. And to the soon-to-be bride and groom, thank you for sharing your special day with us tomorrow." His gaze shifted to Christina, whose arm was in a sling from a gunshot wound, according to the story Lizzie had heard. Grey held out his hand, and Christina joined him. "We didn't want to intrude on Lizzie and Charlie's time, but if it's okay with them, we'd like to add to the celebration."

Lizzie grinned up at Charlie. She had a feeling she knew what was coming. "Go ahead. There can never be enough good news."

Grey tugged Christina onto his lap, careful of her healing arm. "This beautiful woman and I have finally set a date for our wedding."

"And?" Olivia urged.

The entire group had waited for Christina and Grey to get their act together and set a date. No one knew why they'd waited so long, but Lizzie had an idea. Lack of communication and misunderstandings had detrimental effects on relationships.

Christina's smile lit up her face. "How would you all feel about moving this party to Grey's parents' house for a New Year's Eve wedding?"

Mid sip of her drink, Lizzie choked. "As in this year?"

Grey leaned around Christina and addressed Lizzie directly. "Yes. As in next week."

"It's about time," Quinn muttered. Maddy elbowed him in the ribs. "What?"

Laughter filled the air.

Charlie tightened his hold on Lizzie. "Put us down for a family of three. We'll be there."

Oh, how Lizzie liked the sound of his answer. Her gaze drifted to the Christmas tree and her special gift for Charlie. Waiting for Christmas Day no longer had the same meaning. She'd give it to him as a wedding present.

Mind made up, she turned her attention to Christina and Grey and held up her glass. "Here's to the growing Elite Guardians family."

A chorus of "Hear! Hear!" and the click of glasses ensued.

"Come with me." Charlie laced his fingers with hers and led her onto the front porch. He wrapped her in his arms from behind, and she stared at the night sky.

Lizzie rested her head against his chest. "It's beautiful."

"That it is."

She glanced up and found him staring down at her. "Charlie?"

"You are beautiful, inside and out."

Lizzie turned in his arms and kissed him. "You're good for me."

"I know." He smirked.

That was her Charlie, and she wouldn't change a thing.

SEVEN

Today Charlie had the privilege of marrying Lizzie, and the choice of venue, even after all the chaos with Simon, was perfect.

The ranch had transformed into something out of a magazine. Mr. and Mrs. Price had outdone themselves.

He'd peeked at the interior of the buildings twenty minutes ago. The flowers and decorations flowed from inside the barn for the ceremony to the one for the reception. The Prices had guaranteed the perfect winter wedding, and they'd delivered. They'd even placed plywood under the carpet runner for stability, to accommodate Grey's wheelchair and provide solid ground for Laila to walk on.

Charlie paced the dressing room. This was it. A life with Lizzie and Addy awaited him. And he couldn't be happier.

Anxious to see Lizzie in her wedding dress, he tugged on the sleeves of his dress shirt under his tux jacket and glanced at the clock. He sighed. Only two lousy minutes had passed.

"Would you stop? You're making me nervous, and I'm

already married." Quinn ran a finger under his collar. "Why do they have to make these monkey suits so uncomfortable?"

Charlie rolled his eyes. "Dude, you're my best man. You're supposed to help calm me down."

"Oh, yeah, right." The man didn't look at all remorseful.

Mr. Price, who not only ran the ranch but happened to be an ordained minister, walked in. "Are you ready to get hitched?"

Quinn choked back a laugh.

Charlie backhanded him across the chest. "Knock it off." He moved to Harold. "I sure am."

"Then let's go see that girl of yours." Harold smiled and led them out the door.

Charlie strode down the hallway, ready to marry Lizzie, when the depths of the commitment he was about to make slammed into him. His steps faltered.

Quinn's hand landed on his shoulder. "You okay there, buddy?"

Was he?

God, I can't fail. Lizzie's too important for me to botch this marriage.

A warmth spread through him, and he knew. With God at the center of their marriage, he wouldn't fail. Oh, he wasn't disillusioned. They'd have tough moments, but they'd be okay as long as they relied on God.

"Couldn't be better." With a sense of peace and confidence, Charlie continued his trek behind Harold.

The music started, and Charlie and Quinn took their places by the altar.

The reality of the moment hit Charlie hard. Tears swam in his eyes as his gaze swept around the room. The Elite Guardians, their significant others and families, and his mom and dad. The guests were few, but he and Lizzie had wanted it that way.

His only regret...the absence of his sister Shana, a country music star who'd died years ago at the hands of her fans.

A vise tightened around his lungs, and he struggled to catch his breath. Charlie tipped his face to the ceiling, and a lone tear slid down his cheek. He quickly wiped it away.

I wish you were here, sis. You'd love Lizzie and Addy, and you would've been the best sister-in-law and aunt ever. I miss you so much.

He lowered his chin, and his gaze connected with Olivia's.

Her husband Wade handed her a tissue, and she dabbed at the tears streaming down her face.

She knew where his thoughts had gone. She nodded her understanding, then mouthed, *She's here,* and patted her chest.

Charlie mimicked her and patted his chest in response. Yes, Shana might not be there physically, but she'd always be with him in his heart.

A murmur of *ohs* and *ahs* pulled him from his thoughts.

Addy slowly walked down the aisle in her light-blue dress with a bouquet of bright-colored flowers that sparkled with glitter. When her gaze landed on him, she smiled. His daughter. Well, as soon as the adoption paperwork he'd signed weeks ago went through, but either way, she was his to help raise and love.

Next, Lizzie's best friend from Savannah, Noelle Burton, who'd arrived just in time for the wedding, followed Addy in a dark-blue gown with a bouquet of the same beautiful flowers. Once Noelle took her place next to Addy, the music changed to the wedding march.

Charlie straightened and tugged at the hem of his tux.

Lizzie appeared at the entrance like an angel in white. Her brown hair flowed over her shoulders, and her wedding dress fit perfectly in all the right places, making him happy that she would soon be his wife.

Her eyes met his, and his knees almost buckled at the love shining behind her gaze.

Helen, Lizzie's mother, walked Lizzie down the aisle and

straight into his arms. Resisting was worthless. He pulled her close and kissed her.

Quinn cleared his throat. "Wrong part, dude."

Lizzie eased back and smiled. "I beg to differ. I think it was perfect."

Their friends and family laughed at the verbal exchange.

Harold grinned. "If you two are finished, maybe we can get you married."

"Let's do this." Charlie took Lizzie's hand and faced Mr. Price.

He had a difficult time keeping his attention on anything Harold said. His focus was solely on his bride. The woman God had planned for him. His perfect match.

"Lizzie, do you have vows you'd like to say to Charlie?"

She faced him and smiled. "Charlie, I love you. You are my best friend. Today I give myself to you in marriage. I promise to encourage you, to laugh with you, and to comfort you. I promise to love you in good times and in bad, when life seems easy and when it seems hard. I promise these things today and all the days of our lives."

"Charlie." Harold motioned for him to say his vows.

Charlie cleared the emotion from his throat. "Lizzie, you know me better than anyone else in this world, and somehow still, you manage to love me." Quinn chuckled beside him, but Charlie ignored the man and continued. "You are my best friend and one true love. There is still a part of me that can't believe I'm the one who gets to marry you. I love you, Lizzie. I promise to do my best to be the husband you need."

Tears dripped from Lizzie's chin, and he reached over and swiped them away with his thumb.

She cupped his face, and only then did Charlie realize his own tears had escaped his lashes and trailed down his cheek.

Harold addressed the two of them. "I now pronounce you husband and wife. You may kiss the bride."

Charlie didn't need another invitation. He wrapped his arms around Lizzie and lowered his lips to hers. The soft, gentle kiss held a passion simmering beneath the surface that he'd explore once they were alone, but he'd made a promise to himself to keep the kiss rated G in front of their family and friends.

He rested his forehead on hers. "Well, Mrs. Lee, are you ready for a future together?"

"More than."

Charlie couldn't tear his gaze from his wife. *His wife.* The words warmed the center of his chest.

Forget formality and his previous promise. He tugged Lizzie close, then dipped her and laid a kiss on her that left no doubt about his plans for later.

The catcalls and whistles grabbed his attention. He lifted Lizzie to a standing position and pressed one more kiss to her lips, enjoying her dazed expression.

His heart exploded with joy. He'd married the woman of his dreams.

Arm tucked in Charlie's elbow, Lizzie steadied herself from the passionate kiss he'd planted on her and faced her family and friends.

They'd done it. Husband and wife. It was as if the world settled into place, and peace sprinkled over her like pixie dust.

She had a lot of thanking God to do, but for now, she'd enjoy the moment. He understood.

"Are you ready, Mrs. Lee?"

She smiled. "Yes."

"Then your carriage awaits."

She and Charlie walked down the aisle to the front entrance of the barn and drew in a deep breath of the fresh, cool air.

Mary draped a beautiful white coat over Lizzie's shoulder and leaned in. "It's in the pocket."

Lizzie hugged the woman. "Thank you."

Charlie donned his coat while the others filed out of the barn to join them.

She slipped her hand into his. "We did it."

"We sure did." He gave her a reassuring squeeze.

Addy squealed, forcing Lizzie's attention to the edge of the hay barn.

She gasped.

Two stallions pulled a carriage draped with white roses and silver bells, like something out of a fairy tale. Phil, who'd received ten stitches, a dose of antibiotics, and been released from the hospital, sat high on the driver's seat in a black tux and top hat, looking regal.

Lizzie leaned against Charlie's arm. "It's perfect."

The carriage stopped, and Charlie assisted Lizzie onto the passenger bench, then slid in beside her. He grabbed the folded blanket on the carriage floor and placed it over their laps.

Phil glanced over his shoulder, and Charlie nodded.

The horses whinnied, and the carriage jostled to a start. The plan was to circle the ranch once by themselves. Then after Addy had a turn, the ride would open for everyone else during the reception. And she had a feeling that her friends would take advantage of the romantic opportunity.

Lizzie snuggled in close to Charlie and took in the scenery. The snowstorm had left a thick blanket of pristine, glistening white. A gorgeous backdrop for the day. As if God had gifted them the perfect winter wonderland wedding.

Charlie leaned his head against hers. "What's going through that pretty mind of yours?"

"The whole day has exceeded my dreams." Lizzie straightened and pointed in the distance. "Look."

"Where?"

"The deer. The three standing in the open." She released a contented sigh and snuggled in.

Charlie wound a strand of her hair around his finger and whispered in her ear, "I can't think of anything that would make this day more perfect."

Lizzie patted her pocket and smiled. "I can."

Finger under her chin, he tilted her face to his. A look of confusion flickered in his eyes. "What?"

She cupped his cheek. "Relax. I'm referring to my Christmas present for you."

"Hmmm. I thought that would be tonight."

Her cheeks heated. When would she quit blushing at the thought of their nights together? "Very funny. Now, if you'll be serious, I have something for you." Lizzie extracted the envelope from her pocket. "I received this before we left South Carolina but wanted to give it to you as a special gift on Christmas morning. But I changed my mind."

"Okay."

She handed it to him. "Go ahead. Open it."

Charlie removed his arm from around her and scooted back in his seat. He used care in peeling back the seal and slipped out the piece of paper. He unfolded it and read. His eyes widened. "Lizzie?"

"It's real. The final signed adoption papers for Addy. She's officially yours."

Tears trickled down Charlie's cheeks. "I'm her dad." His gaze lifted to Lizzie. "She's mine. *Ours.*"

Lizzie choked back a sob of joy. "Yes. She is."

He threw his arms around Lizzie and buried his face in the crook of her neck. She felt his warm tears on her skin. Not to mention her own streaming down her face.

Charlie eased back and smiled. "Thank you for taking a chance on me. I promise I'll be the best husband and father possible."

She shook her head. "Charlie, I just want you the way you are. The man I fell in love with."

"But—"

Lizzie placed her finger on his lips. "Just kiss me, Hotshot."

"Demanding little thing, aren't you?" he teased.

"Definitely." She looked forward to a lifetime of banter and happiness with this man.

Her life had taken some hard hits, but God had blessed her with Charlie and Addy. She wouldn't change anything for the world.

Charlie, her husband and now Addy's father, lowered his lips to hers. There was nothing simple about the kiss that took her breath away.

THANK YOU FOR READING CHRISTMAS IN THE CROSSHAIRS.

We hope you the action, adventure, and romance in our anthology. Turn the page for more exciting romantic suspense from Sunrise Publishing!

BRAINS. BEAUTY. BOLDNESS.
THE ELITE GUARDIANS WILL KEEP YOU SAFE.

Start reading the series now!

FIRE. FAMILY. FAITH.
LAST CHANCE FIRE AND RESCUE

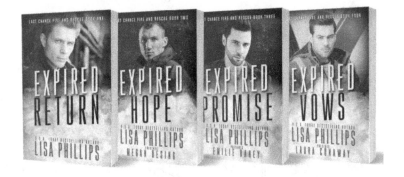

Dive into this thrilling first responder series now!

A SOLDIER, A MALINOIS, AND A STUNT WOMAN WALK ONTO A TV SET . . .

Experience the high-octane thrill ride that is the first book in the A Breed Apart: Legacy series.

FIND THEM ALL AT SUNRISE PUBLISHING!

CONNECT WITH SUNRISE

Thank you so much for reading *Christmas in the Crosshairs*. We hope you enjoyed the stories. If you did, would you be willing to do us a favor and leave a review? It doesn't have to be long—just a few words to help other readers know what they're getting. (But no spoilers! We don't want to wreck the fun!) Thank you again for reading!

We'd love to hear from you—not only about this book, but about any characters or stories you'd like to read in the future. Contact us at www.sunrisepublishing.com/contact.

We also have a monthly update that contains sneak peeks, reviews, upcoming releases, and fun stuff for our reader friends. Sign up at www.sunrisepublishing.com or scan our QR code.

ABOUT THE AUTHORS

Kate Angelo once sold a lion to a circus in Shreveport after her mom realized lions weren't great house pets. Growing up, Kate was a bookworm, dog groomer, exotic pet wrangler, horse trainer, cowgirl, and teenage pool shark. After aging out of foster care, Kate cultivated her inner computer nerd and worked as a web programmer. During a visit to Australia, Kate encountered Jesus and left the corporate world to pursue a life in ministry.

From her home in Southwest Missouri, Kate serves alongside her husband, strengthening and encouraging marriages and families through their nonprofit. After raising 5 children they are now fluent in both sarcasm and eye rolls.

Kate is a romantic suspense author, coffee addict, tech guru, productivity enthusiast, expert knitter, avid boater, dog lover, prayer warrior, and known klutz. With Willow, her long-haired chihuahua, taking up half her desk space, Kate writes thrilling stories with flawed characters who encounter hope and healing while ducking danger along the way. Subscribe to her newsletter to learn more about the pet lion thing at **https:// kateangelo.com/**.

Kelly Underwood's favorite things are reading, writing, and drinking coffee. She was born in New Hampshire, but don't ask her about snow, because she's been a Florida girl since she was twelve. She writes book reviews for her blog **bestinsuspense.com** and is an active member of the Central Florida chapter of the American Christian Fiction Writers. She's a sucker for a good suspense novel, the kind you have to read cover-to-cover until the mystery is solved and the bad guys are in handcuffs. If you're looking for her, she's probably on her back patio with a Kindle in one hand and a cup of coffee in the other.

Visit Kelly at **https://kellyunderwoodauthor.com**

Award-winning, Bestselling author **Sami A. Abrams** grew up hating to read. It wasn't until her 30's that she found authors that captured her attention. Now, most evenings, you can find her engrossed in a Romantic Suspense. In her opinion, a crime with a little romance is the recipe for a great story. Sami lives in Northern California, but she will always be a Kansas girl at heart. She has a love of sports, family, and travel. However, a cabin at Lake Tahoe writing her next story is definitely at the top of her list. Visit her at **https://www.samiaabrams.com.**

MORE ELITE GUARDIANS

Printed in the USA
CPSIA information can be obtained
at www.ICGtesting.com
LVHW040551031023
759759LV00053B/795

9 781953 783561